IT'S A VERY *TIMELY* PHASE FOR—

PERRY RHODAN—The First Administrator, who journeys on a "ghost ship" into time

ATLAN—The Imperator, who is recognized where least expected

Reginald Bell—The Solar First Deputy misses the zaniest adventure of his career . . . but not in vain!

Allan D. Mercant—and *Col. Nike Quinto*—Planners of the "Last Ditch" Operation

Epetran—The Master Mind of Arkon has a very long reach

Homer G. Adams—Head of General Cosmic Corporation

Gen. Freyt—The "home front" Solar Marshal

Gen. Kosnov & Gen. Deringhouse—Also on the "home" staff with Freyt

Lt. Brazo Alkher—A renegade Terran commander of fighting forces

Prof. Kalup—Terra's chief hyper-physicist

Capt. Tresta—Commander of the *Sotala*

Maj. Heintz—Second officer of the *Sotala*

Lt. Pinch—Duty officer on the *Sotala*

Artol of Fenoral—Akon scientist who makes a critical experiment

Adm. Notath—Commander of Arkon's Intergalactic Task Force

Col. Oberst—Officer of the *Ironduke*

Adm. Aichot—One of the ancient High Command

Capt. Usaph—Aichot's First Adjutant

Telater—A temporary disguise for Rhodan

Aday—A temporary disguise for the Chief of the Mutant Corps

Auris of Las Toor—The beautiful Akon woman crosses more than one line that was never meant to be!

AND OUR MUTANT CORPS

John Marshall, Pucky, Kitai Ishibashi, Tako Kakuta, Wuriu Sengu, Betty Toufry, Andre Noir
   . . . and the spaceships *Sotala* & *Ironduke*

AN ADVENTURE YOU'LL SAVOR FOR A LONG TIME TO COME

PERRY RHODAN: Peacelord of the Universe

Series and characters created and directed by Karl-
Herbert Scheer and Walter Ernsting.

ACE BOOKS EDITION

Managing Editor: FORREST J ACKERMAN

WENDAYNE ACKERMAN
Translator-in-Chief
& Series Coordinator

CHARLES VOLPE
Art Director

PAT LOBRUTTO
Editor

Sig Wahrman
Stuart J. Byrne
Associate Translators

Perry Rhodan

117

SAVIOR OF THE EMPIRE

by K. H. Scheer

ace books
A Division of Charter Communications Inc.
A GROSSET & DUNLAP COMPANY
1120 Avenue of the Americas
New York, New York 10036

This Issue Dedicated to
ROGER ADAY
CYNTHIA J. WESLEY
HENRY DAVIS JR.
A Trio of
Especially Dedicated
Rhofans.
"Shahntel, Karani"
Dankon, Amikoj
Thanx, Friends

GUIDE TO THE ACTION
SAVIOR OF THE EMPIRE
PERRY RHODAN # 117
SPECIAL ANNOUNCEMENT!
Calling All Rhofans!
page 7

TIME TRIPS
10 Issues from Now. 50! 100!
page 127

THE SHADOWS ATTACK
PERRY RHODAN # 118

FLASH! FLASH! FLASH!
THORA LIVES!
KHREST ALIVE!
ATLAN AT LAST!

A DREAM COME TRUE!

PERRY'S beloved wife THORA is alive & well next month in WASP-MEN ATTACK, first of the famous Missing Episodes in the Future Diaries of the Peacelord of the Universe. In place of adventures 119/120 you will get instead this previously unpublished novel, the story that follows Kurt Mahr's BASE ON VENUS (PR #4). The Mutant Corps meets the Challenge of the Mind Snatchers in this Tale with a Sting in its Tail.

Plus! The First ATLAN Adventure!

Together! In one book!

WASP-MEN ATTACK, starring Perry & All His People, and Swords & Science in a story of Pure Sorcery; the Lure & Lore of Ancient Atlantis and its Fabulous Son, Atlan, in—SPIDER DESERT!

To be followed the following month by MENACE OF ATOMIGEDDON by Kurt Mahr (the missing novel following PR 14, VENUS IN DANGER) and ATLAN, *The Ancient Astronaut*, #2 in FLIGHT FROM TAR-KIHL.

Then—the Horror of the Iron Horde as Rhodan & His Mutant Corps face the Menace of the Would-be

Metal Masters of Manhattan in ROBOT THREAT: NEW YORK, the adventure that relates the missing events between PERIL ON ICE PLANET (#23) and INFINITY FLIGHT (#24). Plus! Atlan Adventure #3, PURSUIT THRU THE PALE LAND.

And Other Pleasant Surprises in Months to Come!

You'll want to buy at least 2 copies each of these Collectors Items. And introduce Perry & Atlan—*together, in one package*—to a friend and prove yourself *A Friend to Fankind!*

KHREST, WHO WAS PERRY RHODAN'S FIRST ARKONIDE FRIEND, HAD PREDICTED IN HIS TIME THAT THE BOLD AND ENERGETIC TERRANS WOULD ONE DAY TAKE OVER THE CRUMBLING ARKONIDE IMPERIUM IN ORDER TO ERECT FROM ITS RUINS THE STELLAR EMPIRE OF HUMANITY.

HAS THE DAY ALREADY ARRIVED IN WHICH KHREST'S PREDICTION IS TO BE FULFILLED . . . ? IN THE YEAR 2105—NOT YET A CENTURY AND A HALF SINCE EARTHMEN FIRST VENTURED INTO SPACE—IS THE SOLAR IMPERIUM STRONG ENOUGH BY NOW TO RELIEVE THE ARKONIDES OF THEIR RULERSHIP OVER THE KNOWN SECTIONS OF THE GALAXY? IMPERATOR ATLAN, WHO HAS NEVER BEEN ACCEPTED BY HIS DECADENT COURTIERS AND SYCOPHANTS, IS FACED WITH SO MANY DIFFICULTIES THAT HE HAS FOR SOME TIME BEEN ABLE TO MAINTAIN HIS POSITION ONLY WITH THE HELP OF THE TERRANS—TOGETHER WITH THE AID OF THE POWERFUL ROBOT REGENT!

AT THE BEGINNING OF THE YEAR 2106 THE ROBOT REGENT SUDDENLY WITHDREW ALL SUPPORT FROM ATLAN AND INSISTED THAT HE SUBMIT TO A "MENTO DUEL" WHICH WAS TO DECIDE WHO THE NEW IMPERATOR

SHOULD BE. ATLAN FAILED IN THIS DUEL
AND WAS REMOVED BY THE POSITRONICON,
IN FAVOR OF CARBA.

BUT NEITHER ATLAN NOR PERRY RHODAN
ARE MEN WHO TOSS THEIR WEAPONS AWAY
JUST BECAUSE THEY'VE HAD A SETBACK.
THEY STILL SEARCH FOR A WAY TO REVERSE
THE COURSE OF EVENTS—AND THUS THEY
FIND THE IMPERIUM SAVER . . .

1/ THE BRAIN MUST DIE!

"THE JUMP!

"Please, sir, you should let *me* make it! This is my kind of job, not yours!"

I waved my hand in a signal of refusal. Ras Tschubai, a teleporter of the Terran Mutant Corps, had called to me over the helmet phone. He looked at me once more imploringly and then went out.

The energy arc of the matter transmitter took form. Blue fire streamed up from the twin floor projectors, turning to a flaming red at the apex of the arc. The thundering of the nuclear power generator drowned out all other sounds, which had forced Ras to use his radio. Between the fiery legs of the arc a darkness yawned, representing the extra-dimensional dematerializing field. I clutched the bomb that was suspended from my neck. It had been constructed in the atomic laboratories of Terra and was of a thermonuclear design. Its detonator had a built-in time delay which would allow me time to get out of the danger zone, if everything went according to plan.

"IF—!" said my logic sector.

I had already closed the helmet of my Arkonide combatsuit. The oxygen supply and the air-conditioning were functioning properly. I was ready except that I could not activate my defense screen as it would cause interference with the lines of force in the Akon transmitter.

The Akons! They were the unseen masterminds behind the galactic stage. Without their help and technology it would have been impossible for a certain treasonous Arkonide to deceive the robot Regent.

11

About 3 months had passed since my escape. Now I was once more in star cluster M-13 but this time, instead of being the ruling Imperator, I had come here as a dethroned outcast.

"Full power in 42 seconds," I heard somebody say over the radio and I recognized Perry Rhodan's voice. He was in the Control Central of the *Ironduke*.

The Terran linear-drive ship had emerged but a minute before from the semispace generated by the Kalup fields. We were within 20 light-years of the outer defense ring of the Arkon System but could not risk coming any closer. In fact we had probably been tracked already by the robot Brain's fortresses.

"It's disgraceful!" I thought bitterly.

"*Nonsense!*" retorted my extra-brain. "*It's a tactical necessity.*"

The sound of the reactors became deafening. I was alone in the transmitter room. In the few seconds remaining before the start of "Operation Last Ditch", as we had called it, recent events ran thru my mind as in a fast-motion film.

Three months before, a contest between myself and Carba from the insignificant ancestral House of Minterol had ended in a check-mate situation but he had been named Imperator Minterol I. Meanwhile the Solar Secret Service had reported that Carba's reason had been wavering because of an over-driven brain activation and that he was probably on the brink of a mental collapse by now.

Which was all the more convenient for those who had used him for seizing power in the Arkonide Imperium. *Those* masterminds were the ones who manipulated the robot Regent thru this puppet ruler whom the brain recognized. The vast Positronicon was unable to differentiate between Carba's voluntary and involuntary commands.

In the construction of their super robot my venerable ancestors had sought to prevent the very situation which had now developed: the Empire was being taken over by aliens; it was being split up and divided among various interest factions. It was the end of a 20,000-year stellar imperium and perhaps it also meant doom for Earthmen. Rhodan had already performed miracles in the buildup of the Solar Imperium but he was not a magician. Without the support of the robot fleet, Terra was lost.

From all indications an offensive was being planned, and apparently the Regent's fleet would not be operating alone. There were only a few intelligent races who were favorably inclined toward the Terrans, who had become all too irksome or troublesome to others. Most aliens hated them, in particular the Galactic Traders, the Aras, the Antis and of late the Akons, who had suffered the greatest defeat in their history because of Rhodan.

My own power was gone. My alliance with the Earth might have been gratifying to the Terrans but it was no longer to their advantage. In fact a deposed Arkonide imperator was more of a burden than a support to their extra-terrestrial political structure and policy.

Rhodan had been fully aware of my mental and emotional distress. He had not brought up the question or placed any pressure on me until I myself had made the proposal to blow up the Regent. It was then that I learned that Solar Intelligence had already made all the preparations.

Once the Brain was eliminated it would be up to me and the Terrans to save the Imperium. I hardly dared think of the magnitude of such a task at the moment. The Regent controlled industry, the entire food and supply administration and the military might of the Empire. If these controls suddenly vanished it would cause a catastrophe. However, we had conscientiously asked ourselves if those revolts and petty wars which would come as a result could be worse than the present splinterings and divisions caused by the greedy powers of the galaxy.

I had to do it! The criminal augmentation of Carba's intelligence was leading to destruction. By nefarious means the Regent had been convinced that Carba's supercharged mind entitled him to the position of Imperator. During a mental duel, which was carried out on an almost incomprehensible plane of robot logic, my opponents had been able to "prove" that I had become an incompetent ruler. The claimed that I had violated the doctrines of our ancestors by supporting the development of the Terrans, that I had furnished them with technical secrets and had thus enhanced the advancement of an almost invincible enemy.

The Robot had not understood my real concerns for the Imperium. It had responded to the ancient catastrophe program "Ephethus", according to which an Imperator was to be removed immediately as soon as he was not exclusively concerned with the well-being of the Empire. I had not succeeded in giving a purely logical proof that the friendship of the alert and highly intelligent Terrans would be of great benefit to the State. In the end, Carba had been named Imperator and I had been forced to escape.

"Transmission in 3 seconds," Rhodan announced. "Good luck, friend."

It shocked me back to the present and I was aware of the stark reality of the bomb. I would have to ignite it within the inner circuits of the Regent.

"You should have sent a Terran mutant," my logic sector informed me.

Certainly a teleporter would be able to help himself better in a dangerous emergency. However, this destruction of the most magnificent creation of my ancestors was strictly *my* affair. By virtue of my heritage and my office it was *I* who must make the attempt to preserve the Imperium.

"Very heroic!" retorted my extra-brain.

I ignored it. My synthetically activated logic sector had little use for sentiment or feelings. Actually it was an organic computer which transmitted its conclusions or perceptions. But it was up to me to either respond to its admonishments or to reject them.

The energy field had thickened visibly and the transmitter arc was high enough to admit a man. When the violet signal lamp began to flicker I advanced toward the yawning darkness between the rising legs of the arc. One more step and I would emerge inside the Brain 20 light-years away. The Terrans had been able to analyze this Akon technology so that the formerly long-range transmitter no longer held any secrets for them.

I felt the pull of the dematerializing field. Taking a deep breath I cast aside all thoughts of the pros and cons of my actions and prepared myself for the "jump".

"Stop—get back!" somebody shouted. "Danger, Atlan! The receiver station's been short-circuited!"

I responded without thinking, as had become my habit in recent years. When a person is continuously threatened by assassins he develops a 6th sense. Before I had consciously registered the warning cry I had already leapt back but I still fell to the deck within a yard or so of the transmitter arc. My heavy equipment prevented me from moving swiftly. I had to crawl back into the room until I was beyond the marked-out danger zone and could take shelter behind the thermal defense screen.

The hatch swung open and 2 men rushed in with Ras Tschubai in the lead. Without a word they snatched me from the transmitter room and set me on my feet out-side.

"Are you alright, sir?" asked the second man, who was younger than the African teleporter.

I recognized Lt. Brazo Alkher, one of the backup cadre of officers who would one day have a voice in the destiny of the Solar Imperium.

"Yes, thank you," I answered. "What happened?" But I had not spoken loudly enough because of the thundering of the converter, so I repeated the question.

Alkher pressed the release button on my helmet and it glided back onto my shoulders, where it was magnet-ically anchored. Ras Tschubai smiled apologetically and relieved me of the bomb. He seemed to concentrate for a moment and then he disappeared in a bright flash of shimmering air. It was all happening too fast and my brain refused to register the events in their proper se-quence.

Rhodan and the commander put in an appearance. Jefe Claudrin had turned off his micro-grav generator and came along the passage in mighty strides, just as if there were no gravity at all on board the *Ironduke*.

Once more I received no answer. They led me away as tho I were a child. Apparently they had recognized my state of confusion as a form of temporary stupor. In fact I was becoming drowsy by the time Rhodan brought me into the Control Central and bedded me down on a contour couch.

Here it was more calm and quiet. The humming of the equipment and instruments was more pacifying than disturbing. I was wondering about my condition. Normally I should have been fairly agitated under the circumstances but in this case I could barely move. It was similar to a state of shock. I had been torn abruptly from a condition of high concentration and weeks of nervous tension.

A medico gave me an injection and after a few moments I felt more collected and able to move. Perry was squatting beside me, surrounded by the officers of the *Ironduke*. I sat up, staring at them, unable to miss Prof. Kalup's heavy figure in their midst.

"Maybe old soldiers never die," he said ironically, "but you came very close to fading away. Do you happen to know, sir, that you were already within the range of the dematerializing field? How did you manage to jump back just in the nick of time like that?"

"Instinct, self-preservation—I don't know . . ."

"Most likely instinct. The transmitter was short-circuited just as you were about to enter it—which meant that the other end of the line wasn't able to receive you. Anything going into a mess like that would have been shuttled back and forth about a hundred thousand times per microsecond."

Rhodan chuckled unconvincingly and clapped me on the shoulder, hoping to reassure me. "Forget it, friend. We caught it just in time."

However, my thoughts were racing. During the considerable period of my office as Imperator Gonozal VIII, I had succeeded in setting up a transmitter station in the subterranean section of the robot Regent. The Brain had never become suspicious because it was not equipped to detect the equipment's extra-dimensional forcefield. Moreover the device had been built by Terran specialists and it contained security circuits which were unknown even to the Akons.

Who had caused it to short circuit? Who would have been capable of it?

A strange sound gripped my attention. It sounded like the whining of a hound. Rhodan was staring at a viewscreen which revealed the inner room of the ship's transmitter station. Within moments the sound became shriller until it resembled the shrieking of a power-saw.

Rhodan was shouting to me. "We've sent a robot into the field! There—take a look at *that!*"

I jumped up. Once more my legs seemed to move involuntarily and I realized that I must have become frightfully pale.

The dematerialization field between the bases of the energy arc was normally black but at present it was aglow with a greenish flame. Within it was silhouetted a nebulous shape which appeared to become more deformed with each passing second.

Jefe Claudrin gave an order and the transmitter was shut off. There was a lightning flash from the aperture, followed by something that struck the armorplate bulkhead of the sending room and remained fastened to it.

When the thunder of the power pile subsided we were still staring at the viewscreen. The robot had apparently been compressed to a lump of metal the size of a fist. The densified mass clung to the steel plate, glowing white hot and seeming to pulsate like something alive.

I couldn't utter a word. Everyone in the Control Central could well imagine what I would have looked like by now if I had not jumped back in time. Rhodan cleared his throat but also said nothing.

Kalup wiped his bald head with a handkerchief. "The atomic regrouping there doesn't seem to be very tidy," he said. "Could you give me an idea, sir, of what's happened to your transmitter receiver? I thought you had concealed it."

I suppressed my excitement, realizing that this whole thing had become futile. No one said anything until after I had struggled to express what was really on my mind. "A good question, Professor! The Regent could never have found it. Nor could Carba, either. So it means that somebody must have penetrated the robot who is familiar with Akon transmitters."

"*Terran* transmitters," corrected Kalup irritably, "based on the Akon principle."

I shrugged . "Have it your way. I know you and your experts took special pains with it. Nevertheless the equipment has been discovered and evidently somebody was able to understand the technology involved. They were waiting for our sending station to beam out the ready signal and that's when they caused the short circuit. So it seems I've escaped once again. But how to destroy the Brain now is a whole new problem."

Kalup turned away. I watched his portly figure until he disappeared thru the door to the tracking central. His gruff tone did not disturb me anymore. I knew it was only an expression of his choleric nature and that he was not half as formidable as he sounded.

Rhodan was leaning with both hands on a map table. His gaze seemed to bore thru the top of it. Without looking up he made a statement that I could not refute. "That was the last possibility of attacking the Brain with relative safety or at least a minimum of risk. Now Akon scientists have penetrated the situation and they are allowed to do things that we were always prevented from doing. It's certain that the Regent's basic security circuits have been reprogrammed; therefore the machine has become a general menace. Our observations indicate that a large part of the robot fleet has been deployed into the Arkon System. An open attack would not only be hopeless but it would also threaten the existence of humanity. And since our mutants can't enter the Brain's interior it would appear that the tele-transmitter is the only solution."

The idea startled me. The special transmitter was located on board the Fleet flagship. "It's been proved that the Brain's honeycomb screen is impenetrable," I said. "The Akons have modernized the defense weapons. Besides that they also have linear-drive spaceships. What do you have in mind?"

He looked at me cautiously. Jefe Claudrin avoided my gaze. That's when I realized that the Terrans had been discussing something that I was not aware of as yet.

"Nothing, Atlan. Or at least nothing yet! It would have to depend on your decision . . . "

"Pertaining to what . . . ?"

"It would require your agreement to strike Arkon 3 with nuclear fire—it would mean the destruction of the planet. Wait!" He raised a hand and I checked my angry reaction. "Let me finish. We're quite aware that the delicate gravitational balance of the three Arkon worlds would be disturbed. Without the mass of the war planet, the tri-planet configuration created by your ancestors might fall apart. The synthetic orbits would be destroyed. The Crystal World of Arkon 1 and the industrial planet, Arkon 2, would be ravaged by annihilating earthquakes and catastrophic floods. To say the least the climatic conditions would undergo a violent change. This much must be admitted."

I turned to go into the tracking center, struck to the core by Rhodan's words.

"I am against the plan," he said.

When I turned to look at him his face was expressionless. "Thanks for that," I told him. "It won't work. Billions of Arkonides would be sacrificed. I might go along with the destruction of Arkon 3 since hardly anyone lives there. An evacuation would be possible. The Crystal World and #2, however, must not be disturbed. I haven't given up yet."

The armored hatch opened and I stepped thru. I knew that we had reached out wit's end in the matter. Rhodan

followed me and we came to a stop before the echo
screens of the energy sensor. Jefe Claudrin's voice
reached us from the Control Central. He was ordering
an engine warmup.

The sudden roaring of the hypersensors did not come
as a surprise to me: I had expected an enemy sighting.
Rhodan interpreted my weary smile correctly.

We had come here to destroy the Regent. If it ceased
to exist, Carba's plans would come to nought. The alien
power groups would lose their interest in him. Far more
importantly, however, about 100,000 ships of the Arkonide robot fleet would be put out of operation.

"If!" said my logic sector.

I ignored the interjection. The Akons had been behind the revolt of the degenerated Arkonides and now
they had reached their goal. The Regent was acting
illogically, which proved that they had been able to
influence it decisively.

The sensor rumblings indicated transitions. Therefore, we were being attacked by the Brain. I hardly paid
any attention to the howl of alarm sirens. The *Ironduke*
was in battle readiness. Within seconds after the first
long-distance sighting, the warship had begun to pick
up speed. As usual in such moments, the commands
seemed to come so fast that they overlapped each other.
The off-duty crews were hurrying to their combat positions. The heavy gun turrets emerged from the hull as if
to say that Terra was not as helpless now as it had been
100 years ago.

Following the hyperspace entry maneuver of the
detected warships the hypersensors registered a second
set of shockwaves. On the mass-sensor's echo screens
appeared 4 green blips, and seconds later the evaluation
came thru. The Terran translight sensor-tracking system worked on the principle of hypercom-reflex
analysis. The equipment could also pick up return

echoes from physical objects in normal space, so the state of the art was no longer dependent upon tracing energy contrails from the impulse engines of other vessels. Altho the latter technique served to determine range and bearing, the new features permitted an estimate of the size of the tracked objects as well.

The voice of the O.D. rang from the speakers. Presently the *Ironduke* was hurtling into deep space with an acceleration of 600 km per second squared. "Four superbattleships, Imperium class, in close formation—red 33.467, vertical 7.274. Broadside action—turn about and open fire."

I frowned, realizing that the robot-controlled space giants had unquestionably received orders to destroy the *Ironduke*. What astonished me was that our main positronicon had responded to the open fire without an override. The 4 battleships had emerged from hyperspace at a distance of about 10 million km and their speed was close to that of light itself. It was ridiculous to assume we were in effective range for a hit. The distance was also too great for overtaking a swift opponent.

Rhodan did not concern himself with the invisible energy beams sweeping past us.

"Broadside pattern sustaining," came a voice from tracking. "Lousy, too—excuse me, sir!"

I ran to the Control Central where the bogie blips were more discernible on the larger screens. The Imperium-class ships were in a braking maneuver. Even the Regent would not be able to handle the complex factors this introduced to the firing coordinate data. The thunder of our engines made normal communication impossible. I snatched up a radio helmet, slapped the earphones to my head and switched the receiver on. And at once I was aware of Rhodan's shouted orders. He was sitting in the commodore's flight seat while next to him the commander monitored the navigation and defense controls.

" . . . should give it a try," I heard Perry say. "Fire when ready!"

I looked in surprise at the outboard monitor as something leapt away from one of the launching domes. It was an old-fashioned rocket of the type we had used in our fight against the Antis. For a brief moment its micro-impulse engine flamed brilliantly as it broke thru the reverse-polarity field laminations of our defense screens, and then it vanished. But we could still see a green blip on the energy-sensor screen. The missile was accelerating at a maximum rate of 800 km per second squared. It was self-guided, employing 3 different principles which a robotship would find it difficult to recognize. For thousands of years, projectiles had not been used as weapon carriers.

"Do you think it'll work?" I asked.

"The proof is in the pudding, as they used to say on Earth. We're working just now with the mass detector. If it's jammed out the energy sensor will take over. That in turn becomes ineffective if they cut their engines. Residual radiation is too weak for long-range tracking. The crudest method is used by the laser-amplified echo-tracer. It starts working when it comes within range of the return beams reflected from the ships. I don't think they'll try damping the echoes. At any rate, the missile will home in on the leading vessel."

I was impressed. These men never hesitated to use any weapon they had to, from situation to situation, even if it involved such an archaic device that any other intelligences would have haughtily rejected the thought of employing it.

The robotships were still firing at us. Their courses were approaching ours altho they had broken up their formation. Before we penetrated into the Kalup-generated semispace zone, tracking announced a massive energy burst at a range of 8 million km. One of the echo blips disappeared and in its place appeared a glowing orange-red fleck of light.

"Approximately 40,000 megatons," announced the duty officer in the tracking center. "A dead hit—total destruction. Their nuclear fuel helped amplify the chain reaction."

Rhodan leaned back in his seat while I fairly trembled in reaction. Had the Regent become so sloppy that its ships could be destroyed by a primitive nuclear projectile? I myself could have figured out at least 10 different ways of handling the clearly detectable rocket, either by weapons fire or by outmaneuvering it. I avoided Rhodan's gaze.

The howling of the compensating converter died away. The star-strewn firmament of the normal void disappeared from the viewscreens and once more I was captivated by the phenomenon of translight linear flight.

Rhodan's voice rang in my headphones. "The Brain is at the end of its rope. I wouldn't have thought I could hit an Imperium-class battleship this way, much less destroy it. It's time to wipe out that machine. It's a source of growing disaster. Within a few months the galaxy will be in an uproar and by that time Carba will probably have gone mad. From then on the Akons will try to tighten the reins, whereas at present they still have to move cautiously. Can you imagine what will happen when they have a free hand?"

I nodded dejectedly. Yes, I could well imagine. Even tho these 4 robotships had acted erratically the Terran fleet could not hold out against 100,000 of them. The Springer fleet units would also penetrate into the Sol System, in addition to the ships of countless colonial races who would still be in support of the Arkonide Imperium as ever before.

In spite of this, however, I still believed that I could shut off the Regent. In our case the mammoth Brain was the sword with which the Gordian knot could be cut.

2/ A "GHOST" OF A CHANCE

I was prepared for many surprises from the "Little Man", as everyone called the slightly built Chief of Solar Intelligence, but this time the Solar Marshal had proposed the craziest plan I had ever heard of.

With their advancing technology the Terrans appeared to have a penchant for trying the impossible. I had known the human race for 10,000 years. They had always shown themselves to be intelligent, resolute and frighteningly acquisitive when it came to knowledge. These were characteristics which had caused me some apprehension as a former Arkonide admiral. In those days when I first set foot on Earth, in view of my training, my rank and my Arkonide outlook I had pondered at length how I was to compose my field report. I had been inclined to inform those who might follow me that here on an insignificant world in the 10-planet system of Sol a race was developing that would bear watching.

Now the Terrans had become a major power. They were fighting for their life which was something that could not be avoided ever since their official emergence into the political macrocosmos of the galaxy.

A significant figure in the Rhodan game of recognition, expansion and swift retaliation was Allan D. Mercant, a semi-mutant with slight telepathic capabilities and the brain of a genius. He had formerly been chief of NATO intelligence and Rhodan was indebted to him for the fact that the "New Power", founded toward the end of the 20th century, had not suffered still greater difficulties than it had been forced to face.

Mercant's "hobby", as he called it, was secret ser-

26

vice and espionage activity. To my way of thinking the work of such an organization was of course indispensable altho not always neat and clean. While orchestrating such instruments, no intelligence chief can avoid an occasional sour note or discord.

We had landed 2 days ago in Terrania. The city had increased still more in size and modernity. Even Rhodan did not know exactly how many inhabitants were in Terrania.

In response to Mercant's invitation we had gathered together in the conference chamber of Defense-Intelligence Headquarters. The security measures were sobering if not alarming. In addition to robot guards, soundproof walls and the unobtrusive presence of mutants, the small briefing hall was enclosed in a protective energy field. Here there was no "officious" atmosphere, however, no horse-shoe shaped green-top tables. We sat unrestrainedly beside each other as if at a social gathering, placed at our ease by an awareness that no one could eavesdrop on our conversation.

The most important leaders of the Solar Imperium were present. I noted that there wasn't a man among them who had not received the life-prolonging cell-shower treatment.

Even Homer G. Adams, the powerful but never conspicuous Chief of the solar GCC, had put in an appearance. GCC—General Cosmic Corporation—was conceived in a century that hardly knew anything about manned spaceflight until Rhodan flew to the moon. That had been the beginning of a cosmic gamble whose most important phase had now been reached.

I continued to take count of the notables present. Solar Marshals Mercant and Freyt were in attendance as well as generals Deringhouse and Kosnov. Rhodan of course was there, as well as Reginald Bell in the capacity of Defense Minister, in addition to leading scientists and other men I had only heard about but had never met personally.

A man who was veiled in considerable mystery was Col. Nike Quinto, a chief of one of the Intelligence Department's divisions. It was said of him that he was a master of secretive operations. Unquestionably Mercant's wild idea had come partially from Quinto, who sat perspiring in a corner and informed anyone who cared to listen about his imagined illnesses.

So I found myself in the midst of a task team which was capable of shaking the galaxy itself. Here was Homer G. Adams with his GCC, whose financial power was such that his signature alone could authorize a subsidy amount of up to 500 billion Solars. And there was Mercant with his unfathomable Security and Intelligence resources, plus of course Rhodan himself and his whole Solar Fleet, the actual strength of which he had never divulged.

For several minutes a tense silence had fallen upon the room. Mercant's proposal had sounded too incredible. Even Rhodan seemed perplexed. "My friend—are you sure you're sober?" he asked.

Mercant glanced at Quinto. I knew that courteous smile of the Intelligence Chief. I had never known a dangerous man with such a harmless appearance. "With your permission—I am quite in possession of my faculties," he replied.

Rhodan seemed to stiffen as if a cold shock had run thru him. In fact I too could feel cold perspiration starting down my back. "Mercant—but that's insane!" he protested.

Yet at the same time I was surprised to detect a fire of enthusiasm rising within me. Mercant, shrewd psychologist that he was, winked at me knowingly. He seemed to interpret the gleam in my eye correctly.

"Now there are two of us who have rocked off," observed Bell.

"How is that?" interjected Prof. Kalup in his loud voice. "I find myself fascinated."

Rhodan chuckled dryly. "Seems to be quite a difference of opinion here. Quinto, are you the one who suggested this audacious idea to our Chief of Intelligence?"

Nike Quinto stirred his short, rounded figure and puffed out his cheeks. "Sir, in view of my high blood-pressure I'd never permit myself to agitate my superiors because that only develops other difficulties for me. However, since my bloodpressure at present isn't up to its usual—"

"If we're lucky you'll explode on us one of these days," grumbled Kalup. His fat cheeks trembled visibly.

Quinto feigned offense but finally smiled. It helped me to find my inner calm again. When Rhodan looked at me I discovered that same old expression in his features which he had always displayed at the inception of a daring venture.

"Well, old pirate?" I said to him. "I see you're getting the itch, right?"

He laughed. We understood each other.

"Well, that puts it together," commented Bell sarcastically. "Two nuts at the highest level—if Your 'Retired' Excellence will forgive me . . ."

When he bowed mockingly I began to feel impatient. Turning to Mercant, I inquired without preamble: "Have you made a thorough analysis of the data I gave you? You know that the slightest mistake can be fatal for all of us, granting that your plan even gets off the ground."

The marshal made a sign to Quinto and the chief of the so-called "Brain Trust"—otherwise referred to as

Division 3—got up from his chair with a grunt of exertion. He acted as if it wcrc hazardous for him to place both feet on the floor at the same time, yet he maneuvered himself quite agilely to the control console. The seat creaked audibly under his weight when he sat down at the panel.

The snap of a switch was heard. The lights in the windowless room were darkened. A wall-sized viewscreen brightened with the 3-D color image of a spaceship.

I sprang to my feet, clinging with both hands to the table before me. I stared in utter amazement. This could not be real unless the Terrans had become magicians!

"Mercant . . . !" I groaned aloud. "Take it easy, will you? Even Arkonides can only stand so much shock treatment!"

"You are looking at reality, sir. This film was taken early today. You are looking at His Highness Tutmor VI's heavy cruiser *Sotala*, commanded by Capt. Tresta of the distinguished House of Efelith. On the 10th of February of 2106 it will be exactly 6023 years since a hypercom message from the *Sotala* reached the Supreme Council of Arkon. The news was so important that it was brought to the attention of the ruling Imperator at that time, Tutmor VI. In the nebula sector, Capt. Tresta had succeeded in simultaneously liberating two worlds from the enemy—but in the process his cruiser was destroyed. The *Sotala* never returned to Arkon. Capt. Tresta went down in the history of his people as a hero, sir."

"The spaceship you see has been converted by using every branch of technology and science available to us while sparing no expense, and now it resembles the old *Sotala* down to the last detail. Nothing was overlooked. That is guaranteed by Solar Intelligence. During the conversion many details had to be considered. The outer hull had to be reduced in its measurements by 189 meters. The modern full-scale positronicon had to be replaced by the kind that was in use at that time. Engines, power plants, weapons, power circuits and conduits, the computer central, officers' and crew quarters—all this and about 10,000 other details had to be copied. Even the propulsion rating of the original engines was simulated. Any Arkonide technologist from the time of Imperator Tutmor VI could go over the ship to his heart's content and not discover the slightest difference from the original. We thoroughly familiarized ourselves with the construction plans that we found in the microfilms you salvaged.''

I trembled almost feverishly. My extra-brain came to life, activating my photographic memory. I knew how my ancestors had built their ships. Like one hypnotized I walked up to the viewscreen and began to inspect the vessel. The name *Sotala* had been painted in 2 places on the spherical hull in Arkonide letters. Here the same flaming red had been used as was employed then.

''The composition of the color is correct,'' commented Mercant, just as casually as if he were chatting about the weather.

To me it was almost frightening. The Terrans were masters of camouflage but here Mercant had outdone himself. The sharply wedge-shaped engine ring bulge was typical of the *Sotala* class. The personnel airlocks were hexagonal—also correct! The lower sections of the landing struts also had the typical bulges containing the auxiliary hydraulic units. The gun turrets displayed their sensor antennas for individual precision firing. In those days they had not relied completely on remote control from the fire command central.

I looked closely at every last detail but couldn't find

an error. "Does the inside of the ship look like this, Mercant? I mean—copied to such a degree of exactness?"

"You have my word for it, sir," Quinto assured me. So he had been involved with this, after all.

"A real counterfeiter," observed Kalup. "Nevertheless—my compliments!"

My mind was fairly swimming as I went back to my form chair and sat down. The cell activator hanging on my chest was pulsing louder than usual, reminding me once again of my extreme age. Under my present state of excitement it was evident that some extra cell-regeneration was necessary.

Rhodan handed me a refreshment. "Satisfied?" he asked. "No defects?"

"None," I confessed. "Of course I'd still have to take a look at the inside. Mercant—what's it all add up to?"

So far the Intelligence Chief had done very little explaining but we had already been flabbergasted by his plan, which had to do with "time-line alteration for penetration into the brain". What followed now caused me to hold my breath occasionally.

Mercant remained quietly objective. He did not even raise his voice when he came to particularly spectacular and vital points of his exposition. In fact his telegraphic style of delivery made it almost too impersonal—yet for that very reason the whole thing sounded extremely impressive. At no time did we have the impression of listening to a visionary.

"After transmitting her victory message the *Sotala* was not heard from again. Later reports from Arkonide Fleet Headquarters confirm that the cruiser was destroyed. So we are taking over the role of the *Sotala* and will return to the Arkon System 3 days after the reception of its last known message. Atlan is to play the part of the commander. We have also provided uniforms, all types of documents and credentials—even provisions in the form of dehydrated foods and conserves, such as were used at the time. The munitions supplies correspond to the number series issued by the ordnance chief of 'Base T-187'. Nothing is missing, gentlemen. Even the manufacturer's mark inside the collars of the combatsuits will be found to coincide with the facts. The Arkonides were very thorough and all the old data are completely at our disposal. When you land on Arkon 3 you will *be* the crew of the *Sotala*. There are no margins of error.''

''*Land*, did you say?'' Rhodan emphasized the word deliberately. ''When? Don't tell me that this talk about 'time-line alterations' is tied in to *that!*''

''It is the basic condition necessary to the success of the plan, sir,'' replied Mercant, as pleasantly as before. ''The conversion of a Terran cruiser and transforming the crew into Arkonides of the time of Tutmor VI could only make sense if we can succeed in penetrating the corresponding historical epoch.''

''I can't believe it!'' I exclaimed.

''But it's true, sir. I recall the attack on the robot Regent shortly after the discovery of the planet Sphynx. At that time an attempt was made to alter the lines of time. The phantom fleet started to attack the Earth until we succeeded in destroying the converter equipment. A second machine of this type is located on the central world of the Akons.''

''Time displacement?'' asked Rhodan, leaning forward.

''In a way, sir. Certainly not time travel in the tradition of your fantasy tales. The device generates a 5th dimensional absorption field in which relative phases of 'time' can be altered. It is impossible to actually leave one's own time reference and live some-

where else. One can't just travel about as he pleases and
act the part of the visitor from the future. However, the
narrow radius of action this offers us should be sufficient for our purpose.''

Kalup went into some of the technical aspects. The
principle involved was understandable even tho no one
could explain how the Akons had influenced the present lines of time. Mercant waited patiently. The conference gradually took on the semblance of a casual
gathering, breaking down into separate discussion
groups. Everybody came to attention again when Rhodan sought to bring the meeting to order.

"Continue your presentation, Mercant. We're just
about ready for anything by now."

"Thank you, sir. We have learned that the machine
is stationary. It would have to be transported in a
spaceship and transferred in outer space to the converted cruiser . . . The converter's operating crew is
known to us. It consists of 4 Akon scientists who are
still able to operate the equipment. But they aren't
capable of handling repairs in case of a breakdown. The
secret construction details have been lost. However,
there is no particular danger involved in case of equipment failure. No one can be cut off in another period of
time. As soon as the energy field collapses, everything
becomes stabilized again. Our commando force on
Sphynx has already been instructed to keep the 4 Akons
under surveillance. The mutants will make sure that
these men will be in the vicinity of the converter at the
proper time. The device is kept in a museum but any
practical use of it is forbidden, subject to punishment
by death. Only experiments under government control
are permitted. And that gives us our point of attack,
thru the 4 Akon scientists. You must acquire the
machine and get it installed in the simulated *Sotala*.
Once you are in the Arkon System the time-field is to be

activated. The phasing has to be very exact. Once you have picked up and registered the famous hypercom message of the original *Sotala* you will be able to make a vernier time-line adjustment. Wait 2 days and then announce your victorious return over local telecom. It's certain that the genuine cruiser won't be able to cause you any trouble. By the time you will have made your landing, the old *Sotala* will have already been destroyed.''

I almost forgot to breathe. Mercant *had* to be insane. Of course a virtual trip thru time was equally crazy but even this idea of a time-displacement field presented problems that neither the Terrans nor myself would be able to resolve. The ancient science of Akon had left a machine behind that no one really understood anymore. Just the operation of the controls alone would be a gamble which could neither guarantee a trouble-free performance nor any security at all for our task force.

On top of these difficulties we had to face the problem of stealing the machine along with the 4 scientists. No doubt the latter had learned more or less which switches to activate, as a result of years of experimenting, in order to achieve this or that effect but this was still not in the realm of professional operation. I couldn't even imagine what effect a rephasing of time would have on us.

If we should actually manage to land on Arkon 3, 6023 years prior to present time, we would still be energy components of our own temporal plane or epoch. Mercant had admitted that it was impossible to achieve a stable entry into the era of Tutmor VI. The plan was senseless.

Mercant's voice pulled me out of my stupor. It was evident from his concluding remarks that the scientists of the Intelligence staff were aware of the difficulties.

"At the maximum output of the converter the effective range of the phasing field is about 200 km. No one should venture more than 100 km from the generator. Granted, that's a tight squeeze. Everything will depend on landing the false *Sotala* as close as possible to the Brain. At that time the Regent's last sections were being completed and there wasn't any defense screen. You will have to use your ingenuity, with the help of the mutants, to get into the lower labyrinths and conceal a nuclear bomb in such a manner as to prevent its subsequent discovery. The weapon has a time-fuse based on a Uranium clocking device. Exactly 6023 years later the fusion process will be activated. That will be on February 15, which is a few days from now.''

Rhodan got to his feet. He thrust his hands into the pockets of his uniform, walked over to the film projector and came to a stop. ''Mercant, this time you're going too far out on a limb. If the bomb is to detonate on the 15th of February, that means theoretically that it's already located somewhere inside the Brain.''

''A relativistic conclusion,'' interjected Kalup. ''It shouldn't be but it can be! The function of the Akon device is an unknown factor.''

''Professor, I believe I have a fair reasoning faculty but you've lost me somewhere.''

''Me, too, sir,'' Mercant admitted. ''Nevertheless the attempt should be made. I don't see any other possibility of destroying the Brain. Recent events have proved how dangerous the Robot has become because of a reprogramming of its most vital circuits and installations. Members of the Akon Energy Command were detected in the security section. It would have been possible to capture the 8 scientists of that team if the Brain hadn't jumped the gun, so to speak, and opened fire. Atlan couldn't use his transmitter, and to use our most powerful weapon would mean the destruction of the Arkon System. Nor can mutants get thru the modernized honeycomb screen. So I'm asking *you*—how are you going to ward off this menacing situation?''

Quinto spoke up. "Division 3 is of the opinion that something must be risked. Unusual situations require unusual methods. We've worked out a plan of action and it tells us what we have to do. You will be able to contact the greatest Arkonide scientist, the great councillor *Epetran*. He died 8 years later. Perhaps Epetran can be influenced to reprogram the robot Brain—fresh from the start.''

"Nonsense!" retorted Rhodan. "If that were possible the Robot would be acting differently now!" I had to agree with him.

"That's hard to say. The present situation indicates everything and nothing. We still can't tell whether or not you've been back 6023 years or not, or whether you then reached the Brain. We would have to wait for February 15 to determine that.''

"Then let's wait!" I cried out in desperation.

Mercant made a gesture of rejection. Suddenly he seemed to be very resolute. "Impossible, Your Eminence. You would miss the precise point in time. It was on the 10th of February, 6023 years ago, that the hypercom message was received from the *Sotala*. Her commander received orders to return home immediately. So the arrival in the Arkon System would have to be 2 days later, which would be February 12th by Earth reckoning. Of course you will have the conversion tables with the Arkonide units of time to go by. You will have 2 or maybe 2½ days at the most to conceal the bomb—or to influence the chief builder, Epetran, to build in some security circuits that will satisfy our requirements in the present. Otherwise the bomb must explode on the 15th of February. So if you miss the decisive moment there will no longer be any chance of landing you on Arkon in the era of Imperator Tutmor VI. That the *Sotala* sent a victory message but failed to return is a very unique circumstance. There is no other spaceship you can copy.''

''Why so? Thousands of Arkon ships were destroyed in the battles of that time.''

''Of course, sir, but within the few days that are important to us, this only applies to the *Sotala*.''

My extra-brain interceded. Mercant had made a mistake in his reasoning. When I stood up, Rhodan looked at me questioningly.

''Mercant, you know how long it will take to program the robot fleet. An attack is imminent but it isn't going to happen tomorrow or even in the next 3 weeks. So I ask you: why should the 15th of February, the cruiser *Sotala* and all these other things be so critical and decisive? Also you know that the Akon converter enables us to alter time. If we started this operation later we could *still* follow the necessary schedule.'' I believed I had given a logical argument but I was wrong. These Terrans could think!

''Certainly you could start 4 weeks from now and still reach the right moment in time, sir. That still means the 12th of February for your landing on Arkon 3. This cannot be changed by any machine. But to make the plan work, the *Sotala* would have to be used and none other.''

''I don't understand.''

''Sir, during those specific days, 6023 years ago, the last controls of the Regent were being completed. If you arrive only a short time after that, the honeycomb screen will be there. So you have to select a time for your landing that is *prior* to the activation of the screen and which coincides with the arrival of the *Sotala*. The loss of that ship was a fortunate coincidence for us. As for the 15th of February, that is an arbitrary point that was determined by mathematics—pertaining to the Uranium timing device of the bomb. It was quite a problem to calculate the exact detonation time, based on the half-life rate of radioactive decay. Why should we alter that and have to start all over again? You would still be able to steal the Akon machine and begin your operations—but there is no getting around the schedule of the *Sotala.*"

I felt that I had been taught a lesson by the Security Chief—but he was right! If the honeycomb screen was activated only a few days later, any delay in our schedule would be catastrophic. The Terrans had thought of everything. Rhodan went back to his seat and I also sat down again. We looked at each other searchingly. The room became silent.

When I finally nodded to him he seemed visibly to be relieved. "Mr. Mercant, run the film thru again. We want to take a look at the interior of the cruiser."

I was filled with new courage. Rhodan had decided. The operation was "go". My extra-brain prodded me mentally but I couldn't quite make out the signal. It was probably calling me a fool.

The image of the *Sotala* appeared again on the screen just as Reginald Bell remarked resignedly: "Ever since the start of the New Power I've seen everything but this is the zaniest operation I've been involved in!"

"Wrong!" Rhodan corrected him. "You will take command of the Fleet and wait until the Regent is destroyed. When that happens, you will begin immediately to capture the Brain's robotships, which will have become helpless."

"What . . . ?"

"That's right, you are to begin with the task without delay, once the Regent's control has been eliminated. We have the advantage of knowing that something is going to happen. Before other intelligences realize how easy it is to take over the valuable ships of the Regent's fleet, we will have had to beat them to it. It's your task right now to find out where the larger formations can be located. They will be the first to be taken over. The lone wolves way out in deep space will have their turn later. Mercant—switch reels. I want to see the inside of the cruiser.''

I finally felt relaxed. The die was cast. Rhodan had begun to take over with his usual drive. He was already thinking of things that hadn't occurred to me yet at the moment. Naturally, if the Brain should be destroyed, about 100,000 warships would be incapacitated. Unless we acted first, anybody would be able to take them in tow without resistance.

''If!'' said my logic sector again. I lost track of how many times it had used this word in recent days.

Two hours later the towering buildings that housed the facilities of Solar Defense and Intelligence were like one big madhouse. Rhodan was too busy to be reached. He sat in a control room surrounded by at least 50 communicators. Next door to him the Fleet's General Staff was in session. I felt lost in all this hustle and bustle, which was only possible on Terra. A small but tremendously energetic stellar empire was preparing to strike a major blow. A way had been found to achieve the objective, consequently that way was followed. This was what I admired about these Terrans. Once they made a decision they never gave up until they had reached their goal.

I withdrew to my quarters. Almost hourly I was contacted by videophone for information. They wanted to know even the social status of an Arkonide captain of the rank I was to portray. A uniform tailor from Intelligence wanted my exact measurements. Weapons experts wanted to know if officers of the Arkonide fleet in those days were permitted to carry beautifully engraved private sidearms.

For 2 whole days I was busy trying to satisfy the Terrans' thirst for knowledge. But I became increasingly impressed with the feeling that I was dealing with realists rather than visionaries. These men were experts and specialists who considered details which ordinarily wouldn't have been thought of.

Then at last I fell to waiting again. However, I avoided any attempt to influence Rhodan's decisions with any advice of my own. There was still time for that should anything occur to me that might be significant.

3/ THEFT OF THE EPOTRON

Event was heaped upon event until it was time to go. We were accompanied by the simulated *Sotala* as we took off in the Ironduke to pay the Ruling Council of Akon an official "courtesy call". The deputy commander of the Arkonide cruiser was Maj. Heintz, a cosmonautics expert from Solar Intelligence. His crew consisted of 750 men as was the custom on heavy cruisers of the Imperium. In those days we still had sufficient manpower because the degeneration of the ruling race had only just begun.

It was only later that I and Rhodan were to transfer to the cruiser along with Jefe Claudrin and several other staff officers from the *Ironduke*. Our special equipment was already on board the *Sotala*, such as our uniforms, documents, weapons and whatever went with them.

The *Ironduke* proceeded in direct linear flight to the near center of the galaxy where we sent out a message to the Ruling Council. The giant blue sun of Akon, whose 5th planet was the home world of the Akons, had already illuminated our viewscreens when the answering dispatch was received.

Within 10 hours Claudrin started his braking maneuvers and once more I had an opportunity to admire the beauty of Akon 5. Rhodan had named it Sphynx altho the natives referred to it as Drorah.

The reception by several delegates from the Council had been noticeably cool. We were happy to withdraw to the Terran commercial base where almost all the members of the Mutant Corps had assembled.

Two days were taken up with festivities and inspection tours. The Akons had no choice but to show a proper amount of attentiveness to the ruling chief of the Solar Imperium but at the same time it became increasingly evident that the members of the Ruling Council were supporters of the Arkonide rebels. They had given me to understand that my presence on Sphynx could be tolerated for the moment but that it would be in the best interests of their relationship with the new Imperator for me to cut my visit short.

The radio monitoring station at our base had intercepted several hypercom dispatches and decoded them. My successor, Minterol I, was advised that my appearance on Sphynx was unfortunately something that could not very well be hindered, inasmuch as I was in the "retinue" of the Terrans' Chief of State.

I was no longer concerned about what they thought of me or what conclusions they might draw. I knew that the *Sotala* was waiting for us at a distance of 10,000 light-years in an almost unknown sector of space. All that remained was for us to steal the time converter.

The mutants had made all the necessary preparations. Rhodan had just returned an hour before from another reception and now he was relaxing in a contour chair while he listened to a report from Corps Chief John Marshall.

Mousebeaver Pucky had gone on a mission with the mutant Kitai Ishibashi, by means of teleportation. It was the latter's assignment to "prepare" the 4 Akon scientists. Ishibashi's talent enabled him to use a kind of remote hypnosis to force his will upon other individuals. The resulting mental block or suggestion was hardly noticeable but of long duration. To this extent everything had been done to enable us to "appropriate" the secret device. However, a few problematical items still had to be clarified.

The so-called trading settlement was actually a modern and fully equipped base for Solar Intelligence. On

the viewscreens the structures of the main spaceport of
Sphynx were discernible. After Perry Rhodan's discovery of the Blue System the Akons had been forced to
take up space flight again. Now as before, however,
they still managed their interstellar traffic by means of
gigantic matter transmitters, altho these were not adequate in a military sense. It had not been too difficult for
Rhodan and the Terran Fleet to overcome the system's
defenses—after due provocation—and to destroy the
satellite power stations. After that the system-wide blue
defense screen had ceased to exist.

The Akons had clearly recognized the fact that in
spite of their perfected transport technology they would
not be able to have any role in galactic affairs unless
they built up their space travel once more. Doubtlessly
they wouldn't have been so peaceful if they had been
able to call in 10,000 warships to their aid. The Terrans
were considered to be intruders. I well knew their
opinion of me, the former ruler of a rebellious colonial
race. By Akon values the Arkonides were degenerate
savages, comparable to galactic vermin, undeserving
of notice.

It was calm and peaceful at the city's new spaceport.
There were no robotships of the Regent's fleet to be
seen. Merchant ships of other races were not allowed to
land. The Akons maintained a zealous surveillance of
their zone of influence which included an unknown
number of colonial worlds. All such planets were contacted and supplied exclusively with the help of the
giant transmitters. They had set up a communications
system which had functioned well until Rhodan discovered the Blue System.

He had startled the Akons out of their calm compla-
cency and now we were feeling the effects of it. The
Terran agents had informed us that the Ruling Council
maintained relations with the rebels on Arkon. A few

months before this, that fact had been denied, but meanwhile conditions had changed.

Rhodan had followed my gaze and become pensive. "It looks quite deserted out there. In a few years it will be swarming with spaceships of every type and description. The Akon ship-building industry will soon be on its way. Considering the high state of science and technology here I'd say we can expect to see some pretty sensational products."

"We won't have to wait for that, sir," interjected Marshall. "They are already setting their trap for us. Imperator Minterol has been officially recognized. Of course they know he's only a shadow figure. Our latest investigations have revealed that the Akon government has sent scientific teams to Arkon. Guerilla actions have come to a stop. Within a few months the Regent will be so completely reprogrammed that it will be nothing more than a super computer, stripped of all command functions. This will enable the Akons to become the first nation in the galaxy. They are already making preparations for taking over the Regent's fleet. The new shipyards represent a heavy expenditure but their chief purpose is to convert the robotships. Things are getting serious, sir."

Rhodan got to his feet. Bordering the territorial region of the Terran settlement the gleaming force lines of the energy screen could be seen. Our hypersensors were reacting continuously. The Akon long-range transmitters were functioning again.

"They're sending crews to Arkon and the Brain is allowing it," remarked Rhodan. "Well, John, what have you accomplished? 'Operation Last Ditch' is becoming critical."

I observed the *Ironduke* with interest. It was parked in the port sector, which still belonged to the Terran sphere of influence. Jefe Claudrin and the crew were on board. The big warship was in battle readiness. There was still no space vessel on the planets of the Blue System that could have offered it any resistance. The few smaller spaceships of the Akon Energy Command had been destroyed in December of 2102. At that time we knew that the Akons would not take such a blow lying down. On the other hand we had counted on a breathing space of at least 30 years. Even with the Akon state of technology a major fleet-building program could not be realized earlier.

But now thanks to my rebellious countrymen they had found a better way. The Imperium possessed about 100,000 modern robot units which could be quickly converted for human crews. It was a diabolical plan which was characteristic of the Akons.

Marshall's strategic report was brief. All that was still necessary was to tie down the final details. "The time converter is located at Impton. Akon pride in the accomplishments of their ancestors has led to the erection of a museum city which is called Impton in honor of a famous physicist. The device is cubical and measures 8.3 meters on each side. It rests on a platform that is 5 meters high, which contains the power plant. The latter consists of high-powered reactors of an alien design. A fusion principle is used in it which could not be simulated by present-day Akon scientists. Its power capacity is an unknown factor but we estimate it to be about 50 million kw."

I was impressed. Such power outputs were not unusual, in fact quite commonplace on board the major spaceships, but in such a relatively small machine this was enormous.

"The museum town is closed off by energy barriers and the air space is closely monitored. The only way to take the machine is by putting it to work. That is, the mutants will have to get in unobserved and turn it on.

The museum complex was built around 3000 years ago, so we'll have to go back about 4000 years where we'll probably be in an open area. We'll have to bring anti-grav transporters with us. In the converter field we'll be able to move the time-phaser to the place where 4000 years later the Terran trading base is located. That way we'll have the machine right here. The museum has to be destroyed by means of a nuclear explosion—which will help to explain the sudden disappearance of the time converter."

"How will it be accomplished?" asked Rhodan.

"A special commando detail is standing by. For several days now the Akon service posts have been informed that unknown agents have been wanting to get into Impton to study the products of the ancient Akons. Moreover, according to local security officials, the Terrans are suspected of having something to do with it."

"No wonder!" I muttered aloud to myself.

Rhodan chuckled.

After checking his watch, Marshall continued. "The scientists who are familiar with the operation of the time-converter will arrive punctually. Kitai is already at work on them. And that's about it, sir."

I looked about me. The tracking room looked like a military encampment except that the warriors present were not carrying swords and spears. They were equipped with the most modern energy weapons in the Milky Way. I wore a Terran uniform and my white-blond Arkonide hair was concealed by a radio helmet. The best experts of Terra were poised on the threshold of a mission which could decide the fate of the Solar System.

It was beginning to get dark. The blue sun of the system sank behind the horizon. The dense maze of stars here in the center of the galaxy appeared so suddenly that it seemed an invisible hand had raised a cosmic curtain.

"Synchronize your watches," said Rhodan. "The scientists will arrive in 2 hours."

My extra-brain was bothering me again. Undoubtedly the men here had worked very thoroughly but nevertheless I was apprehensive. The whole plan was somewhat too bold, especially since nobody could say what the effects of a time-displacement would be. Even if everything succeeded, could the theft of the machine be covered by an explosion so cleverly that no one would guess the truth?

I learned later that I had underestimated Mercant once more. This man knew how to play a double game behind the scenes. It had been an ingenious idea to inform the Akon defense posts of the activity of the Terran agents.

*   *   *   *

The commando detail consisted of 20 men who were led by the telepath John Marshall. Rhodan and I were the last to make the jump. Our teleporters were Pucky and Tako Kakuta. The gravity neutralizer had already gone ahead of us. The combined powers of 3 teleporters had been necessary to bring it to the museum city.

We were wearing Terran combat suits which had been designed after the Arkonide pattern except that the Earthmen had built in some improvements. For example the deflector screens were no longer detectable by instruments because the energy radiations were damped by special absorbers.

Pucky was looking at me with his loyal hound-dog eyes. "Are you nervous?" he asked in his shrill little voice.

"What else would he be?" Rhodan cut in, sounding more harsh than he intended.

The little fellow wrinkled his mouselike snout in an obvious expression of injury.. "Why is everybody so uptight? We got here safely, didn't we? Sure the Akons have set up extra guard details and they even have snooper gadgets at every entrance but there are a thousand rooms alone in the physical section of the museum. They can't all be watched at once, you know."

"How about the room where the converter is located? Is that strongly guarded?"

"No more and no less than others. They probably think we wouldn't know what to do with the machine if we had it."

"They'll soon change their minds about that," commented Rhodan. "Are you ready, Atlan?"

I nodded and bent down to take up Pucky into my arms. He wore a custom-made combatsuit that even accommodated his tail. The little fellow patted my nose. We understood each other.

Moments later came the sensation of dematerialization. It was the same as ever. Before I could fully register the pulling pain of teleportation I arrived at my destination. Automatically I turned on my deflector field and the micro-reactor responded soundlessly. Pucky still clung to me but he was the only living thing I could see at the moment. The other men of the commando detail who were present were already under the protection of their screens. They were invisible.

My pulse raced almost audibly. In this empty-seeming stillness the weapon in my hand appeared a bit ludicrous. I holstered it and looked around. We had landed in a giant hall that was filled with machinery and equipment that was strange to me. However, all items were provided with nameplates in ancient Arkonide, explaining what each had been used for.

"Use your absorption filter," whispered Pucky.

I reached up to my helmet and swung down the special viewing device. Without affecting normal vision it eliminated the optical effects of the deflector screens. Now I could see the other men who had deployed themselves in a semi-circle in front of an arched doorway.

I carefully placed Pucky on the floor. Ras Tschubai and the third teleporter of the Corps, Tako Kakuta, were beckoning to us. Rhodan moved silently to Marshall, who was standing by an oblong machine. We communicated only by signs and gestures. As for our mutant ''seer''—Wuriu Sengu was standing before the partition wall that separated us from the adjacent room. It was there that the converter had been installed. Films previously taken by the mutants indicated that the device had been given a special location. The room was comparatively small and contained no other displays of equipment.

Sengu concentrated his gaze on the wall. The illumination from the few glow tubes on the ceiling seemed to disturb him. After a few moments he raised his hand. His 4 outstretched fingers told us that Akon security had posted a stronger guard than expected around this device which was probably the most valued legacy of their ancestors.

Pucky nudged me. Before I joined Rhodan I noted that the mousebeaver had vanished along with the other teleporters. They had gotten their orders to go fetch the 4 scientists who were familiar with the converter. If everything had gone according to plan, these men would be meeting together about now in order to discuss some things that Ishibashi had previously suggested to them.

What we had in mind wasn't especially difficult when regarded from the purely practical side; however, the psychological factors involved were by far more important. We had to avoid letting anyone know that the machine had actually disappeared. Otherwise conclusions as to our further intent would be inevitable.

A second "psycho-point", as John Marshall called it, was the 4 scientists. Solar Intelligence had decided to bring them into the museum by force. Their abduction was to be made known to the Akon secret service as soon as the machine was ready to operate. For this purpose it had been arranged for Marshall to be in telepathiccontact with a mutant waiting on the outside. The result of such a "tipoff" from unknown sources would be an immediate occupation of the museum area. By that time we should have disappeared with the machine but special combat robots would start a mock battle, during which the nuclear explosion would occur.

It was a complicated plan. It contained many elements of danger that we had to consider. Above all, the abduction of the 4 scientists must not be discovered prematurely. They were presently meeting in the country home of a physicist named Artol of Penoral. There they were to be overpowered and teleported secretly to the museum site.

Perry pointed to the interconnecting passageway. We heard a loud, commanding voice. Another voice answered.

Marshall gave us a signal. It was apparent that he had picked up the thoughts of the Akons. "The guards have permission to fire on sight," he whispered. "The tipoff strategy is working."

Rhodan checked his shock-gun. We were not to make our move until the scientists were on hand. Without their help the use of the time-phaser would be impossible. The second hand of my watch seemed to have stopped. As always in such situations, time stood still.

A red-headed sergeant moved carefully to the arched doorway. Sengu passed him a small diagram which indicated the position of the Akon sentinels. Other specialists of the commando group examined their sensor and tracking devices. Beyond the intervening wall there were no signs of a surprise buildup of energy, as in preparation for an attack. They actually seemed not to expect a move in the direction of the time-phasing machine.

It was another 20 minutes before the teleporters appeared. In 2 separate jumps they brought the scientists along with Kitai Ishibashi, whose suggestive influence had made the Akons think that their arrival here was quite normal and proper.

When Tako Kakuta approached us the soles of his boots were squeaking. It was hardly audible and yet it seemed to me that it could be heard in every room of the museum. Rhodan raised a hand and Kakuta paused long enough to wipe his soles with a cloth. Evidently he had come in contact with some kind of wax material used in floor maintenance.

When he moved again his footsteps were as silent as those of the other men. "Sorry!" he whispered. "The kidnaping worked out alright. Betty Toufry has been advised. We can begin."

I observed the Akons more closely. They were wearing robelike shoulder capes as a sign of their dignified stations. There was still a slightly blank expression in their eyes, which would soon change, however. I was wondering if a total suggestive block in their minds might not have undesirable repercussions. If these experts did not operate the controls correctly the whole mission would be unfeasible. The only thing left would be flight.

Rhodan came out from behind the machine where he and Marshall had been standing. His signal sent the commando detail into action. I joined Marshall as we entered the adjacent hall. It was a large, vaulted room which contained the strangest apparatus I had ever seen. It was a large cube resting on a platform that was several meters high. On one side of this square "foundation" there was a built-in staircase. Nearby a steel door could be seen which gave entrance into the power room beneath the assembly.

When I looked about for the guards I saw two of them standing at the other entrance. One was crouched down at the staircase but the fourth man was so close to me that I could have touched him.

The Terrans operated smoothly and soundlessly. A team of two attacked each sentry and prevented him from crying out, while a third man pressed an anesthesia mask over his face. Finally the unconscious Akons were placed in deep sleep by a doctor.

Once more no word was spoken aloud. Kitai Ishibashi had the scientists fully under his control. I could imagine the challenge it must have been for his paramental faculties to force them to disregard the surrounding circumstances. They were under the impression that they had come here of their own free will to carry out an experiment that had been authorized by the Ruling Council. They moved with the assurance of men who were being escorted by the highest of official dignitaries.

Moreover they did not speak with one another. Marshall and Pucky led them over to the machine. One of the Akons—it was Artol of Penoral—extracted a code-signal device from his pocket and inactivated the energy screen that surrounded the machine. I nodded appreciatively. The Terrans had thought of everything. How quickly a plan like ours could go wrong because of details like this.

I remained in the hall until the intricately worked-out

steps had run their course. The technicians came in with the powerful grav-neutralizer and anchored it magnetically to the converter floor plates. Twenty robots took up positions at the entrances. They were armed with heavy energy weapons. Their special programming was equivalent to a kamikaze assignment. They were to hold the site until we had disappeared with the time-phaser and then the bomb was to explode. For Rhodan the 20 robots were a small price to pay when the salvation of the Earth was at stake.

Only a few commandos remained outside. I went up the stairs of the machine and passed thru an airlock. I heard voices in the connecting passage. John Marshall was briefing his men.

"This way, sir," said the red-haired sergeant. "Please turn off your deflector screen."

I depressed the control button and the hum of the projector died away. When I shoved up my filter I could again see quite normally. The passage led to the control room which was additionally secured by hermetic hatches. This was also a cubically-shaped room which was filled with a maze of equipment of every description. Not too much room was available for extra personnel.

No one paid any attention to me so I drew back into a protected angle between 2 triangular viewscreens where I was able to watch the operations of the Akons. Apparently they had no intention of violating Ishibashi's instructions. Moreover, they really seemed to be familiar with the intricate controls.

When I heard the machine start to hum, my extra-brain immediately sent me a warning signal.

"I'd hold off with that until the Akons attack," I said aloud. "They could get an energy trace on us."

Rhodan nodded and ordered the machine to be turned down again. Ishibashi passed the order along to the

Akons. Moments later a telepathic message was received. Marshall and Pucky detected it simultaneously.

"It's Betty calling us," said the little one. "The local security boys have found out about the kidnaped scientists. Airborne commandos are on their way. Red alert for the museum town."

He had not quite finished speaking before we heard a racket outside. It was the typical thundering of impulse weapons. Rhodan looked at his watch. The scientists were finally allowed to speak and they began at once to discuss the problems of activating the time field. I only understood a fraction of the conversation. They thought that Kitai was the chairman of the Ruling Council but they took no heed of the commando troops.

Outside we heard the sounds of heavy firing. The rumbling of the powerful robot weapons indicated that the Akon defenders had responded as we had expected.

"Get ready!" Rhodan called out. "Ras, go plant the bomb."

The swarthy-skinned Terran nodded. Around his neck was suspended a micro-bomb of Earthly design. Ras Tschubai dematerialized. When he came back he told us he had planted the device outside the hall in an adjacent chamber. This time I looked at my own watch. We still had 10 minutes. The robots would have to hold their line until then.

Out hypno-mutant was very silent. I was worried about the drops of sweat that had appeared on his forehead during the past few minutes. Unquestionably it must be a terrible strain on him to keep the 4 Akons continuously under his mental control.

"Activate!" said Perry almost too swiftly. "Have them build up the phaser field so that it just encloses the machine."

The last of the commando troops came on board. The hatches closed automatically. Under our feet the nuclear pile of the power plant came to life. The indicator needles began to rise on the scales. I was more or less familiar with such power controls since the same kind of arrangement had been used on the old Arkonide spaceships. I noted that the reactors were only operating at 2% of their capacity. The physicist Artol appeared to be the leader of his group. We could all hear his instructions but for the most part he was explaining things that we could only grasp by using our imaginations.

"Speed it up!" urged Rhodan. His blanched face revealed the extent of his inner turmoil.

I attempted to monitor the activity of the Akons. The power step-up control of the converter was operated by contact buttons. So far only the power plant itself had been fired up. Current feed for a field projector, regardless of what kind, had a much different sound.

Kitai suddenly groped about for support. I leapt forward, pushing a Terran technician out of the way, and grasped the slightly-built mutant under his arms. Marshall saw what was going on and understood.

I was waiting for something that I could neither explain nor even estimate. A displacement or conversion of the applicable time lines was so much to conceive of that the brain failed to produce the normal thinking processes for comprehension. All I could do was struggle for some mental image that might reasonably match the situation that was to come.

When the phaser field came on, the converter did not move from its position. This meant that many things were happening in the same place but separated by different planes of reference. The determining factor here, however, was time rather than distance.

Ishibashi groaned. I gripped him more firmly but his glassy-eyed look told me he had reached the end of his stamina. He had been working for days to produce the suggestive mental block in his subjects. If he should collapse now there was no telling what the Akons would do. Naturally we could force them by other means. The only question was, how long would we have to do it to keep them tractable for our purposes.

The humming of the power plant irritated me. It was a steady, monotonous sound—too normal, in fact, to indicate the technical wonder we were anticipating. Rhodan was bending over the shoulders of the Akons while they concentrated on their control panels. The viewscreens were functioning by now, revealing both the outside world and the machine itself.

"Pucky!" said Rhodan suddenly. "Get ready to dispose of that bomb!"

This startled me as I realized the demolition device would explode in 2 minutes. If we hadn't pulled out of the present time frame by then we could be caught in a fire of annihilation.

"Hold on another minute," Marshall interjected. "Jump within 30 seconds of ignition."

The red-haired sergeant pointedly checked his impulse beamer. Breaking out of the museum could bring on a catastrophe. It would precipitate incalculable political complications. If only one wounded Terran should be found here it would mean more than a lost battle for Rhodan.

The mousebeaver was standing beside me. Kitai's knees began to tremble. Outside we could hear the thunder of the robots' weapons. Mingled with this were frequent bursts of metallic sounds, usually followed by an explosion. It was obvious that our combat machines were being shot down. It had only been intended that they would have to provide a brief holding action. The fighting force had been adequate for our planned schedule except that by now we should have vanished from the present time plane.

"Pucky . . . !"

The little one glanced at Rhodan. In 5 seconds it would be time for his teleport jump. Everyone stared at him entranced as he concentrated—except for myself. My attention was occupied by Kitai, who slumped against my chest.

But in that instance I happened to see the viewscreens. The battling robots had disappeared from view while under my feet I felt and heard the rumbling of another apparatus.

Without thinking I cried out: "Stop—come back! We're pulling out. Stay here, Pucky!"

I shoved the mutant into Marshall's arms and sprang forward. The Akons were busy discussing their work, apparently fascinated by what was happening to the machine. Artol of Penoral was bent forward intensely concentrating on a circular screen above the controls of the phaser field. I reached the mousebeaver just as he came out of his fixation but I jerked him off his feet and shook him roughly.

"Snap out of it!" I shouted. "Pucky, don't jump—it would be the end of you!"

Pucky understood. Without a word he leaned his head on my shoulder and closed his eyes. I realized that even mousebeavers have nervous systems.

By now Ishibashi was lying on the floor and the medico of our commando team was taking care of him. Rhodan and the other mutants were watching the scientists. Apparently their mental blocks were very deepseated because they had not yet become aware of Kitai's withdrawal.

"Can they come out of their trance?" asked Rhodan quickly.

Our other hypno mutant, Andre Noir, seemed calm about it. "Kitai did his work well. They still don't know what's going on here. If they start to get edgy I'll move in on them. No sweat, sir."

I couldn't take my eyes from the viewscreens. The bomb must have detonated a minute or so ago but we had not felt any repercussions from it. It was hard to imagine that the exhibit hall that we were looking at as tho in a fast-motion film had already been destroyed.

I finally followed Artol's gaze. The digital counter over the control panel seemed to be measuring the rate of reversal of relative time. It was impossible to read the flickering numbers, however, to determine how many years we had returned into the past.

Within a few moments my logic sector reacted. It reminded me that the impression of "time travel" was confusing and false. The counter was only measuring the increasing strength of the phaser field. But somewhere there would have to be a synchronously operating device to convert that indication into equivalent years of time. When I shared this thought with Rhodan we soon found the computer that was doing this work. It stood behind me. We'd have to figure out the schematics later. Apparently Artol could read them and interpret the output data.

The pictures on the screens were changing in such rapid succession that we could hardly distinguish one from the other. It was like a runaway film. The cultural periods were rolling past while the exhibit hall remained unchanged.

Then suddenly it was gone. We saw open country that was bordered to the north by a long stretch of forest. We had reached a time period when the museum town of Impton had not yet come into being. A bell sounded. The maximum power of the phaser field was being held constant by an automatic program control. It meant that we had come to a "stop". I awoke as if from a dream. Rhodan kept looking at the screens.

"Success, Your Eminence," said Artol. But his eyes were still glazed and vacant looking. Andre nodded to me. I realized that Kitai's suggestive block was stronger than we had anticipated.

I stepped forward since I spoke the ancient Arkonide language better than the Terrans. Apparently the physicist was now considering me to be the chairman of the Council.

"Hold the machine steady where it is," I said. "How big is the radius of the phaser field?"

"20 meters, Excellence. It only encloses the *epotron*."

I realized this was the Arkonide name for the machine. "Is it possible to go out on the platform without being exposed to any danger?"

"Yes, it's possible but it would be advantageous to intensify the phaser field in that case."

"Why?"

The scientist seemed strangely reserved. "You have the research data, Your Eminence," he replied.

Rhodan cleared his throat warningly. I did not follow up the remark. Naturally, Artol would have prepared and submitted the results of his studies. I knew it would be useless to bring him out of his state of hypnosis.

Andre pressed me aside. "I'll take over," he whispered. "Get on with the transport operation."

I followed Rhodan, who was already at the outer airlock. Certainly the atmospheric conditions of the planet Sphynx could be no worse than those of our own "present" time. We could open the outer hatch without any special preparations. When we stepped out onto the platform we experienced something that it took me a few seconds to analyze.

"Illogical!" warned my extra-brain. *"Something is not right. If the phasing field's radius is so limited—how is it that you don't see the surroundings of your own time frame beyond its effective range?"*

I grasped Rhodan's arm. My logic sector was right! When I told him my thoughts he cleared his throat as if embarrassed.

"This is over my head," he answered. "We should have brought Kalup along. I would presume that a person inside the field could not see the normal world."

"Especially when the field only encompasses a fraction of the other time plane. Perry, this disturbs me. We were told this wasn't to be a regular trip thru time —merely a distortion of the reference point. I imagine I'm seeing everything that exists within the distortion zone. What lies beyond it should either not be seen or it should be only shadowy and vague. Actually what we should be seeing out there is our *own* plane of time!"

If the other men were as confused as I was they didn't show it. They were only concerned about the antigrav transporter which had apparently come thru the strange journey unharmed.

"We'll discuss it later," said Rhodan, changing the subject. "Right now what we have to do first is to get this thing to the *Ironduke*."

I withdrew and strolled around the platform. To the east of our real position lay the museum town—that is, in our own time reference. In that sense one could say that we were in the exhibit hall which had already been ripped asunder by the nuclear bomb.

"Enough to drive you donk," commented Pucky.

I turned to see the little fellow standing at the top of the stairs. He was looking down uncertainly. Directly before us was a growth of Akon air-root trees. Far and wide, no one was to be seen.

"If I had my druthers, Atlan, I'd take a jump right

now," he said. "Then we'd really know what it looks like out there."

"That you will not do."

"I could make it." The little fellow's incisor tooth gleamed enterprisingly.

Wordlessly I took his hand and drew him back from the stairs. If I myself couldn't understand what physical laws were affecting us at the moment I could at least imagine the consequences of suddenly leaving the phaser zone.

The commando troops had taken up defensive positions along the edges of the platform. Their weapons bristled menacingly. The technicians activated the antigrav transporter and adjusted its field to the mass of the converter machine.

"Whether or not it'll bear up under the phaser field we'll soon find out," said a young engineer almost indifferently.

Rhodan was listening at the entrance passage. He had sent somebody back inside to keep an eye on the scientists. They were still under the impression that they were carrying out an authorized experiment.

An unexpected jolt threw me to the deck of the platform. I clung to the railing and waited. The transformer bank of the antigrav was in an uproar. The time-phaser lifted uncertainly from the ground, reeling and jerking, finally hovering at an elevation of 3 meters while the antigrav took its measure. I remained lying in the same position altho I turned on my back to look over at Rhodan. His features were trembling visibly with agitation and then I knew that someone had miscalculated. The antigrav field was just barely sufficient to neutralize the weight of the machine.

I waited patiently until our 2 small propulsion units started whistling. Their base plates had been welded to the platform. The converter slowly began to move. I didn't try to calculate the effects of the air resistance nor did I think in terms of how fast the entire mass could move. Certainly our speed would not be very great. The propulsion units had a thrust capability of 150 kilos per unit.

It was enough for me that the whole structure moved at all. We glided around a group of low hills where a new view presented itself. The tops of high buildings could be seen beyond the horizon. The blue sun of the Akon System had just risen. It was early morning.

"Now all that's left is to make a precision landing at our own settlement in the extra-territorial zone," said Rhodan.

I laughed ironically. "All that's left . . . " How simple it sounded! Wuriu Sengu smirked but he refrained from commenting. The nervous stamina of these Terrans was astonishing. I never stopped marveling at their spirit of enterprise.

I finally got to my feet and dusted off my uniform while trying to be casual in my observation of the "non-existent" landscape. After about 10 minutes a ground vehicle put in an appearance. I waited curiously to see the reaction of its occupants. They only noticed us when we were close upon them. They looked up in surprise. Somebody shouted something I couldn't make out. Rhodan casually waved at them. We knew then that we could make contact with the inhabitants of a specific era thru the displaced time lines of the phaser.

"Those 2 men have been dead for thousands of years," said Wuriu.

I said nothing. My eyes burned as I watched their figures grow smaller in the distance. Far ahead the first of the buildings of the city rose completely above the horizon. They were considerably smaller than those of the time reference we belonged to. And of course the spaceport was not yet in existence.

We flew toward the familiar group of hills where Terran engineers had erected the trading base. The tall limestone cliffs had not changed. This was our goal. The *Ironduke* was scheduled to come back to the base in time to meet us, so we knew that if we landed exactly in a certain relationship to the hills we would be about 30 meters from the warship's nearest landing strut —that is, from where it would be located in our own time.

We were sighted twice again by the "local" inhabitants. I made a note to check Akon history to see if anything would be noted there concerning our strange advent.

Rhodan went back into the time-phaser. I remained on the platform until we sank softly to the ground. The howling of the over-burdened antigrav subsided. The men's faces had grown tense. The plan called now for an immediate return to the regular time plane. How would this come about?

The transition was so sudden that it struck me like a shockwave. I felt a painful pulling sensation while a red mist welled up before my eyes. When I could see clearly again, it was night. Above us shone the stars of the Milky Way and to our right the contours of the battleship loomed into the sky.

A blood-red nuclear flare illumined the horizon. Our bomb! Rhodan joined me. Shadowy figures rushed toward us. They were troops from the *Ironduke*. Colonel Claudrin was the first to pound his way up the staircase, which trembled under the Epsalian's weight.

As usual his voice was thunderous. I groped my way toward him and stretched out my hand. He shoved his weapon into its holster and gripped me. A sudden pain shot thru me. When this giant shook hands with enthusiasm it could be felt.

"Relax, sir," he said. "You'll have to excuse me

but I thought I should let you know for sure that you're back here again.''

"It's been a mad dream," commented Rhodan. "You'd better give me the same treatment, Jefe." I had to laugh when the tall Terran sank to his knees with a groan. "Alright! Don't overdo it!''

The warship's commander desisted at last. "You're ahead of schedule, sir. We figured you'd be an hour yet getting back. About an hour ago the Akon guard patrol wanted to talk to you. I held them off—and then the bomb hit.''

"When it happened, Jefe, we were about 4000 years in the past," I told him. "So you say we've hit the bullseye? No time displacement? Our preparations for departure took about 30 minutes. I'd say that the flight itself lasted about 45 minutes.''

"That fits the picture exactly, sir. It proves that when the field is shut off there's an immediate return to the true plane of reference. So timing of operations on our side can take that into account. From that standpoint there's no danger. Knowing that, you can't ever go wrong.''

Somebody shouted. When I turned around I caught sight of a slender figure darting out of the sliding hatchway. The lock door closed again with a dull thud and the light from inside was cut off. Sengu had just come out of the inner chamber of the time-phaser. He spoke in a calm and objective manner. "The 4 scientists have pulled out of their trance, sir. What are your instructions?''

Rhodan pondered swiftly. Men were moving about under the giant spherical hull of the ship in the darkness. The cargo lock slid open. It was big enough to have taken in 2 converters. Everything was carried out silently and under cover of the night. Rhodan delayed answering until somebody announced that the ship's tractor beam was ready. Now it would be easy to handle the mass of the machine.

"Make an official arrest," he finally ordered. "Bring them into the *Ironduke.*"

"Arrest—?!" I echoed in surprise.

"That's right—it's an arrest," he confirmed. "Intelligence information indicates that the physicist Artol of Penoral had a great deal to do with the reprogramming of the robot Regent. That means he violated the non-aggression pact between Terra and the Akon Empire."

"He was only following orders, Perry."

"Probably, but that doesn't change my position in the matter. The other 3 scientists were pretty high up in the Blue System and they also had their hands in the operation. Carry out my instructions, Col. Claudrin."

As Rhodan turned away my extra-brain came thru to me again: *"Fool! Is that so important—when the existence of an entire race is at stake?"*

I looked around uneasily as if the admonishment might have been overheard. Then I hastily got off the platform. The machine was grappled by the loading equipment and drawn into the lower cargo hold of the *Ironduke.*

"Let's go," cried Pucky. "Some class, eh? Man, was that ever a caper we pulled!"

The mousebeaver emitted a shrill chuckle. I went with him to the ground-lock entrance. The arching hull above us blocked out the starry firmament. The only lingering sign of strange happenings was the red glow hanging over the museum town of Impton. What had become of the people we had seen back there 4000 years ago?

4000 years? For me it had been but a moment. I shuddered at the thought of this machine, which was to be my means of destroying the robot Regent.

4/ AURIS CROSSES THE LINE

She had arrived 15 minutes earlier in an aircar and she had quietly spoken to the officer of the watch, requesting an audience with Perry Rhodan. We had no other choice but to invite the young woman into the Control Central of the battleship. And now she stood before us.

Auris of Las Toor fascinated me. Her dark eyes contrasted with the coppery red of her hair. It seemed to me that she had seen thru some of our actions. Naturally she had no proof but that was a mere superfluity. She knew the Terrans and she knew Perry Rhodan. Auris suspected that there was a definite connection between our sudden arrival and the events in the museum city. She wore the 2-piece uniform of the Akon Energy Command. But her billowing shoulder cape was an indication of her distinguished position as a scientist among a great race of advanced people.

Perry looked at me imploringly. This ingenious man became somewhat uncertain in the presence of women, especially when such a beautiful woman was involved. Auris was not only beautiful but very intelligent. I knew that she harbored certain strong sympathies for Perry. She had only favored me with a smile, to which I responded with a courtly bow.

She frowned slightly in some surprise at this customary Terran form of courtesy, to which I replied ironically: "For those who are merely tolerated it's fitting that they should adopt the customs of their host. I trust you will forgive me."

She had only nodded to me while declining the invitation to be seated in one of the form chairs. The

personnel of the Control Central had withdrawn from
our vicinity. The only ones remaining with us were
Col. Claudrin and John Marshall. I was disturbed when
I noted the barely perceptible quivering of her nostrils.
The satin-brown skin over her high cheekbones had
paled under tension. Auris of Las Toor was not making
a routine courtesy call.

When she brushed back her voluminous hair it was as
if she had made a decision. She apparently refused to
continue with this vapid form of conversation. Rhodan
felt himself under sharp surveillance. He cleared his
throat uncomfortably but manned the ramparts of his
emotions behind a cold mask of indifference. He
passed me a look that urged me to take the lead in the
conversation.

My mind raced for a few seconds until I perceived
only one way of getting Perry off of a hot spot. Winking
surreptitiously at Claudrin, I stepped forward. I noted
at the same time that Auris was only a few centimeters
shorter than I.

"Welcome on board my ship, Your Eminence—or
may I call you Auris?"

She looked at me for a long moment. Her young lips
trembled slightly. Colonel Oberst caught on in time to
suppress a surprised reaction.

"Are you the commander, Excellency?" she asked.
"Or may I call you Atlan?"

I smiled at her. "I request that you do so, Auris. Yes,
I am the commander of this battleship as well as
commander-in-chief of the Solar Fleet's 480th battle
cruiser task force. Your visit comes at an unexpected
hour. Unfortunately I must advise you that we are
taking off in 15 minutes."

"That's a matter for the First Administrator to decide."

Rhodan avoided her gaze. "My orders stand," he

said. "I am urgently required to return home. According to Terran custom it is not my place to influence the decisions of a unit chief and ship's commander. I am a guest here, nothing more."

She still managed to control herself. I looked at her more closely and noticed again how desirable she was. When our eyes met she abruptly changed the subject and came to the point of her visit.

"Alright, then carry on with your schedule. But first I must request that you free my uncle along with his 3 assistants, and that you unload a certain piece of equipment. In which case I will pledge myself to silence regarding this situation. I have considerable influence with the members of the Ruling Council."

Rhodan raised his brows deliberately in surprise. I looked about me in feigned wonderment.

"How is that? I don't believe anyone here understands what you're saying."

She remained self-controlled. "I thought as much. My uncle is the hyper-physicist Artol of Penoral. The device I mentioned has presumably been destroyed in an atomic explosion. I have come here alone without the knowledge of the proper defense authorities in order to avoid complications on both sides. Or do you perhaps assume that I regard these happenings as mere coincidence? The reason for your landing on Drorah is quite apparent."

"I still fail to understand you, Auris."

She tried to bypass me. "I'd like very much to negotiate this with the Administrator."

"Admiral Atlan has my fullest confidence," Perry interjected.

Her eyes darkened in anger and alarm. I looked over at Marshall, who was monitoring the conversation with his paranormal faculties. He seemed to catch his breath tensely when she touched her wrist just a bit too incon-

spicuously to adjust a bracelet. Rhodan suddenly
tensed also but I forced myself to be calm. Appearing to
be merely pensive I went up to her so closely that I
caught the seductive scent of her hair.

Without saying a word I grasped her hand and
banged it against the cabinet of a computer console.
The bracelet shattered and fell from her wrist. I was
indifferent to her outcry because I knew the blow had
not been painful.

Rhodan bent down and retrieved the broad-banded
piece of jewelry. Auris leaned back against the bulkhead, pale and trembling. I waited, knowing well that
my expression was anything but friendly now. I heard a
tinkling sound and turned to see Rhodan bending open
the precious metal casing of the bracelet. A crevice was
revealed in which there were micro-elements of an
electronic nature.

"Not bad," he said. "You should have activated the
transmitter immediately, Auris."

"Barbarian!" she fumed at him. "I wish to leave
now!"

I took the camouflaged device and examined it. It
was a high-powered transmitter. I next checked my
watch but before I could say anything Rhodan took the
initiative.

"Col. Claudrin—you are cleared for emergency
takeoff. Advise the Akon Energy Central. Tell them to
open the screen. Auris of Las Toor remains here."

He gave us an impersonal nod and strode over to the
armorplate entrance hatch. The *Ironduke* was filled
with the howl of sirens. Crewmen ran to their stations.
Three minutes later the machinery was warming up.
During this time I was standing beside the young
woman who had made no effort to resist Rhodan's
decision. Nor was there anything left to conceal from
her. She had seen thru our plan.

"I'm sorry, Auris. You will have to go with us. But it's not the firsttime, is it? The lasttime we were your guests so now we have the honor to offer our hospitality to a bewitching young lady."

She governed herself in an exemplary manner. Only the paleness of her cheeks revealed her inner turmoil. "You are going too far, Atlan! The Ruling Council suspects you of having stolen the time-phaser. There are storm clouds on the political horizon which are straining to the breaking point."

I considered her declaration to be honest and forthright until I caught Marshall's derisive expression. Apparently he had been able to break thru the Akon woman's natural mental screen.

"I must inform you," he said, "that *no one* suspects us of having brought the machine into our possession. They are merely of the opinion that we wanted to penetrate the museum in order to obtain certain technological information. They believe further that they were able to apprehend our agents and that the latter were killed by the nuclear explosion. You have come here without the knowledge of either the Council or your Security forces."

"You're dreaming!"

"I'm sorry but I believe not. The purpose of your micro-transmitter was to record your conversation and to beam it out. You planned to have the discussion picked up by an automatic receiver station. After leaving the ship you were intending to use the tape to force us to hand over the phaser machine. We're grateful for your cooperation."

Now I understood! This wonderful woman had offered us a chance; or rather, she had not wished to make difficulties for Rhodan. Her face revealed her real desperation now. Her fleeting glance told me that she was looking for a way out of her predicament.

The men of the Control Central had taken their flight positions. Intelligence and Security officers were discussing Auris' presence here.

I placed a hand on her arm and whispered to her. "The stellar empire of Terra is at stake, Auris. You should realize that we can't let you go now. Your suspicion is too well-founded for us to take the risk of letting you speak with your very shrewd countrymen. They think the converter has been destroyed. Your uncle is in good health. I must ask you to resign yourself to this journey and to wait for the outcome of our operation."

She pushed my hand away as her gaze shifted to Rhodan, who was just strapping himself into the commodore's seat. "You are forcing me to be a traitor!"

"Nonsense! Besides, there's nothing you can prove. Or do you believe Perry would be agreeable to your searching the *Ironduke?*"

Marshall seemed to be reading her thoughts again. I wasn't quite sure whether or not Auris was deliberately lowering her paranormal screen so that John could perceive what she was thinking.

"A formation of warships from the Regent's fleet is approaching, sir," said the telepath. "It's advisable to make a forced takeoff."

Perry overheard it and turned to Auris with a strange smile on his lips. She tossed her hair back with a quick movement of her head and finally sat down in a form chair. I knew then that she had consciously revealed the information to John.

I cleared my throat gently and sat down next to her. "Many thanks, Auris. How was the Regent notified? Our radio monitors didn't pick up any such message."

"They sent a courier by transmitter, sir," announced

Marshall. It finally seemed to be painful for him to keep probing the young woman's wide-open thoughts.

When I gave him a signal he bowed and left us. Auris of Las Toor said nothing more. We sat there and listened to the intercom voice traffic from the sector chiefs. Rhodan made a personal contact with the Akons. They tried to detain the warship but didn't dare to do it forcefully.

Rhodan expressed his sympathies concerning events at Impton and asked if there had been any casualties. The spokesman for the Ruling Council briskly cut off the videophone contact. It was obvious they suspected Terran agent activity in the case but had not been able to pinpoint the evidence.

Minutes later the giant battleship thundered into the sky. The still glowing crater of the explosion appeared on the viewscreens. It wasn't too large. Only a minor portion of the museum city had been destroyed.

I only breathed a sigh of relief when we had gotten out of range of the Akon defense fortresses. We hurtled out into space at full acceleration, where we soon detected the entrance shockwaves of about 20 heavy-class ships. No one paid much attention to the roaring of the hypersensors. The Regent's robots had arrived too late.

Rhodan came and joined us.

Claudrin was busy preparing for linear flight. "Why didn't you relate your suspicions to Akon Intelligence, Auris?" he asked.

She stared at him silently. I gave him a sarcastic look which he also couldn't fail to catch. This Terran might be an outstanding statesman and an even better fleet commander but he understood nothing about women. He looked at me in sudden confusion and reddened visibly like a schoolboy. Then he stammered and excused himself.

When he left I chuckled softly. "He'll soon comprehend, Auris," I said to her casually. "If we hadn't discovered your wrist transmitter in time, what would have happened then?"

She lowered her gaze. Apparently she was suffering from certain pangs of remorse or a twinge of conscience but was leaving the decision to fate. She had attempted to be loyal to her people yet she had hoped that something would happen that would not corroborate her suspicions. Now I could guess why she had grasped her camouflaged wrist transmitter so quickly. It was probably true that no one knew she was on board the *Ironduke*. Rhodan had counted on it when he spoke to the chairman of the Council, since he did not mention a word about her presence. Nor was he questioned concerning Auris.

She sat there staring into a corner of the room. Altho her face was still tense I had the impression that a faint smile touched her lips. I sighed and got up. My place was with the men at the flight controls. Marshall gave me a nod. He would continue to monitor the situation.

Before I left her, however, she spoke quietly: "Atlan—who is this new Imperator?"

I stopped abruptly. Without any preamble she had reminded me of why I was here. "He's a deranged scoundrel who is being misused by Akon madmen."

"Do you believe the Imperium will collapse or fall into the wrong hands?"

"If Minterol I is not deposed—absolutely!"

"Does that mean your robot Regent has failed you?"

"Yes it does. The Brain was tampered with. And that's where your uncle played an important part. He is here on board as a prisoner of war."

"What are you planning to do with the time converter?"

I finally turned back to her. Her eyes were bright and alert. She wanted to know the truth.

"Auris, you did the right thing. If you want to keep peace in the galaxy, don't question our actions. I have decided to destroy the most ingenious creation of my ancestors. A robot that starts acting up and making mistakes isn't usable anymore. In fact the Regent has become dangerous. It has to be destroyed or the races of the Milky Way—"

"Yes, I know."

The loudspeakers announced a sighting on the tracking monitors. We were approaching the realms of relative light-speed. The echo screens of the remote scanners were showing green bogie blips. The robotships were in a retropulsion mode. A few coded pulse messages were intercepted but we were no longer concerned about them.

A few minutes later we entered semispace under the protective field envelope of the Kalup compensator. A strange, greenish sun glowed suddenly on the target screen of the para-tracker. It marked the location of an imitation cruiser of the Imperium. There the *Sotala* was waiting for us.

I slanted my seat back. Auris seemed to be brooding. Once in awhile she appeared to shudder slightly. She had given us to understand that she belonged to us.

To us? I looked across at Rhodan.

"To him, you fool!" retorted my logic sector.

I nodded involuntarily. Years had passed since Rhodan had met this young woman. Meanwhile her feelings for him had ripened. I had given up all hope of ever winning her for myself.

Finally I fell to wondering again what might have happened if the Ruling Council or Akon Security had gotten the slightest suspicion of our real activity. Without any question they would have done everything possible to block the takeoff of the *Ironduke*. So far the Terrans' mad plan had succeeded. However, I dared not think of the task ahead of me at the moment. A feeling of apprehension came over me every time I tried to imagine how the time converter would function during the *next* phase of our operation.

The engines rumbled onward. Within a few hours we would reach the *Sotala*. Then our final power move would begin.

I thought of the 4 Akon scientists on board. What conclusions would be drawn from the fact of their disappearance? Our agents on Sphynx had a hint of the possibilities but only after the physicists had already been kidnaped. Probably the general opinion was that they had died in the explosion. On the other hand, such considerations might lead to further thoughts about the time converter.

But if it were really possible to reach another time era of Arkon 3, all counteractions by the Akons would be useless. They could only hinder our attack out of no-where if they should succeed in snatching the device from us in time. At the present state of affairs the rulers of the Blue System had lost. If they did manage to arrive at the right conclusion, however, all they would be able to do was to hope for a failure of the machine.

My eyes felt damp, which was a characteristic of my race under this kind of tension. My broodings were getting me into a state of excitement which was not tolerable in view of the responsibility which faced me now. I had to force myself to remain calm and collected.

"Are you getting nervous?" inquired Auris. Her face was as expressionless as it had been when she arrived on board.

Yes, I was nervous. After all, it wasn't every day that a man prepared to meet his ancestors.

5/ THE ANCIENT HIGH COMMAND

The hypercom loudspeaker emitted a short chirping sound. It signified the reception of a coded pulse message on the special frequency band of the Arkonide Intergalactic Task Force under command of Admiral Notath.

The dispatch was addressed to Fleet High Command on Arkon 3. The call letters were not encoded. We waited until the repeat message stopped coming in. The auto-analyzer shoved the magnatape foil into the depulser unit. After serial arrangement of the input the coded message was fed to the computer in the mathematical section.

The code was known to us. The deciphering process required 12 minutes, which indicated a range of possibly 6 billion variables. My ancestors had known well how to guard their secrets.

By normal Earthly time it was the 10th of February of the year 2106. By use of the time converter we had moved back 6023 years into the past, to await the reception of our historical hypercom message. We were the only ones who knew that within 2 hours the real *Sotala* would be destroyed. We were taking its place.

It was an uncanny experience. Our converted heavy cruiser had been enveloped by a time-distortion field. The thing that was hard for me to grasp was the fact that inside this invisible and insensible mesh of forces we were able to receive a radio message which had been beamed out more than 6000 years ago from a spaceship of my ancestors.

Mercant and Col. Nike Quinto were with us in the

Control Central, which had been perfectly simulated. We were all wearing the gray uniforms which were standard issue in the Arkonide Fleet. On our shoulders and breast flaps glittered the colorful symbols and rank insignia that were in traditional usage at that time.

Rhodan was the "First Officer" and I played the role of Commander. Once more the 750-man crew had been processed thru a session of hypno-training in old Arkonide and the technology of the past. I had attempted to trap them into making incriminating mistakes but they had not been tricked by my questions. In effect they *were* Arkonides of the era of Imperator Tutmor VI.

After coming on board I had even secreted myself in the chemical lab where I had cut up a uniform and subjected it to analysis. When I found out that Solar Intelligence had also carefully simulated the synthetic fibres used in those days, I gave up. These men had made no mistakes!

We had arrived in the vicinity of my home system 24 hours previously. We hovered in space at a distance of 8 light-years from the Arkon sun. We were using the gravity field of a red sun as protection against tracking detection and felt relatively safe. We knew that the outer cordon of satellite fortresses had come into existence by that time.

No one in the Control Central spoke a word but the burden of tension could be seen in the Terrans' faces. Rhodan had again taken refuge behind his expressionless mask. Mercant smiled a bit too fixedly while Quinto streamed rivers of sweat. Everyone had his own way of reacting to the situation. The mutants were gathered in the lower cargo hold of the *Sotala*. The telepaths together with the suggestor Ishibashi and hypno-specialist Noir were monitoring the 4 scientists, upon whose operations the success of the entire enterprise depended.

The phaser field did not waver. The time plane we had reached remained constant. I wasn't quite sure just how the Akons had been coerced to do their work or how they had been convinced of how vital the perfect function of the machine was to us. It would have been impossible to continue keeping the Akons under hypnotic influence although Ishibashi's powers were urgently needed. Apparently the other mutants were merely standing by for the present.

Auris of Las Toor had definitely come over to our side. For her there were no more compromises.

At the moment I wasn't concerned how the scientists had been persuaded to work in our interests. On a computer console before me lay the deciphered message from the man I was supposed to represent, who had actually been dead for more than 6000 years.

As I leaned over to read it, Rhodan was beside me and I noted that his breathing was tense. He was much more nervous than he cared to let on. Perhaps it was the uncanny aspect of our undertaking that tautened the nerves and caused the blood to race.

"CCFK-1919-ABOAT-, Heavy cruiser *Sotala*, Cmdr. Capt. 2d cl. Tresta, to Fleet High Command Ark-3, attention of His Omniscient Eminence Tutmor VI. Task assignment Nebula, special orders 4th phase completed. 4 methane cruisers destroyed, 2 com stations eliminated. Evacuation of numbers 2 and 4 in Ilatzi System follows. Transporter with landing troops requested. Holding position. Signed Tresta, ship *Sotala* . . ."

I read thru the dispatch twice. It agreed with the

historical text that had been handed down. Rhodan
cleared his throat dryly.

Allan D. Mercant reached for the dispatch foil. "In a
few minutes the answer from Fleet High Command
should come thru. Tresta will be instructed to return
home immediately. A new weapon was employed in
the Nebula operation. The war against the methane
breathers is nearing its end."

He spoke of things we knew. We had only a few
more minutes to wait. The fighting men in the time of
Tutmor IV had been swift and logical in their re-
sponses. In those days the signs of the degeneration had
only been seen by the scientists. The fact that they had
immediately begun the construction of a super robot
brain said much for the decisiveness of their leaders.

The answering message came thru as expected and
was deciphered. The contents coincided with our information. Tresta was given orders to return to home
base without delay and submit his battle report. We
continued to hold our receivers open but the *Sotala* was
heard from no more. Mercant looked at his watch.
Finally he straightened his frail frame and looked
around.

"Gentlemen, at present the heavy cruiser is being
destroyed by superior enemy forces. No survivors! No
time to beam out a distress signal."

My voice failed me for a moment. I had to swallow
several times before I could speak. "I'm beginning to
doubt my senses. Did you say—the *Sotala* is being
destroyed *at present* . . . ?"

"Yessir. We are located precisely in its own plane of
time."

I sat down. My legs were shaking. It would have
helped if we could have at least sensed the operation of
the incomprehensible machine but we could feel nothing.

The stars of star cluster M-13 glittered on the viewscreens. Thus I had always known it. Nothing had changed. Of course the short timespan of merely 6000 years was much too negligible to effect any change in the constellations.

Mercant turned to Rhodan. He was as disturbed as I was. So Terrans were also familiar with the feeling of being at the finish line.

"Sir, it would be advisable now to transmit a simulated weak signal to the Fleet High Command—that is, using our prepared message. We have to confirm the reception of their order to return."

"Whatever you say," replied Rhodan huskily. He nodded to the com officer.

Behind the transparent metal partition we could see the communications specialists getting to work. The confirmation was sent out on the same frequency and in the same code.

Mercant nodded his satisfaction. I looked down at my uniform, which was very plain except for the gleaming symbol of the Greater Imperium on my chest.

I tried to shake off the idea of the past. Seconds later I had the impression of actually being a part of this plane of time. It was wrong to think of a present that didn't exist anymore. The year 2106, in Earthly reckoning, had become unreal although "now-time" was out there only a few miles from the false *Sotala*. I had to keep telling myself that this relative reference was only effective *inside* the phaser field.

"Chow time!" Quinto called out. Still perspiring, he went over to the transport chair. These were incorporated in the design of the old Arkonide cruisers, being used to carry men from the Control Central to the officers' mess. It wasn't much more than a simple basket.

When I got up I heard Rhodan clear his throat again.

"You should see the doctor, Terran," I said listlessly.

His answer was incoherent. Everybody on board knew that we now had to wait out a period of 48 hours. The true *Sotala* would not have been able to arrive before the 12th of February by our reckoning. It had been a typical transition-type ship whose earlier design of the nav-hypermatics section made it necessary for long and complex calculations. Still, one might say that not so much had changed on the most modern units of the robot fleet, discounting the first weakness of not having a living and thinking crew on board.

We went to the messhall and there was very little conversation. I had to force down the repulsive-looking synthetic food. It reminded me of a still more remote past—10,000 years ago.

At that time I had flown from Arkon to visit the planets of an unimportant little star. The colonists on the second planet had sent out a call for help. The star had been Earth's sun. I had to restrict my flow of memory so that I wouldn't start fantasizing. One way to do that was to push the reddish-blue mush away from me. On board the old Arkonide fighting ships there had been no other rations than this. When on a mission there were no social differences between officers and crewmen.

I retired to my cabin, where old memories plagued me again. Finally I had to ask the ship's doctor for a deepsleep injection. When he arrived I learned that many men had requested the same. Perry had been among them.

I smiled with relief as I fell asleep. It was the best way to bridge over our period of waiting.

*   *   *   *

We encountered a phenomenon which strengthened Kalup's theory only a few hours after we had rejected his claims. The scientific genius had drawn some conclusions from the fact that outside the phaser field we were looking at the relativistic past instead of at the environment of our present time. He had explained the results of some of his research before we had started out.

He claimed that we—the *Sotala* and every atom inside the conversion field—were components of present time, now as before. He meant specifically February 11 of the year 2106, by Terran reckoning. However, that existence within the frame of "now-time" was relative. To any observers in the plane of reference of the era of Tutmor VI, we were materially stable objects of their own time. And on this basis a remarkable effect was obtained.

Kalup had concluded by saying that to anyone in this past of 6023 years ago the ship was a recognizable physical object—and could continue to be so if the time-phaser should suddenly put us back to 2106 in our own time, that is if we tried to leave the field in some precipitate manner. In the final analysis it showed us what a bewildering time trip this was. Altho we could not actually leave our own present time, to all persons on the outside of the field we were "present" in their own temporal plane.

Shortly after his exposition we finally got under way. Prior to this we had sent out an auxiliary craft to perform a piece of advance strategy. We used its guns to damage one of the engines in our ring-bulge with a precision shot. We wanted to come in with a crippled ship so that we could justify asking for a specific landing site.

After allowing the glowing hole to cool down we had gone into transition, which brought us back into the Einstein continuum in the orbit of the 6th planet of the Arkon System. The maneuver failed to alter any effects of our time-line warpage and this was a positive indication that the nature of the time-phaser's energy was not subject to the laws of the 5th dimension.

It was then that Kalup had his triumph. We were tracked by several patrol cruisers of the inner defense ring and were hailed, even tho our 200-km phaser field did not extend to them. So they could see us and also track us on the radar-echo basis. It proved Kalup's theory. For these long-dead crewmen of the past we *did* exist.

I had ordered a transmission of the *Sotala's* code signal and call letters. The answer had been gratifying because the landing permit had come thru from Fleet Command immediately.

At the moment we were moving at a moderate speed toward Arkon 3. A light cruiser escorted us. For the firstime I had a chance to speak to one of these "ancestor phantoms" out of the past. As the false Tresta I was treated very respectfully by the commander, who was a 4th-class captain. Apparently he already knew of my success in the nebula sector. Since I was a few steps higher in rank and could also boast of more service seniority, the young man addressed me as "Your Excellency".

In the fleets of the old Arkonide Empire, such things were important. No one ignored the order of rank. Over the radio I requested a landing place be assigned to us near the main shipyards. We knew that the robot Regent was being constructed in that immediate area.

The request was processed thru the prescribed service channels. According to regulations it was not my place to personally contact the port authority while under escort of a patrol commander.

While I waited for a confirmation, Rhodan smiled sarcastically. "Long live bureaucracy! Your ancestors must have really had some red tape to contend with."

I took his little barb calmly. Where wasn't there such a thing as bureaucracy? As soon as intelligent beings started to think, the first thing they always did was to entrench themselves in red tape and regulations which were then usually handed out by people who had no idea of the practical applications. I could well remember the heydey of the Imperium. Altho I had been the Crystal Prince and was Commander-in-Chief of a special fleet, I had once had to present 5 signatures before a certain colonial world granted me permission to take on fresh water supplies.

It seemed that here was a similar case. First, the cruiser commander advised me that my request to the port authority had been approved. But it was then necessary for me to call directly and to repeat the request. The port commander referred me to the wharf officer, who then had to determine thru Headquarters if the landing was agreeable. By the time we were already plunging into the atmosphere with our roaring retro-engines ablaze, I was finally advised by a young lieutenant that we should use landing apron KP-176.

"Jumping Jupiter!" exclaimed Maj.. Heintz, the deputy commander. "I'll take everything back that I ever said about red tape in the Terran Services!"

I glared at him unappreciatively but I think all 750 crewmen on board the *Sotala* were starting to grin. These Terrans had a strange sense of humor. Usually it came to the surface when other intelligences were ready to break under the strain. Perhaps this was what was great about this young galactic race.

I looked at the viewscreen tied to the outboard cameras. The commander of the escort cruiser requested permission to withdraw. When I had obliged him he still had to notify the chief of the ground-based defense fortresses that I had authorized his maneuver. It was only then that I was free to bring the spherical warship down thru the inner defense zone.

I didn't know at this moment that the exhausting bureaucracy of the Arkonide officials was helping the Terrans to view our forthcoming task like a spirited bunch of sports enthusiasts. They were amused at me and my tussle with the petty instruments of a petty officialdom.

We flew over the titanic installations of the war planet. The remote-control central took over and guided us into the prescribed flight corridor. My energetic protest resulted in a mild rebuke from the local commandant. This official gave me to understand that my engine damage was "a mere scratch". I told him angrily that this was a matter which he should kindly leave to the judgment of an active service technician such as we were already provided with on board our damaged vessel.

In spite of our perilous situation, Rhodan's grim sense of humor was enough to bring tears of laughter to his eyes. He suddenly found the operation to be quite entertaining.

In every section of the *Sotala*, a final checkout of all personnel was made. The names of the crew members of the genuine cruiser were known to us. Heroes had always been well recorded in Arkonide history. The hypno-training proved itself effective. Every man knew what his name was supposed to be, where he came from and what his background had been. In this case the extensive pedantry of administrating officials had come in handy. Nothing could go wrong now unless we encountered Arkonides who were personally acquainted with the commander or any members of the crew. Then our only salvation would be the quick intervention of the mutants, to control their minds.

Solar Intelligence had thought of everything. Mer-

cant was still giving instructions over the P.A. system
by the time the landing struts had extended. Beneath us
was the main spaceport of Arkon 3. We caught a brief
glimpse of the mammoth building site to the west of the
wharfs. There the robot Regent was being completed
by the top scientists and technicians of my venerable
ancestors. In a few days of relativistic conversion time
the impenetrable energy screen would be in place.

When we touched down and bounced gently on our
hydraulic struts I was intending to bring the special
bomb into the Brain as quickly as possible and then to
take flight. But for that we'd have to find a means of
gaining regulation approval thru official channels for a
takeoff again. Without a takeoff permit we couldn't get
very far with the cruiser. The Arkonides of this age had
been hard and alert. Nobody could get off Arkon 3 if the
commander in charge did not approve. Not even Perry
Rhodan.

When the engines died out I warned Perry again:
"Listen well, little barbarian! When these Arkonides
really were alive, your ancestors were living in smoke-
filled caves and whimpered helplessly at the thunder of
every storm. Don't get the idea that those troops out
there can be compared with the Arkonides of the year
2106 A.D. You would be in for a surprise. You have to
compare my forefathers with your most capable elite
soldiers. Then you will know how to comport yourself."

"Understood, sir," Mercant answered in Perry's
place. "But the operation of the time-phaser is much
more important. If it fails us we'll soon be standing
before the Regent under orders of somebody from the
Akon Energy Command. I'm wondering which could
be worse."

I glanced at him appraisingly. He was a model of
self-control. Major Heintz, who was officially the 2d

officer, handed me the green shoulder mantle I was to wear in my position of commander. I fastened the magnetic clips to my shoulders. My radio helmet was a magnificent piece of workmanship. Captain Tresta had been granted the privilege of wearing such custom gear in his time. Even this detail had been documented in the microvideo tapes covering the crew of the *Sotala*. The Terran experts had simulated the helmet perfectly.

"Should somebody accompany you?" asked Rhodan hesitantly.

"Out of the question! The commander disembarks alone and—according to custom—climbs into a groundcar of the robot reception escort and then reports to Central Command. The crew along with the officers have to remain on board until the captain returns. After that the granting of ground leave for the crew lies within his own jurisdiction."

Perry looked around. The facts were self-evident. "We have to go along with the Arkonide customs," he concluded.

Mercant cleared his throat. "Here's where the difficulties begin, sir. Take care that you don't run into somebody who thinks he knows the real Tresta. Can you use a mento-beamer?"

"No. Arkonide brains don't react to the suggestive frequencies. That weapon was developed for use on alien planets. I believe the Terrans found that out toward the end of the 20th century."

I managed to chuckle, seeing Rhodan's perplexity. Apparently he had forgotten that after his return home in the moon rocket *Stardust*, he had used the beamer to make a decisive impression on Reginald Bell.

Quinto looked at his watch. We didn't yet know exactly how late it was. Within the time distortion we could determine the day but not the hour. Our astronomers were already at work on the problem. The rotation rate of Arkon 3 could not have changed.

Before I left, the correct time of day was announced. It was 13:24. When I stepped into the outer airlock and the ceremonies began, the telepath John Marshall appeared. He reported to me that the Akon scientists were doing what was expected of them. Whether this was of their own free will or not was not mentioned.

20 men of the false *Sotala* had formed a double line out in front. One of them announced me and I walked between them with appropriate salutes. Ahead an escort groundcar was waiting. Shrill robot music started up. The noisy mechanical instruments hadn't changed. Their screeching and fifing were familiar to me from the time of my rulership. They had always been a strain on my eardrums.

In dignified representation of my rank I strode forward to the robots. A uniformed officer straightened up in the car. I wondered if I was supposed to know him! He turned out to be a 1st-class captain. A dark beard obscured his chin. I looked into a pair of red Arkonide eyes. His nearly white hair had been modishly styled. His service helmet did not conceal it entirely.

I came to a stop before the hover glider where I struck my hand flat against the left side of my chest and bowed my head. In rank and seniority the officer was doubtlessly my superior. All Arkonide officers were able to note such fine distinctions. It also went without saying that an appropriate form of address was necessary in such cases.

Thus I said respectfully: "Captain Tresta greets you, Excellency. I am reporting back in accordance with my signal dispatches."

He raised a hand. I shook inwardly. My right hand hovered over the butt of my service weapon. I thought I could deduce from his searching look that he had never seen the real Tresta. And so it turned out.

"My greetings to you, Captain Tresta. Welcome to Arkon 3. I am instructed to transmit the request of the commanding admiral for your immediate presence."

The polite formality of course meant nothing. But thus it had always been in the old fleet. Whenever a superior commander "requested" something it was the same as a binding order.

I bowed my head again and waited until a combat robot opened the vehicle's door. Then I climbed in. I remained silent until the higher-ranked captain had taken his seat again. Above us glared the bright sun of my home system. I felt comfortable under its burning heat, which the Terrans had never seemed to appreciate.

The car started up with a lurch. With shrill alarm whistles going we raced across the spaceport, the borders of which blended hazily with the horizon. I thought I was being unobtrusive when I stole another glance at the major construction site but my companion noticed it. He smiled benevolently.

"The work goes forward without interruption," he told me. "I believe you were 3 years on active duty, were you not?"

"That is correct, Excellency."

"Within a few days the giant robot will be surrounded by a new type of defense screen. Excuse me—I neglected to introduce myself. I am Captain Usaph, 1st Adjutant of the Commanding Admiral. A year ago His Eminence, Admiral Kreto, was relieved. The acting chief now is Admiral Aichot."

I thanked him for the information, which was something I must not forget under any circumstances. Eminent Arkonides expected everyone to know who they were. According to custom I inquired about Admiral

Aichot's family altho I already had the data from the Regent's memory banks. But such trivialities were a part of the mentality of my people. I didn't dare overlook them if I didn't want to be exposed.

I finally ventured to indulge in the usual jokes about the bureaucratic attitude of the port officials, which was a welcome diversion to any officer in active duty. The tacit animosity between front-line officers and the "tinplates", as the civil service type troops of the administration were called, was always a sure source of amusement.

After we had traveled a considerable distance the high buildings of Fleet Command Headquarters loomed into the sky before us. Our conversation kept being interrupted by the thunder of spaceships which were constantly either taking off or landing. In those days Arkon 3 was the center of the universe. There was no other galactic race which could have dared to stand against us. Now and again a formation of warships would take off into space and the roaring was so unbearable that we had to press our hands against our ears.

The car halted and once more I was faced with an honor guard, this time composed of veteran Arkonides. Someone among them could have known Tresta. I kept my head down and strode rapidly to the wide steps of the building.

An antigrav lift took us upstairs. The press of service people in the wide corridors and the general hustle and bustle was fairly breathtaking. I had to wait 2 hours until the commanding officer was ready to receive me.

The interview proceeded fairly well. Acting-Admiral Aichot was a younger man who probably held his present position chiefly on the basis of his distinguished heredity. He commanded the Home Fleet, was a military expert in the Supreme Council and was also a member of the Admiralty Staff of the Commander-in-

Chief. I had to stand stiffly for an hour before this "Top Brass" representative, who nevertheless treated me with a sort of friendly condescension.

I gave him a complete report on the effects of the new weapon. This was a vibration beam which produced certain biological effects and—as I already knew—was soon to be abandoned. The device hadn't held up to its expectations, which I pointed out. I also pointed out that I had destroyed the enemy cruisers with conventional impulse and disintegrator weapons.

I finally ventured to request permission to contact the chief scientist of the Supreme Council, hyper-physicist Epetran. Admiral Aichot expressed his surprise openly. For a commander of my rank it was unusual to wish to speak to such an important personnage.

"Epetran? What do you want with him?"

"I'd like to make certain suggestions concerning a simplified technique for making hyper-transitions."

Aichot stared at me almost pityingly. "Do I understand you correctly? You wish to make suggestions . . . ? You actually mean—technical recommendations?"

"Yes, Your Eminence. My years of research along this line have led to some important observations during actual battle conditions, especially with the last 4 Nebula cruisers. I believe I can offer some interesting recommendations."

Aichot may have been an average commander type but he was also an active Fleet officer. Such men were noted for their swift powers of decision. Within 3 hours I received written permission. Only with that could I dare to enter the palace of the Supreme Council.

With that the interview came to an end. Of course I was ordered to submit the customary task-action report. Aichot couldn't know that meanwhile the report had been prepared by Terran experts.

I then withdrew. A hover glider brought me back to the *Sotala*, where a team from the shipyards was already looking into the engine damage. My First Officer, meaning Rhodan, had received orders to inform me that the overhaul of the cruiser could not be completed in less than 5 or 6 days. During this period I was free to determine the disposition of the crew.

This meant crew leave on Arkon 3 but it was also a big advantage for our operation. The deliberately planned engine damage had been Quinto's idea so when I arrived he was basking in the favor of the men because they hadn't counted on such a break.

I had to throw cold water on their enthusiasm. "Your hypno-training seems to be less effective than we expected. Ground leave in this past era is out of the question. At best you would only be able to spend your free time in the subterranean cities of the planet. You will remain on board. I don't relish the idea of your meeting with Arkonides who might actually know the real members of the crew. In our fleet there were thousands of cross-contacts among the fighting men on active duty. Also, relieving and changing of crews was an everyday occurrence, so they all knew each other. It would be surprising if there were no man among the other crews who wouldn't want to try to contact a buddy from the *Sotala*. So you have to control yourselves."

"That's an order," announced Rhodan over the P.A. "You will govern yourselves accordingly. Major Heintz, post the men at their battle stations."

The Chief of Intelligence gazed reproachfully at the ceiling. "Sir, for many hours now the cruiser has been on standby for action."

Rhodan swallowed, then laughed. "Excuse me, then. I haven't said a word."

I looked wonderingly at this tall Terran. He was the

chief of the Solar Imperium, he commanded thousands
of ships and was practically idolized by 50 billion
Terrans and colonists. He was far above Admiral
Aichot—yet he could laugh about a mistake in his
reasoning without any fear of damaging his prestige or
reputation.

Perry Rhodan was a wonderful human being and
friend. There had been very few like him on Arkon. I
had known a few like Rhodan but they were now long
dead and gone. Then it occurred to me that the Arkonides here in this relativistic conversion time were
actually my descendants. 4000 years earlier I had been
born and in my early manhood I had been sent off into
action. Perry noted my momentary state of confusion
and wanted to be helpful. I felt his hand on my shoulder.

"Don't think about it, Atlan. It's a thing of the past.
Never forget that we are creatures of the year 2106, by
Terra reckoning. What we are experiencing here is an
illusion—a deception under the almighty laws of Nature."

When he walked toward the exit hatch my gaze
followed him pensively.

3 hours previously the sun had gone behind the horizon but night had not come to the war planet. The great spaceport was brilliantly illuminated by countless field lights, revolving search beams and hovering nuclear "suns". Also the jet flames from departing spaceships gave an impression of a continuing fireworks display. There was no end to the thundering and roaring.

The sky had taken on a blood-red hue above the main shipyards, which were the most modern on the planet. There the bellows of the thermonuclear smelters pushed a continuous river of vaporized metal into the cooling slag troughs. Arkon 3 never slept. The robot-operated assembly line of spaceships of every class and description was the nerve-center of the Imperium.

The Terrans and myself were the only ones on this world who knew what it would look like 6000 years later. At this time the throng of Arkonide spacemen was seemingly endless. The cities swarmed with troops from every branch of the service. Altho the prime of the Empire had passed, they could still send 100,000 manned ships into the void. Subordinate races were not permitted on the war planet. They were best employed on the colonial worlds.

Pucky and Ras Tschubai had just returned after reconnoitering the area. The third teleporter was still busy with our suggestor. Kitai Ishibashi had the mission of probing the scientist Epetran.

I had not been able to make my presentation. Epetran did not live in one of the great conical palaces but had quartered himself instead in an officer billet, which would also have been my own way of doing things. My request was politely but firmly rejected by his subordinates. I was informed that at present Epetran had no time for recommendations from an officer back from the fighting front. I was asked to present my suggestions in writing.

When I returned, Mercant had only nodded and said that it was what he had expected. Logically the Arkonides' greatest scientist would have other things to do than to get into a discussion with a second-class fleet captain.

According to our conversion table the date back on Earth was the 13th of February, 2106. We couldn't wait much longer.

Pucky had rolled himself up into a ball on a contour couch, exhausted from his labors. Even Ras Tschubai had come back breathing heavily. We guessed that their excursion hadn't been easy. So we had to wait until these two had recovered from their exertions. In the meantime I paid the 4 Akon scientists a visit.

Artol of Penoral was monitoring the machine as usual. Two telepaths of the Corps were keeping him under surveillance. Auris was also in the cargo hold. For 2 days now she had avoided the Control Central. I inquired after her health.

"Alright, considering the circumstances. When will you take action?"

I couldn't answer her. We exchanged a few more words, which enabled me to see that she was uneasy.

When I returned to the Control Central very much was going on there. Tako had returned with Ishibashi. Pucky reported that the robot Brain already had the appearance of the Regent we knew in our own present day. This meant that it had practically been completed.

"How is the Regent guarded?" asked Quinto.

"The security is very tight, sir," answered Tschubai. "We had to keep on making jumps continuously in order not to be discovered. Twice we tripped off alarm systems and once I was shot at.''

"What with?"

"A disintegrator, sir."

"With a deadly weapon?"

"Yessir. They're playing for keeps. We saw the scientific team. About a hundred men are busy checking out the final circuits. There's no normal way to get in without showing special passes. They are key card devices containing each person's frequency pattern and they are regularly monitored by the guard stations. Any unauthorized entrance seems to be impossible. Even tho the energy screen isn't up yet, the Arkonides have gone to every extreme to tighten the security around the Robot.''

I looked around. The men's faces were grim. Mercant tapped with his fingers on a computer console.

"So there's no other choice," declared Rhodan. "We have to go in with the teleporters. What do you have to report, Kitai?"

The lean-figured mutant wiped sweat from his brow. His imitation bio-hair, which simulated that of an Arkonide, was glistening with dampness. "Nothing, sir—or almost nothing. We located Epetran in the math section. His quarters are close to it. He appeared to be putting special instructions on program tape."

"He's the one who designed and built Security Circuit A-1," put in Quinto.

"It could be that he's working on it now," said the mutant. "I tried to work on him and influence his mind but I don't know if I had any luck. Epetran has an extremely strong voluntary block. Besides—Tako claims that he may have seen us in spite of our deflector screens."

A cold chill ran thru me. When no one else could see thru our disguise, this old scientist was able to. He had an activated brain with special faculties. Rhodan guessed my fears but sought to dismiss them.

"Don't be a pessimist, my friend! Even Epetran isn't omniscient. If he had gotten suspicious we'd know it by now."

I couldn't contradict his argument, yet from moment to moment I became more apprehensive. I deeply regretted that I had asked Admiral Aichot for a permit to visit Epetran. According to the circumstances Kitai had described, it would be better not to meet him.

Mercant looked at his watch. "Soon after sunrise you'll be getting involved with receptions, sir."

I nodded. I already had the invitations. My "colleagues" wanted to see Captain Tresta. The situation was becoming intolerable. Quinto was about to say something when the tracking center put thru a call.

"To the Commander: a strange vehicle has stopped in front of the cruiser."

Rhodan stiffened. Heintz hit the alarm button automatically. The men who were off duty were awakened from their sleep.

Tracking switched circuits so that we could see what they were looking at. On our viewscreens appeared an unwieldy-looking contraption. It had wide caterpillar chains instead of wheels and was equipped with numerous antennas. Before we could really get a good look at it, the heavy vehicle rolled away. It disappeared behind a battleship, became visible once more beyond it, then entered an armored surface lock that led underground.

We looked at each other, nonplussed, until Mercant chuckled heartily. "Could our scientific associates kindly explain what that was supposed to be?" he asked.

Kalup still stared at the viewscreen. His eyes had narrowed so much that they seemed to be lost in the fatty folds of his face. "That was a sensor vehicle," he declared. "No doubt about it. Who guided it to the *Sotala?* Who wanted to find out what?"

"Find out?" asked Quinto hastily. "What do you mean?"

Kalup didn't answer. He stomped swiftly toward the exit but as he went out he was heard to mutter something that sounded like "sensor surveillance".

After he had gone I felt that my activator was louder than usual. Even 6023 years before the present time I was already a very old man. Rhodan was still standing in front of the screens.

"It's useless to try to figure it out," I said. "It seems an impossibility to influence Epetran by any paranormal means. So there's no point in making his acquaintance. From what Kitai has to say, it could be dangerous. We move into action. We'll get into the Brain with the help of the mutants, we'll install the bomb and then get out of here."

"How?" asked Rhodan, now very alert to what I was saying.

"It should be considerably easier to return to the present time-plane of Arkon 3 than it was to enter the era of Tutmor VI. Everyone on board has seen how tight the defenses are here. I vote for alternate 2 of our escape plan. We turn off the time converter. When we get back we may have to face a robot attack but the Fleet under Bell's command can cover our retreat."

"That's also my opinion," declared Mercant. "But before that there's a lot to be done. Of course if I had my preferences I would have felt better if we could have handled this thing with Epetran's help."

"What should I tell the man?" I asked sarcastically. "That I've come from the future to save my people?"

He regarded me soberly. "Sir, perhaps that still might not be as crazy as you think."

"Mercant, you're dreaming!" exclaimed Rhodan.

"No sir, I don't quite see it that way. This scientist was the first Arkonide to detect the beginnings of the degeneration and to perceive its outcome. Moreover, he's expert enough to be able to conceive of such a device as the time-phaser. I'm playing with the idea of informing Epetran."

Rhodan bluntly rejected this. When my extra-brain signaled me I was astonished that it seconded Mercant's plan. Nevertheless I was also in favor of dropping the idea of getting any cooperation from Epetran.

Rhodan got up and went over to the main computer, where he began to press the input keys.

I interrupted him. "It would be useless to try to get a logic evaluation. Mr. Mercant, I must also reject your proposition. The bomb can be relied upon to explode as planned. We have no way of knowing what Epetran's reaction would be and we can't take the risk of being arrested or maybe even shot in case he sounds an alarm. We move as planned. I'll install the bomb."

The Chief of Intelligence bowed resignedly. The decision was made. Possibly we could be mistaken —no one could say.

The computer made a clicking sound. While I was still waiting for its output a message came thru from the duty officer at the ground lock. His face appeared on the intercom screen.

"Lt. Pinch here, sir. A letter has been delivered for you."

"What . . . ?"

"An oblong envelope, sir. It was brought over by a robot."

Rhodan stopped his computer work. We looked at each other tensely.

"Another invitation?" asked Maj. Heintz. His voice sounded apprehensive.

I shook my head. If that were the case it would not come to me this way. Such matters were customarily handled over the radio. The letter arrived in the Control Central. The envelope was of fluorescent foil and it bore the seal of the Supreme Council. Rhodan's hand was tense when he handed it to me. I ripped it open and the letter fell out.

"It's in handwriting!" said Quinto. "Who's it from?"

I thought that my heart stopped for a moment. The signature and seal were unmistakable. After reading it I lowered the letter and looked at the others. "It's an invitation, alright! Epetran asks me to visit him since he's heard from Admiral Aichot that I had some recommendations to make for the improvement of transition techniques."

Rhodan also read the message. "It says other officers familiar with the subject are also welcome . . . Well, I'll be! What is he up to?"

"Danger!" signaled my extra-brain.

Almost against my will I declared: "The invitation can't be avoided. When Epetran makes a request it's the same as an order. Who will go with me?"

Rhodan called his service robot to him. "My extra uniform—fast!" he ordered.

Within 30 minutes a vehicle was waiting for us at the cruiser's ground lock.

"So he took it for granted that we'd be ready in half an hour," observed Rhodan grimly. "Alright, let's go. No, Kitai, I'm sorry, we won't be taking you with us. Anyway, if this scientist is equipped with an activated brain your efforts will be useless."

Our suggestor mutant remained behind. We descended in the antigrav and climbed into the robotcar. It was emblazoned with the escutcheon of the Supreme Council. The third man in our team was John Marshall, who was to attempt to read the scholar's mind. Officially he was joining us as the Chief Engineer of the *Sotala*.

We started off, not knowing what awaited us in Epetran's quarters. Certainly he wasn't thinking of any gala reception. Apparently the interview was to be a very sober one. Arkonides of Epetran's rank had been very clear thinkers. They were only interested in facts. It was said especially of the chief scientist of the Supreme Council that he very seldon took part in noisy festivities altho he stood well in the Imperator's favor.

We drove into the control zone close to the main construction site. Long hangar-like structures loomed before us. Apparently Epetran didn't consider it unusual to be requesting a visit from us in the middle of the night. He was one of those Arkonides who believed that soldiers should be ready at any hour to serve the Empire.

Rhodan was uneasy when no inspections occurred. We were allowed to pass thru the energy barriers without hindrance. My extra-brain remained silent. My skull felt as if it were held in an iron band. We knew that Epetran had been the greatest man in Arkonide history. It was quite an ordeal to be facing such a personality.

"Captain Tresta?" queried an officer of the guard. He belonged to the famous elite troops of the Tentons.

"That I am," I confirmed, introducing Rhodan and Marshall as officers "Telater and Aday".

"His Eminence is expecting you. Your visit will be limited to one hour."

He saluted, I nodded, and the car moved on a bit farther. We got out in front of a tower-like structure. We had arrived.

* * * *

Marshall's face had blanched conspicuously. I caught a signal from him and understood. It was dangerous to attempt to probe Epetran's mind. It was almost as if the telepath were trying to tell me that the scientist may have detected the paramental interference.

However, if this was true the great man did not reveal it in any way. He was a tall Arkonide with snow-white hair that hung down to his shoulders. I had never seen a man with such a high forehead nor such a benevolent expression. For a moment, as we came in, this kindly look darkened. I felt as if the Supreme Council had secretly condemned us to death. Then—quite strangely—his threatening aspect vanished.

My presentation took 2 hours. His questions fairly exhausted my technical knowledge. Within the first few minutes he had understood how the transition computations had to be processed in order to accelerate succeeding hyperjumps and make them more accurate in terms of the navigational course. Arkonide history has it that shortly before his death he had introduced considerable improvements in this regard. If I wasn't entirely mistaken, we the "yet unborn" had provided the impetus.

Even Rhodan and Marshall did some talking. In fact Perry had gone so far as to allude to the possibility of linear spacedrive. This seemed to fascinate Epetran still more. He regarded Rhodan closely as if he were seeking to penetrate his thoughts. His deep voice trembled with an inner excitement when he questioned us.

We found ourselves in a laboratory where the equipment appeared to be dedicated to computer programming. We were fairly surrounded by instruments and consoles. It was quite clear that Epetran had not been planning a gala reception.

When Rhodan finally stopped giving hints and reassumed his regular role, to my great relief the old man's quiet smile returned. He wore the uniform of the practical working scientist. Only the symbol of the Supreme Council indicated his high position.

"I thank you, Major Telater," he said. "Your statements have been very interesting. But I believe it would be more advantageous to us to first try your commander's recommendations for improving our existing propulsion system. You will be hearing from me. How long will you be staying on Arkon 3?"

I assumed he was addressing me. "In any case until my cruiser has been overhauled, Your Excellency. After that I expect to receive new orders."

He nodded thoughtfully. "Are you satisfied with the fighting power of your ship?"

"It could be better, Your Eminence."

The old man frowned as if piqued for the moment. "The *Sotala's* armaments are the very best."

"Which soon may not be enough, Excellency. The enemies of the Imperium are not asleep. I beg you to let me be frank with you."

"Of course, as you wish. But I know of no race in the galaxy that would be capable of defeating our fleet."

"I was thinking about developing intelligences. No one knows what the future will bring."

He rose to his feet by way of dismissing us. But his last words had the heaviest impact on me. "When we are no more, the Imperium will find powerful friends. Then it will all depend on taking the right steps."

We left. The old man gazed after us from amidst his machines. Marshall walked out first and I followed him but then I missed Rhodan. When I turned to look back I saw him standing there tall and straight in the lab room. Epetran's gaze and his seemed to be locked together. Marshall stifled a sigh as we heard Perry's departing words.

"Most assuredly the Imperium will find friends one day, Your Eminence. And they will remember you and your genius." He saluted and finally came out into the corridor. The sliding door closed behind us.

"Was that necessary?" I snapped at him angrily. "Even without that I have a feeling he saw thru us."

"I do, too," he answered, impressed. "Let him make of my words what he will."

"Caution!" whispered the telepath.

Farther ahead 2 soldiers of the guard appeared. My hand touched the butt of my service weapon. But all they had to tell us was that we had gone way over our visiting limit. They emphasized that it wasn't proper to prolong an interview with a man like Epetran with persistent questions.

I was reminded of the hospitality of my race. I had the impression that the old man would not have let himself in for such a lengthy discussion, nevertheless, unless he had wished it so. Unquestioningly he would have dismissed us the minute he ceased to be interested. I made my apologies to the guard officer, who gruffly passed us thru.

A half hour later we again entered the Control Central of the *Sotala*.

"No unusual events, sir," reported Maj. Heintz.

Outside the sun was rising. I wondered if Epetran ever slept. Rhodan checked his watch. According to our conversion table the date must be February 14.

"Tomorrow at 12 noon—our time—the bomb will explode," he said with unusual emphasis. "Pucky and Ras Tschubai, stand by for action. Marshall, your face is still gray. What's wrong?"

The telepath was almost apathetic when he spoke but his words shattered our self-confidence. "Presumably Epetran knows who we are and where we come from. Just after we entered his lab we were monitored by paramental means. For half a minute there, you and Atlan were unconscious. I was able to resist it. But I don't know if Epetran succeeded in breaking thru your mental screens. I don't think it was possible with Atlan. How about you, sir?''

Rhodan sat down. He stared almost dumbfounded at the chief of the Mutant Corps. "Unconscious, you say? You sure you're not mistaken?''

"By no means, sir. I was awake. You and Atlan were asleep with your eyes open. Probably the results are coming thru now from the para-probe. I urgently advise you to conceal the bomb in the Brain at once —and to leave this time plane.''

I glanced involuntarily at the viewscreens. Outside the spaceships of my people were taking off and landing. Personnel vehicles were crossing the area back and forth. No one approached the *Sotala*.

Rhodan turned on the P.A. microphone. "All hands! Red alert is in effect. It's possible that we may be attacked, in which case the time converter will be shut off. If we should unexpectedly enter our own time reference we will be close to the Regent and his robot fleet. Open fire without waiting for orders. Com Central: prepare a distress call to the Fleet. Stand by for emergency takeoff. That is all, thank you . . . ''

He turned off the switch. The ordnance experts appeared with Terran combat suits. They were far superior to the equivalent products of Epetran's epoch. The energy screens were stronger and the deflector projectors were much more advanced.

Pucky and Ras Tschubai reported. We were ready to make our jump. Two weapons technicians brought us the bomb. The uranium timer was already operating. The halflife radiation clock would give the ignition impulse in 6023 years.

Mercant was getting nervous. "I don't think it's wise

for the leaders of both imperiums to place their lives in danger. Since we left our own time on February 10th we don't know if you were still alive on February 14—meaning today.''

"Mercant, don't get me all confused," Rhodan snapped at him edgily. Obviously his sense of humor had failed him at the moment. "By the same token I could just as well claim I've never lived. That would be the case if something were to happen to us now, wouldn't it?''

Mercant turned to look helplessly at Kalup. The scientist said nothing. He was busy studying the micro sound-tape of Epetran's conversation.

"He sounds like an oracle," Kalup said finally. "When you read between the lines you can conclude almost anything. Wait till I get the analysis. At first try I can't prove anything.''

"Request denied. We're teleporting. The bomb must be placed in the Brain. Ready, Atlan?''

I nodded. We had decided to dispense with our pressure helmets. Breathable air would be available where we were going.

Once more I pointed out to the teleporters the remote power room where I wanted to operate. I was familiar with it from my days as Imperator, since at that time I had free access to the Brain.

Then we jumped.

Rematerialization occurred in a fair-sized room containing an emergency-power reactor and a converter bank. Farther to the left were the control panels which were connected to the pile by heavy cables. High tension lines led thru the thermically-glazed rock walls into an adjoining room where the tanks containing pre-catalysts and nuclear fuel were located. There were also the moderator pumps for damping down the reactor with regulated injections.

I knew that the emergency power pile had never been called upon for any current demands. I had found the place during my numerous inspection tours and learned that its installation had been a useless precaution.

Typical of this type of construction, the whole assembly sat on a shoulder-high foundation made of armor-plate plastic metal. One wall was broken by a maintenance hatch. Behind it was a passage thru which one could crawl to the cleanout access holes around the reactor zone. The hatch was no more used than was the power unit itself. Here was the place for our bomb. It could lie here undisturbed for over 6000 years, waiting for the impulse from its uranium timer.

Pucky took a look around in our immediate vicinity, finding only several technicians making routine inspections. They were checking out individual relays. The construction of the giant Robot had required thousands of years. This particular reactor room must have been completed about 20 years ago and there were no further installations being done in this sector. The only thing we would have to fear would be detection by a security patrol, which was unlikely.

I turned off my deflector field. The room was lighted

by a permanently burning emergency lamp. We waited until our eyes had adjusted to the dim illumination. It was warm and it became uncomfortable in our combat-suits but we didn't dare turn on our air-conditioners. To avoid any danger of being traced by instruments it was better if our micro-reactors could remain inactive. Their residual radiations were enough to worry about.

Pucky returned from another teleport jump. Ras Tschubai stood at the closed steel door and listened for sounds outside.

"Everything clear," whispered the little one. He looked around anxiously. "Nobody's there but those technicians."

"Almost a little *too* easy, eh?" remarked Rhodan.

I thought of Epetran and Marshall's story. If the learned scholar had seen thru our game he was certainly reacting strangely. Why hadn't he sounded an alarm? Or didn't he suspect what we were intending to do? Had he merely regarded us as interesting visitors from the future who had come to impart specific knowledge to him? No—Epetran was too shrewd not to realize in that case that we must have come here to destroy his life's work? Would he stand for that?

I was helpless to find an answer. Finally my extra-brain expressed itself. Granted that Epetran had guessed our origin, he wouldn't be able to interpret our thoughts. He would have to rely on the vagaries of machine analysis.

This thought relieved me somewhat. At any rate we hadn't been eliminated so far. No one seemed to suspect our presence down here. Above us lay about 1000 meters of solid rock. The few access passages were heavily guarded. If there were any hint of our presence, all the sentries would have to do was to move in and attack. This was evidently not the case or they would have come looking for us long before now.

Rhodan's voice suddenly tore me from my thoughts. "What are you waiting for?" he asked. I was surprised to see that the Terran was suspicious of me. I could detect it in his eyes. He had always looked this way at other intelligences when he doubted their intentions.

"You Terran barbarian," I retorted angrily, "are you thinking perhaps that I'll lose my nerve at the last minute? Will you never learn any better?"

The Chief of the Solar Imperium suddenly grinned with the ingenuousness of one of his youngest cadets.

Pucky showed his incisor tooth brightly. "Now he's acting human again!"

I released the cylindrical bomb from its carrying straps. Rhodan held it while I opened the maintenance hatch. After I had crawled in, he handed it to me and I attached it to the plastic metal wall with instant-grip fasteners. To check it over would have been superfluous. The weapon was sealed. There was nothing more to attend to here. I carefully emerged from the crawlway and closed the hatch.

Pucky was listening telepathically for thought impulses from the outside.

"Almost too easy to be true, sir," said Ras Tschubai. "Is that all?"

I nodded.

"Then let's jump back," ordered Rhodan. "We can't wait here for 6000 years."

He attempted to laugh but it didn't have the desired effect. Pucky ran to me and I picked him up in my arms. It was the best way for the two of us to teleport.

"Are you sure the reactor definitely won't be inspected?" asked Rhodan again. He had often asked this question.

I couldn't tell him any more than I had previously. The power pile had never been used. The main reactors had never failed.

Ras suddenly groaned and I realized why too late. He and Rhodan were standing several meters away. Before I understood why they both started to collapse I was also attacked by a wave of pain. Pucky screeched and I felt his legs tremble. I felt as if fluid fire were running thru my veins. I squatted down and let the little fellow roll onto the floor.

After 3 seconds it was all over with. The pain faded as swiftly as it had come. Rhodan's reaction was to reach for his weapon immediately. My eyes finally cleared and I was about to ask what happened when Ras let out another groan. His eyes were fairly popping as he stared beyond me. When I turned, I knew why.

The emergency power reactor had changed. Its isolation shielding jacket which had just been so immaculate was now stained and spotted. Here and there were cracks and other signs of decay. A thick layer of dust was on the floor and the equipment. I jumped up. Rhodan was already on his feet. Pucky was still squirming on the floor.

"How can a new reactor become a pile of junk in 3 seconds?" asked Rhodan. His voice sounded hoarse. I declined to answer, since we both knew.

"It's—it's the time field!" stammered Tschubai, horrified. "Sir, we've gotten out of the conversion field. The machine has stopped working."

I helped Pucky to his feet. His mouse face was contorted in a grimace of uncertainty.

"The field is gone," he confirmed. "I'm getting many impulses. We're back in our own time again. But the bomb—!"

I whirled about to look at the hatch that I had just closed. *Just* closed? Perry reassured us.

"Don't get excited. We left the *Sotala* on February 14. We haven't spent more than an hour here. We still have 20 hours."

His last words were drowned out by a nerve-shattering howl. Outside the alarm sirens were sounding. The Regent had detected us. For 6000 years it had been a harmless machine. Now we had to get used to the idea again that it had begun to deteriorate due to the tampering with its A-1 circuits.

Pucky had calmed himself. I took him up in my arms once more. Rhodan took a firm hold of Ras Tschubai.

"Where to?" asked the teleporter confidently. He was accustomed to eluding his enemies thru the paramental planes.

I hesitated. Where could we go? If the time-phaser had ceased functioning, then the cruiser would also be in the present time. That meant a battle which would sooner or later lead to the destruction of the ship. There was no other explanation for our sudden return to our own time. The machine must have failed. Whether by accident or plan was immaterial just now.

"Our target is the *Sotala*," Rhodan decided. "Then we'll see what we should do."

I waited for the dematerialization but it did not occur. Pucky began to tremble. His eyes seemed to grow dim. Ras Tschubai staggered so that Rhodan had to support him. I felt gooseflesh come over me.

"Pucky . . . !"

"Antis!" he exclaimed. "Antis are close by somewhere! I can't concentrate—they absorb my *psi*. Atlan, I can't jump!"

Tschubai confirmed it. I didn't ask any more questions. We knew that the Akons had the support of the Baalol priests. Their mental emanations negated the mutants' para-faculties.

I pulled my minicom set from my equipment belt and turned it on. I sent out a distress call on the hyper-frequency band of the Fleet. We had found that the

Brain's honeycomb screen could be penetrated by relatively weak hyperwaves. If the radio experts of the *Sotala* were alert they would hear me. Of course that depended on whether or not the cruiser had actually returned to present time.

We listened breathlessly. Pucky detected a few brain impulses, then nothing more. So the Antis were also closing in on us. The *Sotala* did not answer but in its place we heard a strange voice. It was a time announcement in English. Someone was broadcasting on our frequency.

"*Ironduke*—it is now 11:43, 15 February 2106 . . . !"

The message was continuously repeated except that the time of day kept changing. I tensed, hardly noting Rhodan's sudden grip.

"The 15th of February, sir," said Ras, nonplussed. "The bomb will explode in less than 17 minutes!"

"But—we came out of the ship on the 14th," protested Rhodan. "The conversion table—"

"Was wrong," I interrupted him. "The time-phaser doesn't work as precisely as we assumed. Friend, I'm getting nervous."

He released his grip on my arm. Pucky announced that his *psi* faculties had surrendered completely. A merciless enemy waited for us outside. We exchanged glances. In a basic sense it made little difference to us which way we would die if it were going to happen. Perhaps an energy beam might be easier to contemplate than being caught up in the sun-hot concussion of a 50-megaton explosion.

"We'll use the emergency exit. All set?"

We turned on our individual defense screens. They were strong enough to absorb the impact of hand weapons fire altho a robot shot might be dangerous.

The deflector screens made us invisible. When I pulled down my absorption filter I could again see my companions.

Ras opened the emergency door in the rear of the chamber. Beyond it was a dimly-lit corridor. There was still no one in sight.

The hypercom message of the *Ironduke* was still giving the countdown. It was now 11:46 . . .

8/ FROM THE TOMB OF AGES

Our deflector screens were machine-generated. Even the mental capacities of the Antis were not sufficient for them to detect these light-diverting lines of energy.

This had been our last hope but then the Akon technicians appeared with their electronic sensors, which homed in on our micro-reactors. The famous Terran radiation-absorption features of our suits proved to be useless. It could not be denied that the Akons were masters of an outstanding technology.

Arkonides were not in evidence, which was a sign that the men of the Blue System had already suppressed my people. We found ourselves in a lengthy hall that I had never seen before. It was an impossibility to get a perspective of this labyrinth of passages and rooms without a construction plan. Also our orientation was all the more difficult because of the complex system of levels. Many of the long chambers were split by 2 to 3 mezzanine decks.

I was lying behind a master relay cabinet from which thick cable conduits led to other switching units. The deep humming sound behind the housing panels indicated that the Regent was working at full power. It seemed to have activated all auxiliary sections. The lighting here was very inadequate. We could hardly see the flitting shadows of our attackers altho thousands of indicator and parity lamps were flickering on and off. It caused a confusion of vision which was unpleasant.

Rhodan was crouched a few meters away behind the base of a transformer. Its rumbling sound covered our whisperings. I noted that he was carrying his heavy impulse beamer over his shoulder. So far we had not used our hand weapons. The Antis' defense screens were reinforced by their mental abilities and were not normally penetrable. We had not brought along any of the new combination "persuaders" which had been designed to combat the Baalols. No one had foreseen that we might be fighting the mysterious priests.

I saw a figure at the end of an aisle. Its outlines seemed to flow and change, which was proof that the god-priest had fully activated his screen. It would be useless to bring him under fire.

I checked my watch which I had synchronized with the Fleet's countdown broadcast so that I would know when the moment of destruction would come. The tolerance limit of the uranium timer lay between plus or minus 3 minutes. I was hoping for a breakdown of the bomb's ignition system, which I knew could not happen.

I was startled by a thundering sound nearby. Ras Tschubai had fired his weapon. The white-hot glow of a thermo-beam lit up the dim twilight around us. Somebody yelled out piercingly and I saw an Akon stumble out from behind a bursting bank of equipment. I did not shoot altho he was apparently only wounded. Two Antis dragged him to cover behind a stack of memory banks.

Ras changed his position. The enemy's greenish weapon beams struck back. Wherever they hit the material was converted to dust. The Regent sounded more alarms. Whenever any part of the installations was destroyed a new battery of sirens became activated.

Rhodan jumped across the aisle and threw himself down beside me. "Let's go back to those mezzanine stairs. We'll work our way to the surface," he said. "Are you ready?"

I beckoned to Pucky and Ras. Then we ran for it. In

that moment the spot I had left was hit by a disintegrator beam. The relay cabinet collapsed under it and meter-long sparks shot out of the cabling and connector housings. The bedlam of sirens increased so that it didn't matter if we shouted to each other. Ahead we saw the stairs. Rhodan yelled at us to take cover once more and we followed his advice.

Our battle tactics developed a set pattern within minutes. We would risk opening fire and then quickly change our location. It always took a new space of time for the Akon sensor equipment to pick up our trail again. I figured we had a good chance as long as they didn't get the idea of concentrating exclusively on our gun muzzles whenever we opened fire. But for that it would be necessary to open a frontal attack, backed up by many marksmen in the background.

We would then be thrown on the defensive and it would make it still easier for them to fire at our blazing muzzles. I knew it wouldn't be long before the Akons started applying such logic to their tactics.

We were now communicating by hand signals. Pucky made it clear that we were surrounded. In the rear of the hall the Regent's combat robots were showing up. They appeared to have been guided to our position by radio. If necessary they could also track us with their own sensor equipment. But by this time it made little difference to me.

On a signal from Rhodan we all began firing again. I shot blindly at the robot Brain's installations. I jumped forward a few meters and opened fire anew. The racket of our energy weapons was greater than that of the alarms. Irreplaceable circuit banks exploded while flying fragments damaged still other equipment.

After this onslaught we gambled everything on one last maneuver. When our abandoned positions were attacked and the smoke clouds obscured the opposition's visibility, we turned on our antigravs and rose above the floor. After adjusting my equipment for negative weight, I placed my hand against the low ceiling and crept along like a fly toward the stairwell opening.

"Stop!" yelled Rhodan.

I had braced my feet against one of the landings but drew them back as the robots brought the spiral stairs under fire. We held onto several refrigeration pipes to keep from being blasted away by the shockwaves. Glowing fragments hammered against the pipes and equipment nearby. Where the stairs had been was a bubbling mass of synthetic metal. Our defense screens reflected the heat so we were able to dart up thru the opening into the next level.

One storey below us everything seemed to be in confusion. The thunder of the robot weapons went on incessantly. Stifling gases shot up out of the stairwell opening.

"They're shooting at the Antis," yelled Ras. "Where next? They're giving us a breather!"

"From here on we fly," I shouted back. "They haven't found out yet that we're on antigravs. Onward! Keep looking for other overhead openings. Somewhere there must be a way out. Don't fire unless we're under specific attack. They may try to force us to show where we are by keeping up random firing, hoping we'll answer back."

Pucky discovered the next opening. Another staircase led upward. We glided thru the stairwell gap and arrived in an arched, domelike chamber which contained the main register banks for a principal memory extension. In these units billions of pieces of data were stored for retrieval.

Just as we thought we were reasonably safe we were

tracked again. Pucky picked up a few thought impulses but they faded away immediately. The Antis were everywhere. They seemed to be exerting every possible effort to counteract the paramental faculties of the mutants.

Then we were finally surrounded. The combat robots and Akon forces appeared simultaneously. I managed to check my watch at that moment and saw that it was 12:04—the 15th of February, 2106.

We could no longer hear the warning countdown from the Fleet of the *Ironduke*. An interference transmitter had come in on the same frequency. All I could hear in my minicom speaker was a faint high squeal.

We let ourselves sink to the floor and took cover behind some equipment racks. Rhodan resignedly hung his heavier weapon over his shoulder and then stared at my watch. The explosion would have to come at any moment. Somebody fired up ahead. Robot weapons came into play. More equipment exploded. We didn't pay much attention to the shockwaves anymore.

I stiffened with alarm when I heard a terrible roaring sound. Ras threw himself to the floor and grasped an upright support. We waited for death but it did not come. The sound increased its volume. The cyclonic howling was not quite like a nuclear explosion. It was as if a hurricane had been unleashed in the labyrinths of the robot Regent.

Tschubai's dark countenance was twisted with tension. Rhodan had grasped both my shoulders. We kept on listening. The shooting had been silenced. Underneath us the floor was shaking. Here and there shockwaves shot thru the armored hatches of the exits. The Regent was opening all its doors. It was obvious that the Brain was being destroyed even tho our bomb had not detonated. We looked at each other in amazement.

Pucky raised up. He listened with his head cocked on one side. Then he cried out: "I'm getting a message! The Antis are dead or they're pulling back."

"Can you jump now?" asked Rhodan. There was a spark of hope in his eyes.

"No, not yet. Watch it! Somebody's coming! He's sending thoughts on a para-plane. He says: 'Don't shoot—I come as a friend.' It keeps repeating itself, the same words . . . ''

Even tho annihilation was raging thru every other area, in our chamber it was still. No machines exploded, except that the memory banks ceased their humming. They had suddenly died out.

A strange object appeared in the connecting passageway. It was a coupled vehicle that slithered its way toward us on tractor treads.

"The transmitter!" cried Pucky excitedly.

We waited until the thing stopped in front of us. The side panel fell open, revealing seats inside. I recognized it as being an inspection vehicle. However, this particular one appeared to be of special design. I didn't hesitate any longer. In this situation it didn't matter what avenue we turned to. I entered the passenger cabin, sat down abruptly and waited for the others to join me.

When they had all come inside, the panel closed. The inspector car was completely automatic. In front of us a viewscreen lit up. I tensed suddenly when I recognized the features of Epetran. His smile was genuine. All of his mysterious inscrutability had vanished. The speaker crackled and his voice was unmistakable.

"This is a visitape which I prepared after the visit of Your Excellencies, Imperator Gonozal VIII and Solar Administrator Perry Rhodan. I won't be able to work out the principle of the time-converter since my life is too short now. Altho I perceived from probing your minds with the mento-monitor where you come from and what you intend, after studying the future I have decided to set up a self-destruct program for the Regent in case it should become influenced by alien powers in a way that is against the interests of the Empire. Thus I am placing the destiny of the Greater Empire in the hands of Your Highnesses.''

Epetran fell silent while bowing his head. Rhodan had turned pale.

''The special vehicle your crew detected in front of the *Sotala* was able to mento-monitor you also. The results proved to me that you have spared yourselves neither dangers nor difficulties in your efforts to preserve the stellar empire in accordance with the ancient traditions. Your thoughts are known to me. I am informed concerning the situation of your own time. When you hear this tape you will be back again in your own plane of reference. In order to hasten that process, shortly after you entered the Brain I had the simulated *Sotala* towed to another part of the landing area. I know that this will place Your Excellencies in danger but I have found no other solution. This robot vehicle has been exclusively designed to bring you and your companions to safety. It is with painful regret that I must destroy my life's work. I took the liberty of removing the time bomb from the base of the reactor. In its place the robot Brain was furnished with an extra safety circuit which would be activated when you arrived —you, the rightful Imperator with truth in your heart and risking life itself in the cause of the Empire. This has now occurred—the 'Insanity Circuit' has taken over. The Regent will self-destruct. I thank you for the new data concerning transition technology. I send greetings to the true friends of the Imperium. What will happen henceforth in your own era is unknown to me. I could only follow your thoughts as far as February of your year 2106. Take now the heritage of your ancestors. I have done my best.''

The voice became silent and the picture vanished. I cried out imploringly, speaking the name of the old scientist, but he did not appear again. Rhodan had to shake me by the arm before I regained control of myself.

Now we knew what that monitor vehicle had been up to. Marshall's guess had been correct. Rhodan and I had been scanned again during our visit without our knowing it. By the time we said goodby to Epetran he had already become informed concerning events of the future milleniums. He had been wise enough not to destroy the Regent beforehand because otherwise he would have changed the course of history. Instead he had chosen our planned date of February 15th as the key point of destiny.

The experience left me shaken. Only now could we fully perceive the man's greatness. What other scientist of the era of Tutmor VI would have been able to make such wide-ranging decisions? Epetran had overlooked nothing. We, the visitors from the future, had been recognized by him. The chain of related factors was mind-staggering. We, the intelligences of the advanced present, had to marvel at the genius of the old man. While we were still trying to figure how we could escape from Arkon 3, he had already worked out a 6000-year plan.

The rumblings and thunderings were still going on outside. Our vehicle traversed unknown halls. After taking an antigravitor upwards it finally brought us to the surface inside an armored dome. The journey was ended. We got out. The steel gates of the dome stood wide open. Before us lay the central spaceport which we had walked upon in another time. There was nothing to be seen of the *Sotala*. Epetran had caused it to be taken to another location. With the increasing distance we had come out of the zone of influence of the time-conversion field. The expedient had been correct even tho it had placed our lives in danger. Apparently the old man had wanted to be positive of the results. If the Regent had not been tampered with by the Akons it would not have activated its own self-destruct circuit. Epetran could not have installed a better security factor for testing the veracity of our thoughts long after his death.

There were thousands of robot spaceships on the landingfield but they had become inactive. Beneath us the ground was still rumbling. The "Insanity Circuit" must have reached out to all sectors of the Regent at once. It meant the total inactivation of the robot fleet as well as the remote-controlled defense fortresses, auto-mated industries and supplies and everything else. At the moment the Imperium had become a scrap heap without the slightest ability to defend itself.

We waited under cover of the armored dome. Here and there the ground cracked and fissured as machines exploded below. I thought I must be dreaming. Operation "Last Ditch" had come to an end. The Akons and Antis on Arkon 3 had lost the battle. Without the Regent they were more helpless than before.

Rhodan put out a call to the *Sotala*, which produced an immediate response. The crew had returned to present time.

"Heintz here, sir. We are attacking an Akon ship but give us your tracking coordinates."

Minutes later there was a distant clap of thunder. A dark point suddenly expanded until it burst into a sun-bright explosion. Then we made out the outlines of the *Sotala*. It came tumbling down toward the ground in our direction. After grazing a robot battleship it bounced to a stop. The lower section was in flames. The cruiser must have received a heavy hit.

Rhodan stared as if entranced toward the West where the planet's atmosphere was beginning to vibrate with rising thunders. The Terran superbattleships were the first to appear. With titanic force they attacked the spaceships of the Akons and the Antis.

An hour later the central spaceport was swarming with Terran landing troops. After another emergency call we were picked up by Bell.

The most daring operation in recent history had been completed. Terra's fleet was circling within the Arkon System. All resistance was crushed. Arkonide officials were removed from their offices. Akons and Antis were captured. It had all been a fantastic conquest. If the Regent had still been in existence, unquestionably the whole thing would have developed into a war of extinction.

20,000 paralyzed robotships were manned by Terran space troops. Large contingents of the fleet were already hurtling into space in order to also appropriate the units which had been posted there by the Regent.

We stood before the gutted wreck of the false *Sotala*. In the decisive action, 82 Terrans had lost their lives.

And the 4 Akon scientists were dead.

And . . .

And—!

My eyes avoided Perry, nor could I trust myself to speak to him. What, under the saddest of circumstances, was there to say? I knew he must be undergoing a terrible emotional trauma. For tho no one could ever replace Thora in his affections, could ever fill the vacuum created by her untimely death; and tho Auris of Las Toor had not yet joined his side officially; still a strong male-female bond had developed between the

Peacelord and the Lady of Las Toor. A chemical attraction heightened by spiritual affinity that, given a different timetrack into a more compassionate parallel world, could have eventuated in—who knows what? Very likely a second marriage for Perry. Perhaps a more satisfactory son. A delightful daughter with her mother's emerald eyes.

But the emerald emanations had faded from those flashing eyes, now.

Laughter would no longer spring from the smooth soft throat.

The magnetic thrill of her accidental electric touch had died.

For the Lady of Las Toor herself had died.

Auris was dead, her spirit fled from the holocaust of the conflagration loosed in the last moments of the disintegrating cruiser.

Well . . . Perry would have to find his inner peace in his own time and in his own way. In the meantime, I was deeply relieved when I heard one piece of good news: the time-converter had been destroyed by the fatal hit. At least the uncanny machine would never be employed again.

The commander of forces landing on Arkon 1 advised over intercom that the mad Imperator Carba had fallen in the battle with the robot guards of the Crystal Palace. I hardly paid any attention to this news. The heatwaves emerging from the *Sotala* singed my hair. We waited a long time until the chief of the rescue troops came and regretfully shrugged his shoulders. There was no trace to be found of Auris and the Akons.

I went with Perry to the *Ironduke*. We were only accompanied by John Marshall. I had briefly given him the basic import of Epetran's message to us but he had only nodded in silence.

Jefe Claudrin was waiting for us at the ground lock.

Reginald Bell had already taken off with a fleet unit, intent upon taking over the patrol cruisers of the Arkonide Home Fleet. From now on Terra would be strong—stronger than ever before.

For the time being I refrained from asking what position I was to hold in the future. Probably I would have to take over the teetering Empire. I didn't want to think of the impending revolts on the colonial planets. Time alone would tell whether or not Terra and Arkon could be welded together into a single entity.

Rhodan withdrew to his cabin. Marshall and I remained standing under the mammoth hull of the *Ironduke*. Major Heintz came and joined us. I made no reproaches for his attack on the fleeing Akons.

"I'm sorry, sir," he said. "Is there anything you want to know?"

"Yes. When did you get the order to move your location?"

"About 40 minutes after you'd gone on the mission. We were flanked by 2 battleships. An antigrav tender towed us to the other end of the field. It would have been senseless to shut off the time-phaser. We didn't know if you had planted the bomb yet or not."

"Thanks. That's all I wanted to know. You'd better get yourself to a doctor."

He saluted and went away. I looked once more at the vast spaceport. More than 500,000 Terrans had come in the transports. Now they were taking over the ships of the Imperium. Who would have imagined this in the late 20th century when a man named Perry Rhodan flew to Earth's moon in a primitive rocket?

I also went to my cabin. It was time to surrender to my need for sleep. As I closed my eyes I thought of the great councillor Epetran. *He* had saved the Imperium—not I . . .

TIME TRAVEL TO TOMORROW

10 ADVENTURES FROM NOW
Join Clark Darlton on
The Solitude Patrol

25 ADVENTURES FROM NOW
They're something special—
The Specialists

50 ADVENTURES FROM NOW
It's breathless Kurt Brand in a
Race Against Time

100 ADVENTURES FROM NOW
Join Kurt Mahr in a
Rendezvous in Outer Space

200 ADVENTURES FROM NOW
It's paradoxes of Chronos in
Time Experiment of the Exiles

300 ADVENTURES FROM NOW
Hans Kneifel describes
The Attack of the Centaurs

400 ADVENTURES FROM NOW
William Voltz describes
The Great Death

500 ADVENTURES FROM NOW
Dare you cross it?
The Null-Time Bridge

600 ADVENTURES FROM NOW
The epic of
The Galactic Alliance

PERRY RHODAN#797 WILL INVOLVE
Earthborns, Solarians, Mutants in
Flight from Intermezzo

RHOFANS RENDEZVOUS

WENDAYNE & FORREST J ACKERMAN, that Perry Rhodanic Pair, will be Guests of Honor at the

7th Annual FANTASY FAIRE
August 12-14
Pasadena Hilton Hotel
Pasadena, Calif.

3 Thrilling, Exciting, Amazing, Fun-Packed Days (& Nites!) You'll Never Forget are promised by Veteran Convention Promoters BILL & PEGGY CRAWFORD.

In addition to FORRY & WENDY such Sci-Fi Celebrities are expected to attend as A.E. "SLAN" VOGT, GEO. "LOGAN'S RUN" JOHNSON, LEIGH (DRAGON-QUEEN OF JUPITER) BRACKETT & Many Many More. At last year's FANTASY FAIRE there were such Stars as RAY BRADBURY, DANTON BURROUGHS, JIM (Super Animator) DANFORTH, RUSS (Tarzan Comix Ace) MANNING & Many Others.

Scientifilms! Panels! Art Show! Costume Party! Hucksters! Special Programming! And the Overall Aura of Thora, Khrest, Perry, Pucky, Atlan et al. The opportunity to Meet Fellow Rhofans, get your Perry Pocketbooks autographed, enjoy a 3-day Whizbang SF Convention!

$10 at the door (150 So. Los Robles, Pasadena, Calif.) or Advance Registrations to FANTASY FAIRE #7, 1855 W. Main St., Alhambra/CA 91801; telephone 218-337-7947.

**FORRY & WENDY
WANT TO SEE *YOU*
AT THE
RHOFANS RENDEZVOUS**

THIS UMBRAGEOUS ADVENTURE IS WAY OUT FOR—

PERRY RHODAN—The Solar First Administrator, who answers a nebulous distress call

Reginald Bell—The Solar First Deputy. He bumps into something he can't handle

Col. Jefe Claudrin—Commander of the flagship *Ironduke*

Col. Kermak—Commander of the *Alderamin*, whose handling of pirates inaugurates a new policy

Lt. Vitali—Chief of boarding crew for the *Alderamin*

Col. Sukril—Commander of the *Caesar*, who starts to hunt robots but finds the unexpected

Maj. Brokov—First Officer of the *Caesar*

PUCKY—The mousebeaver insists he's not old enough to be a "grandpa"

Iltu—The girl mousebeaver sends the teleporter into a transport

Ras Tschubai—The Afroterranian mutant arrives in the nick of time

Capt. Henderson—Nav officer of the *Caesar*

Maj. Borovski, Capt. Delmarin, Lt. Steinwald, Lt. Germa, Sgt. Bering—Commando team leaders for boarding robotships, all under Col. Sukril

Sgt. Brado, Sgt. Gork, Cadets Wilkovski, Lester & Hansen—Prize crew under Lt. Germa, who made first contact with the SHADOWS . . .

. . . And the spaceships *Ironduke, Caesar & Alderamin.*

FUTURE EVENTS CAST OMINOUS SHADOWS

Perry Rhodan

118

THE SHADOWS ATTACK

by Clark Darlton

ace books
A Division of Charter Communications Inc.
A GROSSET & DUNLAP COMPANY
1120 Avenue of the Americas
New York, New York 10036

Printed in U.S.A.

KHREST, *who was Perry Rhodan's first Arkonide friend, had predicted in his time that the bold and energetic Terrans would one day take over the crumbling Arkonide Imperium in order to erect from its ruins the stellar empire of humanity.*

The point in time for this takeover is now in the year 2116 by Earthly reckoning. The robot Regent of Arkon no longer exists and Terran experts take its place.

The robot fleet, consisting of 100,000 spaceships, has been paralyzed by the destruction of the Coordinator, and carefully-trained Terran spacemen are taking over these helplessly drifting vessels.

Also, other stellar races in the Milky Way are hunting for units of the robot fleet—and so a number of conflicts have arisen.

A much more ominous and completely surprising development, however, takes place when THE SHADOWS ATTACK.

1/ THE ROBOT HUNTERS

"BOGIES!

"Sir, we have bogies in sector K1-8-DX. Range 2.3 lisex. Standing by for instructions . . . "

Col. Kermak, commander of Solar class battle-cruiser *Alderamin*, did not so much as turn his head. He stared intently at the main viewscreen of the Control Central, which gave him a very natural reproduction of a section of the outer void. With a swift movement of his hand he brought in the magnification. The 2.3 light-seconds of distance seemed to telescope and the tracked objects became visible.

"Increase retropulsion," he said without taking his eyes from the screen. "Approach maneuver. Boarding crews stand by! Man the battle stations!"

The 1st Officer saluted and left the room in order to transmit the orders and see that they were carried out.

Col. Kermak was looking at 3 ships on the view-screen. They were apparently drifting along thru space without guidance and it was obvious that they were unmanned. They were robot units of the Arkonide Imperium's fleet which had virtually "died" when the robot Regent was destroyed. The Terrans had already succeeded in securing about 90,000 out of a total of 100,000 of them but out there in the unfathomable reaches of space there were still 10,000 heavily armed ships. In the hands of any potential enemy this could represent a force not to be underestimated.

Col. Kermak was among those who had been chosen to prevent this. With his heavy battlecruiser *Alderamin,* a spherical vessel 500 meters in diameter and carrying a normal crew of 800 men, he had been assigned to the task of tracking down the pilotless robotships of Arkon and taking them over with special prize crews.

This was no simple operation because when the robot Regent of Arkon was destroyed the units of the Arkonide Fleet were scattered all over the galaxy. Without a special circuit alteration these ships had responded exclusively to the command signals of the giant positronicon. Thus from one moment to the next they had suddenly become pilotless and they were subject to being confiscated by anyone who knew the secret of how to switch them over to manual control. Within the Milky Way there were numerous races who desired to increase their military power so it was natural for them to seize the opportunity by attempting to capture Arkon's inactivated warships.

But Perry Rhodan sought to prevent this at all costs.

As Col. Kermak continued to observe the 3 drifting vessels he noted that one of them was a superbattleship of the Imperium class, a tremendous sphere measuring almost a mile in diameter whereas the 2 other smaller ships were obviously cruisers. They still flew in their original formation, which was loosely triangular, with the battleship leading and the 2 cruisers following.

The First Officer returned to the Control Central. "Ship ready for combat, sir."

This time Kermak turned toward him. "Probably as superfluous as in all the other cases," he said with a reassuring smile. "Let's secure the battleship first. Who's leading the boarding team?"

"A Lt. Vitali, sir. This is his third ship capture."

"Then he knows what he has to do. Let me know as soon as all 3 ships are secured for manual flight."

"Very good, sir," answered the First Officer, who again exited the room.

Col. Kermak turned back to the viewscreen in order

to follow the forthcoming procedures in every detail. But before the locks of the *Alderamin* could be opened for Lt. Vitali and his men, something unexpected occurred: a message came thru from the duty officer in the tracking section. At least 20 ships ranging from large to small had materialized at a distance of just 5 lisex and were now approaching at top speed. They deployed themselves swiftly so that they quickly surrounded the *Alderamin* and the robotships.

"Energy screen!" roared Col. Kermak. This placed him in a security mode which would protect his spacesphere from eventual raybeam bombardments. And of course Vitali could no longer leave the *Alderamin*.

"Stand by!" he ordered, while watching his screen.

The alien ships were cylindrical in shape. Springers! But after all, what else? Wherever there was trouble the Springers, otherwise known as the Galactic Traders, were never far away. These merchant-pirate offshoots of the Arkonide race were as shrewd and clever as the Terrans. There could be little doubt that their technicians knew how to make the manual override connections on the robotships. The stellar traders had shown up with the intention of grabbing the spoils and dividing the heritage of Arkon between themselves.

"Radio message, sir!" announced the com officer over intercom. "An urgent warning!"

Almost imperceptibly, Kermak composed himself. With outward calm he answered: "Alright, let's have it!"

The Springers' challenge was brief and unmistakable: "Get out of here, Terrans! The 3 ships belong to us because we sighted them first. We'll give you 10 minutes, your time."

Kermak studied the viewscreen thoughtfully. The 20 longships of the fighting nomads had meanwhile firmed up their positions around the *Alderamin*. Within that circle were the 3 robot vessels which were the objective of both sides. He knew that for the moment the 20 Springers were no direct threat to him during their granted period of ''grace'' but on the other hand he was not in a position to drive them off. Under these circumstances he could not order Lt. Vitali to try taking the Arkon vessels. It would be a useless sacrifice. But for the same reason the Springers couldn't send out any boarding crews either, without exposing them to danger. It was a completely messed up situation.

He had the option of beaming out a call for Terran reinforcements, he thought bitterly, but they couldn't arrive before the 10 minutes were up. Probably by then the Springers would open fire in an attempt to break down the *Alderamin's* defense screens. The gamble could turn out to be fatal. Turning the picture around, it seemed out of the question for the *Alderamin* to knock out 20 opponents simultaneously. This was aside from the fact that Kermak was not intending to be the first to fire a shot. There could be no doubt that the Springers were in superior force here. It wouldn't be easy for them to knock out the heavy battlecruiser but with a streak of luck it was possible.

''Only 8 minutes left,'' said the First Officer, who had returned. ''That's damnably short . . . ''

''Long enough to make a decision,'' replied Kermak calmly, altho he was shaking inwardly. ''There's no way they can take those ships in the meantime. On the other hand we're under orders to avoid armed conflict with other races wherever possible. We are to defend ourselves if attacked—and that hasn't happened yet.''

He scanned the viewscreen again. Altho the 3 robot-ships were hurtling thru space at a considerable velocity, they appeared to be standing still. The *Alderamin* and the Springer formation also seemed to hover there motionlessly. It would be quite simple to take deadly aim with all the cruiser's heavy armaments. Anyway, only 3 minutes of the allowed time had been used up.

"The 3 Arkon ships don't have their screens up," muttered Kermak as if to himself. "They could be wiped out with our first broadside."

"But sir . . . !"

"Do you have a better idea for keeping them out of the Springers' hands? You'll have to do better than a shrug of your shoulders. If we can't get control of those robotships, then the Springers shouldn't be allowed to either. That would be the best solution where Terra is concerned."

The First Officer stared at his commander. "If we had a teleporter on board I'd know of another way!"

"Me too," confessed the colonel bitterly. He glanced at the chronometer. "Still 3 minutes left. Get a move on! In the meantime I'll try talking to the Springers."

Which was no particular problem. The Springers spoke Interkosmo as well as the Terrans. It didn't take the com operator more than 30 seconds to establish contact. On Kermak's screen the bearded face of a typical Galactic Trader appeared. He must have been one of the patriarchs because he was certainly more than 100 years of age by Earthly reckoning. The full, thick beard was tinted red and curiously squared, which was obviously a clan identification.

"What do you want, Terran? You have 2 minutes left."

Kermak controlled himself and kept his voice as even as possible. "These 3 Arkon ships belong to us. We have permission from Gonozal VIII . . . "

"Permission, he says!" The Springer began to laugh thunderously. "Who is this Gonozal VIII, anyway? Or are you talking about that pseudo-imperator of Arkon who merely fronted for the robot? If so, then the ships don't belong to you any more than they do to us. They are ownerless—free booty for the first to find them. And we were first in this case. So?''

Kermak knew that he only had another minute to go. ''Gonozal-Atlan was the rightful ruler of Arkon. Perry Rhodan is his rightful successor. Therefore the ships belong to him. If you take them it will be an act of theft. Do you want to tangle with Terra?''

''Terra!'' echoed the Springer, starting to laugh again. He seemed to be genuinely amused. ''What is Terra without the protection of Arkon? And the Imperium doesn't exist anymore.''

The bearded swindler was in for a surprise, thought Col. Kermak heatedly while noting with a quick glance that only 40 seconds were left. His hope of convincing the Springer was fading away. The First Officer had just returned and gave him a nod. This meant that Kermak only had to depress the red firing button to bring the robotships under concentrated fire. Since they were without defense screens they would be destroyed in a matter of seconds.

''So what you are saying is that you are willing to perform an act of piracy and risk open conflict with Terra?'' he asked quietly.

''That's right!'' nodded the Springer, still chuckling. ''What have we got to lose?''

10 seconds to go.

''Very well,'' said Kermak, suddenly returning a very sarcastic smile. ''I might have let myself be talked into letting you have at least one of those cruisers but since you're so greedy you won't have even one of them. Do you understand?''

''Not a word,'' replied the Springer, fingering his beard. ''You Terrans are fond of speaking in riddles.

Besides, your time is up. Get out of here or I'll open fire."

"I'll do it *for* you," retorted Kermak grimly. He shoved in the red button which activated all the guns that had been carefully aimed in the meantime. "You're welcome to the scrap!"

From 3 turret positions the concentrated energy beams of the *Alderamin* shot out and found their targets. They penetrated the hulls of the robotships with ease and bored their way into the vessels' central cores—to the Arkon power piles. The resulting nuclear explosions ripped the ships asunder.

Altho there were actually 3 explosions their effect was that of one gigantic detonation. One of the Springer ships had been too close to the robot super giant and was hurled away into the void by the fury of the blast. Before the remaining 19 longships could take their revenge on the *Alderamin,* Col. Kermak shoved his flight lever forward into full thrust. Immediately the warship started toward a distant nebula and accelerated wildly. It soon reached light velocity and vanished into semispace.

The 19 Springer units were left in helpless dismay. All they could do was attempt to rescue the smaller longship that was plunging out of control into emptiness. They paid no further attention to the glowing nuclear clouds which had been 3 proud Arkon ships. They also knew that it was useless to try pursuing the Terran cruiser with its new linear-drive propulsion.

The *Alderamin* switched course, however, and made a direct flight to the distant Earth, prepared to submit a report to the First Administrator. It was to inaugurate a new phase of the search for Arkon's missing robotships.

* * * *

The *Caesar* was a superbattleship of the Imperium class, also equipped with linear space-drive and also on the hunt for the valuable Arkon robotships.

4 days had passed since the return of the *Alderamin*. Tactics had been changed. In a conference convened by Perry Rhodan it had been decided to distribute the members of the Mutant Corps among a number of the search ships so that even superior forces of Springers, Aras or Ekhonides could be outsmarted. Moreover, all had agreed that no compromise was to be countenanced and that it was preferable to risk combat, if necessary, and to destroy the robotships rather than have them be taken. From now on the search units were going to offer stiffer resistance. In the past few days the Springers especially had demonstrated a ruthless determination to challenge the men of Earth for possession of Arkon's heritage.

Col. Sukril, commander of the *Caesar*, had also been present at the conference. Outwardly he looked very much like Rhodan's second-in-command, Reginald Bell, nor was it to be denied that certain elements of his character reminded people of Bell. This is why it was perhaps not a pure coincidence that Col. Sukril had the distinction of acquiring the mutant services of Pucky the mousebeaver.

Their first meeting had not been without a certain flavor of drama.

It had been Pucky's own fault that he had not been present at the briefing. He had just come back from a strenuous mission and had decided to pass the few hours of his leave at his weekend place at Lake Goshun. Rhodan had told him that his presence at the meeting wasn't mandatory. He said that it only entailed some routine matters that concerned the Fleet commanders.

So it was that Pucky came on board the *Caesar* at the

last moment, after Rhodan had given the mutants their assignments. He was of course familiar with the name of Col. Sukril but he had not yet met him personally. The *Caesar* was like any other ship and, like every one of them engaged in the search activity, it was to have a mutant on board. This was in addition to a special load of 20,000 experienced spacemen, other than regular crews, which the search ships were carrying for the purpose of taking over the robotships and bringing them to Earth.

A young, dark-haired officer was waiting for him in the airlock. "You're flying with us, Lt. Puck," he said. "May I welcome you most heartily on board the *Caesar?*"

"That you may," replied Pucky patronizingly, saluting rather indifferently. He wore his custom-made uniform with the heated case for his beaver tail. Being a telepath, he already knew the officer's name. "By the way, does it happen that I've been assigned to your task unit?"

"You're quite correct, Lt. Puck!"

The mousebeaver stretched out his paw and smiled. "Then you can drop the title of rank. We're buddies in this together."

"Hm-m . . . ah—very well, Puck."

"Pucky!"

"What . . . ?"

"Pucky! That's what I'm called." He looked around. "Where is the commander? A Colonel Sukril, if I understand correctly."

"In the Control Central. We take off in 5 minutes."

"Then I've arrived at just the right time," Pucky grinned. "So up, up and away—to happy hunting!"

"Hm-m," grumbled Germa doubtfully, shrugging vaguely. "I'm not so sure it's going to be all that

happy. The Springers are keeping our search commandos pretty busy.''

''Pah!'' Pucky watched while the heavy main lock
closed and slid in place with a dull thud. ''So far we've
always been able to handle those whisker-faces. We
just have to be faster than they are—and smarter.''

Lt. Germa smiled to himself. He seemed to be
pleased with Pucky's answer. ''Come on, I'll show you
to your cabin. It's right next to mine.''

The mousebeaver waddled after him altho he would
have preferred teleportation. But in the young officer's
mind he had detected some very important indications.
First of all he discovered that Germa liked him very
much. It wasn't the usual respect for his outstanding
para-faculties but a genuine feeling of fondness and
friendship. And secondly Germa had thought of their
forthcoming interim landing—on Mars.

Mars? What did the *Caesar* want on Mars?

Pucky realized that Germa didn't know. If anybody
knew the reason for the Mars touchdown it would most
likely be the commander. So he'd have to ask him,
provided the thought didn't come into his head first.

The cabin reflected Pucky's extraterrestrial preferences and was provided with everything the mousebeaver would have wanted for a lengthy journey. Even
the fridge with a supply of fresh vegetables had not
been forgotten. And even a full-grown man would have
been comfortable in the wide bed.

''Neat!'' chirped Pucky appreciatively, and he
reached up to pat his much larger companion on the
back. ''Very neat. You people must have really put
yourself out. So you live in the cabin to the left of me?
Who's in the other one?''

Germa shrugged. ''No idea. As far as I know, it's
empty.''

"That suits me." Pucky lowered his little dufflebag in which he had collected the things most important to him. "At any rate I guess I was too pessimistic. I sneaked in my own crop when I didn't have to."

He picked up the bag and shook out its contents onto the floor. Nothing but fresh carrots. Lieutenant Germa laughed until it brought tears to his eyes.

At the same time the *Caesar* took off and accelerated at a modest rate into space. Inside the ship the effects were barely noticeable since the gravity fields and inertial absorbers took up the shock. Thus the effects of small course changes were also neutralized.

"You still have to report to the Commander," said Germa somewhat concernedly. "Col. Sukril is a stickler for the rules. It's a wonder he took off without making sure you were present and accounted for."

Pucky made a wry face. "I hate regulations and formalities, Germa. I always get in trouble with people like that. But how is he otherwise?"

"A good officer, pretty daring at times, and he flares up once in awhile—otherwise he's straight and very fair. But I think in your case you'd better not—hm-m . . . "

"I'd better not what . . . ?"

"I mean, maybe you'd better not try a first name basis right away. If you forget rank and title he might blow up at you."

Pucky grinned, revealing his famous incisor tooth. It was a sure sign that the situation was turning into a "fun game" for him. "Alright, you know him better than I do. Why should I make things tough on myself? But watch out if our good friend Sukril plays a one-sided game! If he drops his formality with *me*, he could be in for a surprise! Fine—let's go. Or aren't you coming along?"

"Do you think I'd want to miss it?" retorted Germa with mock indignation, and he led the way out. "The grav is right over there."

"I could get there much faster if I wanted to but there's no need to startle Sukril too soon. Also, it's good to have a walk after eating."

The *Caesar* was a world in itself. With its 1500-meter hull it resembled a Terran submarine modular city with streets and even building-like structures which were connected by antigrav lifts. An untrained person could become irretrievably lost in this maze of ultra-modern installations and never find his way back to the point of exit. Pucky, however, was well acquainted with the interior of such superbattleships. He could still recall the many emergency drills he had gone thru in the days when these "big ones" were still a novelty in the Fleet.

Germa stopped at the door to the Control Central. "It's always like entering the Inner Sanctum," he half-whispered.

Pucky could hardly suppress a giggle. "You're stretching it, Slim. I've never been afraid of any commander. If he's not a nice guy, I sail him thru a couple of corridors and clamp him to the ceiling somewhere. Then they can just get him down with a ladder."

"You and your telekinesis," muttered Germa shakenly. He pointed to the door. "You lead the way this time."

Pucky cautiously concealed his incisor tooth and pressed the automatic release button. The door slid into its niche and gave access to the Control Central. In spite of the maze of consoles and equipment cabinets the room appeared to be semi-circular in shape. Everywhere there were gleaming viewscreens on the walls, surrounded by controls and switches of every description. At one table an officer was studying star charts.

He looked up briefly and grinned at Pucky—then immersed himself again in his work.

Another man sat in the wide seat before the main control board. His back was almost broad enough for 2 men. His hair was cut short and stood up like gleaming silver-gray bristles. He still didn't seem to have noted the intrusion because he was staring intently at the viewscreen, in the middle of which was a reddish star. His vise-like hands were on the console beneath the indicators.

Two other officers turned to discover Pucky and Germa. One of them seemed to know what was on the commander's mind.

"Sir—the mutant."

Col. Sukril did not even turn his head. "You mean this Pucky creature?" he asked. He cleared his throat. "As soon as he shows up he is to come to me. I expect him to report in according to regulations like anyone else." He continued his concentration on the outer space view altho he must have known that the mousebeaver stood directly behind him.

Pucky gave Germa an imploring look but the lieutenant shook his head. Knowing that the mousebeaver could read his mind he suggested mentally that he should "toe the line" just now. It was no use to start any trouble when it wasn't necessary.

Pucky turned his gaze from Germa to contemplate Col. Sukril's broad back. There was something about his figure that was very familiar. Hm-m . . . If his hair were red instead of gray, one might have thought this was Reginald Bell. But Bell was with Rhodan just now on the *Ironduke*, which was the flagship. They, too, were on a mission.

"Lt. Puck reporting for duty, sir," the mousebeaver finally managed to say, while more or less standing at attention.

The man in the pilot's seat folded his hands in his lap before he slowly turned around. He remained seated and it was only the chair that actually turned. His healthy, ruddy face was good-natured but revealed a trace of curiosity. He smiled faintly. ''So this is Pucky, the most notorious of all the mousebeavers. Hm-m . . . Why are you just reporting to me now, Lt. Puck?''

Pucky stared in utter amazement at Col. Sukril. Actually he looked almost like Bell with his hair dyed. If it were not for the completely different brainwave pattern it would be possible to imagine that this was Rhodan's second-in-command. But then upon closer inspection the other differences came to light. The mouth was smaller and more tight-lipped than Bell's, the cheeks somewhat fuller and the chin much heavier. In the gray eyes there was an expression of sternness, courage and justice.

''Well, is this too late?'' was Pucky's counter-question.

Col. Sukril remained motionless. He made an effort to screen his thoughts but of course without experience in such matters he didn't quite succeed. Thus Pucky picked up a few interesting items altho they didn't seem to tie together clearly. So he was going to have to rely on questions to learn the rest.

''Lt. Puck!'' said Sukril sharply. ''I permit no exceptions to the rule on board my ship. You are a member of my crew, with the same rights and the same duties. A lot of commendable stories have been told about you, I'll admit, but don't think that entitles you to any special privileges. Here everybody does his job and you will do yours. Is that understood?''

''No sir,'' replied Pucky while lowering his gaze in mock shame. ''There are some people who say that my intelligence leaves something to be desired and . . . ''

"Military discipline has nothing to do with intelligence!" roared Col. Sukril impatiently but then he calmed himself immediately. "Anyone boarding a ship for duty must report immediately to the commander. Can you understand that?"

"That's what I just did, sir," replied, Pucky, making a weak attempt to defend himself. Inwardly the discussion began to amuse him. "Lt. Germa brought me here right away."

"So? And how do you explain the fact that you're just getting here now? Look there on the viewscreen! We're already passing the moon!"

"Nice view," commented Pucky appreciatively as he watched the cratered landscape pass by. "It always reminds me of Pericles."

Sukril caught his breath, apparently nonplussed. "Of what?"

"Aren't you familiar with Pericles? Too bad —you've missed a lot. It's the 2d moon of the 4th planet of Clara 5, a red sun just left of Cancer. Of course you must know where Cancer is located?"

Col. Sukril's face went thru an interesting process of changes. It became darker, for one thing, but in contrast to Bell's face instead of becoming red it turned blue.

"Are you trying to—?"

"No sir, it's not what you think!" interjected Pucky. "But—to be honest about it, I couldn't report to you any sooner than this."

Sukril appeared to have calmed himself again. "Oh? And just why was that?"

"Because I just got on board before you took off."

Sukril looked at Pucky more closely. "Your top uniform button is unfastened, Lt. Puck."

The mousebeaver nodded negligently. "Why is yours buttoned? Afraid you'll catch cold?"

Col. Sukril swallowed hard and thought of his temper. He told himself to just take it easy and not get excited. To fence with the mutant was a senseless waste of time. He abandoned the hope of getting the best of him, in contrast to all the mousebeaver's other superiors. No one had ever succeeded. Why should he be the one? And yet . . . ?!

"Lieutenant," he said sharply, "you will adhere to the regulations. In your cabin you may do as you please, as far as I am concerned." He took a deep breath. "You are familiar with our orders and your own, as well?"

"We're to catch us some robots, sir."

"You might call it that." Sukril became a trifle friendlier. He leaned forward and looked into the mousebeaver's eyes. "Has Lt. Germa shown you your quarters? Do you have any complaints?"

"None, sir. Just one question: what are we going to Mars for?"

Sukril leaned forward still farther. He grinned broadly. "Aha! So you've already done some telepathic snooping? If not, why would you ask about Mars? Alright then, I'll tell you. Rhodan ordered us to pick up Miss Iltu. From now on she'll be flying on various missions, as occasion demands, and she is to be trained by you."

Pucky forgot his military schooling. Indignantly he placed his small arms akimbo. His expression was one of thunderstruck amazement. "Iltu? That babe in arms?"

Sukril nodded affirmatively. "What do you have against Iltu? She is a cute and capable mousebeaver girl. She can handle telekinesis and is also a telepath. Well, yes—where teleporting is concerned she has some shortcomings, but she'll also learn that—"

"But she's much too young!" persisted Pucky.

"Nevertheless, she's 100 years old, according to what she told us," declared Sukril soberly. "If that's supposed to be young I'd like to know just how old mousebeavers get. How old are you, Lt. Puck?"

It was a delicate question to which Sukril received no more of an answer than had Rhodan or Bell or anyone else.

"Iltu!" Pucky's voice seemed to express complete rejection but deep in his brown eyes was a glimmer of pleasure over the prospect of meeting his special friend whom he had once rescued from Vagabond along with 27 other young mousebeavers. They had all been brought to Earth but had later settled on Mars. "Does she know about this?"

"She was instructed about the mission and has agreed to go."

"She's a brave girl." Pucky nodded appreciatively but then added quickly: "But she's not ready for real work because she has no idea of how to teleport properly. And as for telekinesis she only has playful kid games in her head. Does she really have to come with me?"

"No, it's not mandatory. According to Rhodan's instructions, if you're strictly against it we'll change course and not pick her up." He turned to the officer at the chart table. "Captain, work out the new course. We'll continue to accelerate and bypass Mars."

"Hey!" chirped Pucky in a shrill tone. He waddled past Sukril to the navigator. "If you don't land on Mars I've got news for you!" Then he turned back to Sukril who had become speechless. "Well, don't lose your eyeballs, Sukril. After all, everyone has to make a start sometime."

He nodded patronizingly to Col. Sukril and strutted

out of the Control Central. With a stiff salute, Lt. Germa also took his leave before the thunderstorm could break over his head.

But there was no thunder.

The commander watched Pucky go with his mouth agape but then he got hold of himself. He nodded to the navigations officer. "Steady as she goes," he ordered. "Interim landing on Mars."

The first round, he thought to himself, was undecided. But he didn't realize how wrong he was.

*   *   *   *

The brief landing on Mars occurred according to plan. Iltu was brought on board and taken to her quarters by Lt. Germa where she was received by Pucky. Then the *Caesar* took off again and set course for its assigned sector.

This was a peripheral region of the galaxy where there were very few stars. Atlan had declared it to be a zone of operation for one of the larger fleet formations, which turned out to be the case. Almost daily the search teams of the Terran ships ran across scattered cruisers or major vessels of the Arkonide Imperium. Being cut off from the usual command signals from the robot Regent, they drifted without direction thru the void, the helpless prey of anyone who found them.

Col. Sukril waited until his target star appeared on the screen. It was an unknown giant sun that didn't even have a name, merely an index number. It was to be the point of reference for all operations of the *Caesar*. The ship had long since surpassed the speed of light. Gaining velocity with each passing second it glided toward its goal between Einstein space and the 5th dimension. The target star remained visible even tho part of the universe had disappeared into a zone of darkness.

Rather than a blind flight as in the case of hyper-transitions, it was based on visual navigation.

The *Caesar* was the first super-class spaceship to be equipped with a fully tested propulsion system based on the semispace principle. The *Alderamin* also had this new system but was not considered to be perfect because Prof. Kalup had provided the *Caesar* with certain additional safety factors which had not been applied before. Thus the *Caesar* was the safest and fastest ship in the Terran spacefleet.

Col. Sukril was fully aware of this fact. He sat in front of the screen for another half hour and monitored the flight, the course and the velocity. Then he called his First Officer to him. "Maj. Brokov, you can take over now. Call me if you think it's necessary. All incoming hypercom messages are to be recorded. I'll go thru them later. Well—good night, Major."

"Good night, sir," said Brokov, saluting. He relaxed again only after Sukril had left the Control Central. He had crinkly dark hair, was stockily built, in fact almost too broad in the shoulders, but seemed otherwise to be of an easy-going nature. "The Skipper's sure a stickler for spit and polish, wouldn't you say, Henderson?"

The Navigation officer, Capt. Henderson, placed his hands on the star charts and grinned. "I think he must even sleep with his fingers on his pant seams," he reflected. "But on the other hand I don't believe we could imagine a better commander."

"I'll buy that, Henderson—all the way!" Brokov sat down. "You want to give me the usual poop?"

The other nodded toward the screen. "Course is border zone BM-53-XB. Present speed is 370,000 light units. Acceleration constant at 3X factor. The target area ETA is 50 hours as she goes. So far nothing unusual has come up."

"Thanks, Henderson." Brokov removed his gaze from the screen to look at the captain. "I hear we have the mutant, Pucky, on board."

"He was assigned to us as you know but he only arrived at the last minute. The Old Man almost came apart."

"I can imagine because I know Pucky, actually. We once flew a mission together with Rhodan. As I recall, he doesn't go much for the rule book. Well, he'll have his hands full now that his little Bopeep is with him."

"Come again?"

Brokov grinned significantly. "The little mouse-beaver gal we picked up on Mars. Seems as if having one of them on board isn't enough. I'm afraid on this flight the Colonel may suffer a stroke."

"He can adjust himself to a lot of things," Henderson assured him. And he went back to his work of checking out the ship's course.

At this time a quite different discussion was going on in Pucky's cabin. Pucky sat with his legs drawn under him in the farthest corner of his couch and with his pack pressed against the wall. It seemed as if he would have been happy to go back farther if it had been physically possible. Sitting all neat and proper on the edge of the couch was another mousebeaver.

As seen thru human eyes, at first glance there might have been no observable difference between them altho Iltu only wore a pastel green combination without any rank insignia, instead of a uniform. Also Iltu was slightly smaller and of a more delicate build than Pucky but that was the only outward difference. Even Iltu had an incisor tooth which showed when she laughed but it was not gleaming white like Pucky's. Rather it was a pale pink counterpart. She had the same brown badger eyes and the same flat beaver tail altho it was somewhat smaller. Her suit pants had no special arrangement in the seat but merely a hole. The tail with its silky red-brown fur lay directly in front of Pucky.

He made a disdainful face. "Do you all run around on Mars like that?" As if to change the subject he added: "How's the settlement getting along, anyway?"

Iltu briefly flashed her pink incisor at him. "You've been long overdue for a visit to us, you know. All the children want to see their grandpa."

Pucky stiffened in sudden shock. "Grandpa!" he gasped. "Are they referring to *me* with that name?"

"Who else? There is certainly no one else here."

Pucky slumped despondently. "So that's what those dorky rascals call gratitude! I rescue them from certain death on Vagabond, bring them to Earth, settle them down on Mars and give them a new home—and then they call me a grandpa! How disrespectful can you get?"

Iltu shook her delicately-shaped head. "Haven't you always pointed out what youngsters we were in comparison to you? Haven't you always said that compared to us you were old and wise? Well, then—there you have a grandpa!"

"If Bell heard that he'd die laughing."

"Bell? Is that the fat fellow with the fire-red hair?"

Pucky grinned cheerfully, having forgotten the "grandpa" subject. "Yes, that's him but don't let him hear you call him fat or he'll have you for supper in spite of your pretty eyes."

Iltu moved closer. "Do I have pretty eyes?" she whispered hopefully.

Pucky's incisor vanished as he sought to press himself farther into the corner. "Uh—what I was asking you—how is the colony doing on Mars these days?"

Iltu pouted. "All day long we get schooling or sports. We hardly ever get to play anymore. They've

put an energy dome over the settlement—so that nobody can rob us, they say. But I think they put it there to
keep us from having some real fun.''

Of course by ''fun and play'' Iltu referred to telekinesis. The young mousebeavers used their natural
gift by way of amusement—moving every possible
object—including men—from one place to another
thru the force of their minds. For the officers and
personnel of the Martian base this type of ''fun and
games'' often resulted in some unpleasant surprises
—hence the energy dome.

''But we still play anyway,'' Iltu continued. ''We
can do it inside the dome.'' She sighed. ''But I'm glad
to be flying with you. That's a real nice vacation.''

Pucky frowned sternly. ''This is no vacation,'' he
said. ''You have been assigned to me as a pupil. As it
is, you're far too young—I mean, too inexperienced
—to be of much help to me. But I'll do what I can. How
is your teleportation?''

She seemed to become a bit smaller, as if shrinking
from the subject. ''It's nothing special,'' she finally
answered candidly. ''My telekinesis is great—as well
as telepathy. But I'm still learning teleportation
whenever they give me the chance.''

''We'll have plenty of practice,'' Pucky promised
her grimly, ''before we go into any action. There's
enough room here in the ship but let me tell you one
thing, Iltu: there will be no 'fun and games' on board! It
can cause too much grief. If you just moved one of the
control levers it could be the end of all of us. We could
crash into a sun or maybe even fall into a hole in time.''

''Fall where?'' Iltu raised her ears, which was becoming to her.

''That's a special expression,'' Pucky told her evasively. "Anyway, there'll be no telekinesis unless I order it. Do you understand?"

"Yes," she sighed. Then she got up and began to waddle flirtatiously about the cabin. "How do you like my jumpsuit outfit?"

Pucky shrank back again. If it hadn't been for the bulkhead he would have tumbled to the deck. "Females!" he chirped impatiently. "They're all the same everywhere and in every race or species! But I'm going to tell you this, girl: this is no summer resort—you're on board a warship! Here there is discipline—you'll find that out. I am not your grandpa—I'm your superior officer! You are to do exactly what I order you to do. Is that clear, once and for all?"

Iltu beamed at Pucky with her big mousebeaver eyes. "And what do you order me to do now?" she half-whispered anxiously.

Pucky threw his small arms into the air and whistled in sheer desperation. "I order you to disappear into your cabin at once and to leave me in peace! I want to go to sleep! I'm tired! I've had enough of this children's prattle!"

Instead of pouting, Iltu smiled in submission. "Yes, grandpa," she chirped teasingly. After that she seemed to go into a brief trance while she stared at the cabin wall—and she was gone. She had teleported. Only a momentary shimmering of the air marked the place where she had been.

Pucky sighed and simply fell back on the bed where he stretched himself out and pounded the covers with his fists. "What a little monster!" he muttered angrily. "A sassy little beast, she is!"

But then he suddenly became quite motionless and

listened inwardly. He was receiving Iltu's thoughts. She must also be lying on her bed and reflecting on their meeting.

She was thinking of him, Pucky.

He closed his eyes and began to smile. What Iltu was thinking about him must have been something very delightful.

2/ INVISIBLE INVADERS

For 2 full days Pucky put Iltu thru her training exercises. He would lead her to a specific location where she was instructed to firmly memorize her surroundings. Then he would take her back and order her to teleport to the target area. At first it didn't always work out. Altho she could dematerialize properly she would often land in an entirely different place. Then Pucky would have to make a long search until he found her. Even telepathy didn't help much because Iltu couldn't say where she had landed.

These drills were surprising as well as distressing to the crew of the *Caesar*. Sometimes it was even a shock to the men because it was not an everyday occurrence to suddenly be confronted with a figure that popped right out of the air. And Iltu materialized in machine rooms, gun turrets, cabins and even restrooms.

However, at the end of the second day Pucky had to admit that she was making progress. "That's pretty good now, little one. If you keep on like that you'll be a usable teleporter. There's no doubt that you have the ability."

It was a gross understatement, to which Iltu objected.

"Pucky, you're mean! In the last 2 hours I didn't make one false jump. I *can* teleport!"

"Passable," he minimized. "But now you still have to learn how to get to a place you're not familiar with beforehand. You have to do it by using telepathy. As an example: search out the thoughts of the commander,

161

trace his location and jump. Materialize directly in front of him.''

''I don't want to do that,'' protested Iltu. ''The Colonel is very severe. I'm afraid of him.''

''Hm-m. Then let's take somebody else: Lt. Germa.'' Pucky looked directly at Iltu. ''Where is Germa now?''

Iltu understood what she was supposed to do. She concentrated and attempted to sort out the thought patterns pressing in upon her. It required almost 10 minutes before her eyes suddenly brightened. ''I've got him! He's off duty and in his cabin.''

''Excellent!'' said Pucky with a grudging note of praise in his voice. ''Then follow me now!''

He had jumped almost before completing his sentence. Staring at the spot where he had been, Iltu forgot Pucky and concentrated entirely on Germa's incoming stream of thoughts. Then she jumped.

Germa was sitting in a chair, reading. Thus he had been putting out a clear and constant stream of thoughts which could easily be intercepted by a telepath. He was abruptly interrupted as Pucky materialized near him and let out a shrill whistle to make him aware of his presence.

Germa half rose out of his seat but then sank back again. He had learned not to be startled so much by Pucky anymore. But then he turned pale a second later when Iltu landed right on his stomach and her weight pushed him into the upholstery.

''Is that any way to do?'' he protested indignantly. ''I was just sitting here reading!''

''And we're training,'' replied Pucky. ''Well done, Iltu! That was good measuring. You came right in on target. Of course it wasn't exact precision or you would have landed on top of his head. I'm presuming that's where he keeps his brain.''

Germa straightened up after Iltu slipped out of the chair. "That's just about enough, Pucky! At least you could leave me in peace during the little free time I have off. You know we're getting close to the operation zone and after that we'll hardly have a chance to sleep. We're already on alert here and apparently you have nothing better to do than to spook innocent people —and even bug them. Shame on you, Iltu! I wouldn't have expected this of you."

The girl mousebeaver shyly lowered her eyes and pattered timidly closer to him. She chirped plaintively: "I didn't mean to do it that way, Germa. But we have to practice or otherwise I may fail when things are serious. I'm sorry, too, about landing on your tummy. I meant to just appear in your room. So please don't be angry . . . "

Germa's indignation melted away like butter in the sun. He reached out his hand and drew Iltu toward him. "That's alright, little one. You're not to blame." He looked disapprovingly at Pucky. "But he is big enough and apparently old enough, as well, to cut out this kind of tomfoolery."

Pucky had straightened up stiffly. "I am *not* that old!" he retorted heatedly. He then dematerialized as if he'd been insulted.

Germa stared at the empty spot. "What's the matter with him, anyway?" he said.

Iltu revealed that she was not one to use the opportunity for slandering her fellow creature or making him look ridiculous. "I don't know," she answered, taking her paw from the young officer's hands. "Excuse me—I'll go look after him. Until later . . . "

Then Germa was alone again.

He picked up his book but suddenly he had no more interest in reading.

* * * *

The rest period was over on board the ship when the alarms sounded.

In the Control Central, Capt. Henderson sat before the naviagation screens while he analyzed the data that was coming in from the tracking center. The forward screen's angle of vision narrowed as the view was magnified. Eleven faintly gleaming blips of light became visible.

Col. Sukril had given the alarm as a matter of precaution because he couldn't be sure if these were the sought-after robotships or fighting units of the Springers or some other race. Formations of 10 or more robotships were not unusual. They could have been in a flight group together when the robot Regent ceased functioning—in which case they would now be drifting onward without pilots or propulsion until eternity itself put an end to their course. Or perhaps the search commandos.

"Course and velocity unchanged," said Capt. Henderson after 2 minutes of calculation. "All signs indicate that we're dealing with the ships of Arkon. Your orders, sir?"

Col. Sukril did not take his eyes from the screen. He thought of Col. Kermak's bitter experience. This wasn't going to happen to him. If any Springers appeared he was going to attack them immediately but in no case was he going to destroy the robotships. But aside from the robot units nothing could be detected by the trackers in a surrounding area of 800 light-years. The nearest sun was 800 light-years sternward from the *Caesar.* It seemed that sector BM-53-XB was about the loneliest region a man could imagine.

"Decrease velocity, Captain. Hold our present course. All gun crews on standby. Lt. Germa, report to Control Central!"

Germa was only one among a number of team officers so it was merely by chance that he chose him. He might just as easily have picked out Capt. Delmarin, Maj. Borovski or Lt. Steinwald but he selected Lt. Germa. It was one of those instinctive decisions that often change the course of events. Perhaps also Col. Sukril's knowledge of the good rapport between Germa and the 2 mousebeavers had helped to influence his choice.

"We reach the formation in 10 minutes, sir. Their course is the same. Lt. Germa is on his way."

Sukril only nodded. He observed the screen intently. Something warned him inwardly but it was only an indistinct sort of premonition. By now it was clear that those 11 ships out there were drifting without a crew. All radio calls had remained unanswered. There was no indication that the least robot element was functioning.

"Lt. Germa reporting, sir!"

Col. Sukril seemed to awaken as if from a dream. He swiveled around slowly. "Take a look at those ships, Lieutenant. What can you tell me about them?"

Germa moved closer until he was standing next to the commander. With alert eyes he studied the 11 ships. He followed their steady course and took note of their configurations. Without exception they were spherical vessels, from the smallest 60-meter type to the Imperium-class flagship which was the same size as the *Caesar*. Their relative velocity now was almost zero but actually they were still moving along at a rate of many thousands of km per second. The void beyond them was black. Only a few blurred nebulous specks bore witness to the fact that other galaxies existed across the tremendous abyss. According to present knowledge, nothing lay between but an awesome emptiness; no suns, no planets—and probably also no ships.

"No question about it, sir, they're robotships, no longer in operation."

Col. Sukril nodded. "That's also my analysis, Lieutenant. I think we can take them over. Do you have any reservations?"

"No, sir. After all, it's my job for me and my men to take over one of the ships and bring it back to Earth. Just give the order, sir, and we'll go into action."

Sukril gave him a fleeting smile. "Don't be over-confident, Lieutenant. It's true that there's no trace of enemy units in the immediate area but that can change. The Springers only have to make one long transition to make a sudden appearance." He sighed. "Take a long-range scoutship and 5 men, Lieutenant. You're the advanced guard. You can head for the flagship. The main lock can be opened manually from the outside when the electronic security system is out of operation—and that's the situation now. You will penetrate into the Control Central and from there I will expect to hear your radio report. Is everything clear? Can you get out there and overtake that formation?"

Lt. Germa sought to clear up a certain point. "Then—it's the normal boarding procedure, sir? No special precautions?"

"Not indicated—until after your team has gone on board first."

Germa hesitated.

"Something else, Lieutenant?"

"Just one question, sir. What about the teleporter, Pucky?"

"The mousebeaver?" Sukril wrinkled his forehead. "What do we need him for when everything is in order? We only use the mutants when something unforeseen comes up—more or less like an emergency backup."

"I only thought, sir . . ."

"Do you see any compulsory reason for using him already, Lieutenant?"

"No, certainly not, sir."

"Alright then! You and your men get into the hangar and take one of the Gazelles. Fly it directly into the main lock of the robotship. And now—good luck, Lieutenant."

Germa saluted and went out. He picked out 5 men from his team and hurried with them to the hangar, where the flight personnel were already waiting for them. One of the Gazelles had been made ready for the mission. The disc-shaped scoutship measured 18 meters in height and was almost 30 meters in diameter. It was equipped with a hyper-transition system which allowed a jump-range of up to 5 light-years.

Germa was the last one into the airlock but as the hatch was about to be closed the mousebeaver materialized directly in front of him in the hangar. Pucky beckoned to Germa and waddled up closer.

"So it seems I'm not needed," he remarked.

"Nonsense, Pucky! The commander only wants to use you in case of danger—more or less like an emergency brake, you might say."

"I don't happen to be a brake—and besides, I overheard your conversation. I'd like to know why it was decided at that supposedly important conference that mutants were to come along. What did I train Iltu for? So we can sit around now and twiddle our thumbs . . . ?"

Germa looked worriedly at his watch. "I don't have any more time. The takeoff order can come any second now."

Pucky looked intently at the lieutenant. "Be careful, Germa. There's something that isn't right about those ships. I can feel it."

Even Col. Sukril had sensed this but he refused to react to indefinite impulses. Pucky, who had watched Sukril telepathically, could not shake off his uneasy feeling so readily. It had led him to make a quick *esp*-scan of the robotships. The lack of results by no means reassured him. It was evident that no intelligences were on board the ships, yet something was wrong.

"I'll call you if something happens, little buddy."

"I'll be there," Pucky promised. He had determined to get thru this mission without clashing with regulations. Otherwise he would have simply teleported on board the robotships long before this in order to check them over personally. At any rate he had decided to have a serious word with Col. Sukril since he needed a broader range of authority. "You only have to think 'Help!'—nothing more."

The hatch closed. Seconds later the Gazelle glided into the launching lock and from there it shot outward into the void.

Col. Sukril had given the order for takeoff.

*   *   *   *

The control room of the Gazelle was on top of the disc-shaped hull. Its "roof" was transparent. Germa could clearly observe the 11 robotships. He approached them slowly with his right hand next to the flight lever, which he only needed to shove forward in order to hurtle away at tremendous speed. Actually the assumption that aliens could have boarded the ships in the meantime was purely absurd because if that had happened the aliens wouldn't be waiting around until somebody discovered them. Of course it was also possible that such strangers might not be able to operate the robot controls and this could explain why they were waiting.

But even if that were so, the ships they had arrived in would have to be somewhere in the vicinity. In that case the tracking instruments would have detected them long before this. Pucky had warned him, however, and Germa still had an uneasy feeling in the pit of his stomach. The mousebeaver would not have said anything like that without a reason.

The outer hull of the superbattleship had become so large that it almost embraced the entire field of view. Germa could clearly make out the outlines of the airlocks, the great ring-bulge of the engines and the gunturret hatches. The viewscreen revealed these details with an increasing clarity but Germa preferred to examine the approaching colossus directly. An uncanny aura of menace seemed to exude from the robotship, which had originally been assigned to guarding the outer limits of the Arkonide Imperium.

''Brado!'' One of the 5 men in the control room came away from his companions and approached him. ''What do you think, Sergeant? Where the devil is the main hatch to the hangar?''

From 100 meters away one might have seen that Brado was Mexican or Spanish. His black hair appeared to be glued to his head with pomade. He was nervously turning his space helmet around in his hands. They all wore the lightweight protective suits which could enable them to work in the outer vacuum. The helmet could be put on in a matter of seconds.

''I'm familiar with the Imperium class, sir,'' he said, ''but they have such a big surface area that I don't know at first glance . . . ''

''Same with me,'' admitted Germa. But suddenly he saw the small control wheel next to the outlines of a hatch door that must have measured 50 meters in depth. ''There it is!''

The problem was solved more quickly than he had

first expected. He carefully maneuvered the Gazelle closer to the ship and then brought it to a relative standstill. They were now no more than 20 meters away from the towering wall of the hull, which at this proximity hardly revealed any curvature.

Germa turned to the others. "Who's going?" he asked.

An oppressive silence answered him. No one volunteered. It was so unheard of that Germa was speechless for several moments. He could sense the uneasiness of these men whom he knew he could ordinarily depend upon. It was an unrest that seemed to be contagious, because he felt it himself. It was as if he were no longer *alone* with these 5 men in the ship.

"Sgt. Gork! Take Cadet Wilkovski with you and open that hatch. If necessary we'll cover you with the weapons—but get a move on!"

The 2 men nodded wordlessly, donned their helmets and secured them with magnetic clamps. Then they turned on their air supply and checked out their radio systems.

"Sgt. Gork ready."

"Cadet Wilkovski ready."

Germa confirmed and gave them their signal. He remained at the controls and activated the airlock mechanism. One minute later they were visible outside the ship. They shoved away from the Gazelle and landed softly a few seconds later on the hull of the superwarship, which had enough mass attraction to work its effect on them.

It was a familiar enough scene for Germa. Two ships stood next to each other, apparently motionless, separated only by a few meters. The jump from one to another was very short but the abyss beneath extended for billions of light-years. Yet a man couldn't fall into it under such circumstances. Forces of inertia and local mass attraction prevented it. From awesome distances the other island universes sent their shimmering light, beyond human reach—or so it seemed.

Sgt. Gork found the control wheel and began to turn it.

On a robot-operated ship a control wheel was as primitive as it was indispensable. Without a mechanical provision of this nature it would be impossible for a man to enter in case the automatic system failed. The purpose of the wheel was to open a small adjacent manlock. Once inside, an operator could start the semi-automatic machinery which was energized by a power bank.

Over Germa's head a loudspeaker crackled and Col. Sukril's voice rang out: "How it is, Lieutenant? Everything alright?"

"I've sent 2 men over to the lock, sir. As soon as they raise the hatch I'll move the Gazelle inside."

"We have you on the screens. Report to me every 2 minutes."

"Very well, sir."

The ship-com speaker fell silent but then the space-com came to life. It was Sgt. Gork. "The wheel's stuck, sir. It made only 2 turns and no more. What should I do?"

Germa cursed softly to himself before answering. "Maybe that's all that's required. Just give it a try, Sergeant!"

"Sir . . . ?" This time it was Cadet Lester, who stood behind him in the control room with Brado and Hansen. "Sir . . . ?"

Germa swung around. "Well, what is it? Can't you see I'm—"

"Sir—here in the ship—there's something . . . "

Germa was aware of a rash of gooseflesh which only confirmed that he had sensed the same thing. He and

the other 3 men were not alone in the Gazelle. More
accurately stated, they were not alone right here in the
control room!

The chamber was not very large and offered no
concealment. Even Pucky would have found it difficult
to hide here. And also Germa knew the mousebeaver's
presence would not have caused the aura of fear and
horror that was undeniably here now.

It was a mental current that came from somewhere
and seemed to be concentrating on him. Germa was no
telepath or he might have grasped more of what was
happening. He could only react instinctively to the
unknown presence.

"Keep your beamers ready," he ordered, not knowing any other way to calm his men. Then he turned his
attention again to the other two outside.

Meanwhile Sgt. Gork had succeeded in opening the
manlock. "I'm going in, sir," Gork reported.

"Wilkovski is to go with you," replied Germa
hoarsely. "Both of you stay together. Give an alarm if
you run into anybody."

Gork didn't answer. He and Wilkovski disappeared
into the small opening.

The seconds seemed an eternity.

Germa recalled a mission he had been on long ago.
Five hundred light-years from Earth they had found a
derelict in the void. The design of the ship had been
completely unknown, indicating that it had been built
by a race that Terra had never contacted before. After
the hull had been opened with cutting beams a prize
crew went on board. He himself had been a member of
the boarding team.

He remembered being gripped by the same feeling he
was experiencing now. It had seemed to him as if
someone were watching him from unseen eyes and
following every move he made. But the wreck had been

found to be completely empty. Its builders must have abandoned it long before then, whoever they might have been or whatever they might have looked like. Neither the Arkonides nor the Springers nor the Aras had been able to give any indication of where it had come from. Still today it remained one of the unsolved riddles that the universe seemed to be full of.

Germa came back to the present. He reasoned that he certainly couldn't compare this robotship with the derelict. Besides, he was sensing the presence of an alien not there but right here in the control room of the Gazelle—someone who could not be seen.

"Sir . . . ! The controls!"

Germa tensed. The voice of his second sergeant, Brado, had been touched with horror. The flight lever was moving by itself in slow little jerks.

He suddenly saw the hull of the giant battleship recede while the *Caesar* appeared at one side of his field of vision. The Gazelle picked up speed and with ever-increasing acceleration swept away in an opposite direction. Both of the big warships dwindled rapidly in size; 10 seconds later the smaller companion ships were no longer visible to the naked eye.

It was only then that Germa overcame his momentary paralysis.

His hand gripped the flight lever. Shifting it to the reverse slot, he pulled back. The ship obediently slowed down and described a wide curve. It was on a course that would bring them back to where they had started from.

But then an invisible hand shoved it forward again, slowly but steadily. When Germa grasped it firmly again it seemed to be immovable as if it had been welded in place. It could not be budged.

The inertial forces had been absorbed automatically. Sgt. Brado had thrown himself against the door as if he

feared that someone might enter the control room
—perhaps somebody who might be lurking outside in
the corridor. He didn't realize how useless this was
because if any invisible alien were on board the Gazelle
he would have to be right here in the room with them.

The 2 cadets Hansen and Lester leaned with
blanched faces against the wall near the communications console, unable to move a muscle. They stared in
wide-eyed bewilderment at the bewitched flight lever.

Germa gave up his struggles. He was faced with
something for which there was simply no explanation.
Because if it were merely an invisible person grasping
the lever he should have been able to feel his hand. He
had been struggling with it at the same time and yet had
not contacted a thing. If there *were* a stranger here he
would have to be not only invisible but immaterial as
well.

The *Caesar* was only a dimly glimmering point of
light in the immensity when Col. Sukril reacted. Al-
together about 15 seconds had passed at the most.

"What's wrong with you, Germa? Have you lost
your mind?"

"Sir, we've lost control of the Gazelle. Somebody is
changing the flight settings—and they're invisible!"

5 seconds of silence ensued. During that 5 seconds
the *Caesar* and the group of robotships faded completely from Germa's range of vision. The shimmering
band of the Milky Way and a few isolated giant suns
was all he could see.

"Try to bring the ship back under control, Germa.
Keep sending us your tracking coordinates. We'll get
you back. Over and out!"

No question, no amazement or surprise, nothing.
Why not?

Lt. Germa stared at the flight lever, which was
shoved out to the last notch. The Gazelle was at its top

acceleration. If the present situation weren't changed they would soon be in the realm of relativistic velocities. The course had shifted again. Now if they continued straight on they would reach a dimly shining nebulous mass that was barely distinguishable from the black background of the absolute void.

An island universe? A star cluster between the galaxies? Or actually a nebula?

The Gazelle was racing toward it.

If one were to discount the possibility of making a transition—or more likely a thousand or a hundred thousand hyper-jumps—it might take a few million years to reach it.

In sudden anger Germa grasped the flight lever again. He encountered a motionless piece of metal.

"Pucky!" he said aloud. "Help me now!"

*   *   *   *

Sgt. Gork and Cadet Wilkovski knew nothing about what was happening outside the airlock. They had penetrated the giant launch chamber and immediately located the mechanical controls. A few manipulations of switches served to turn on the automatic sequence and they waited.

Almost a full minute went by. Within that minute Germa and the 3 men with him traversed a distance of more than 10,000 km. Under their feet a dull rumbling began. They felt the deckplates vibrating. There were unintelligible sounds in their headphones.

Then the main hatch began to open and to slide into its retainer well. The gulf of the outer darkness began to be visible. But the mighty lock door only opened halfway before it stopped. The rumbling ceased and all was still.

Sgt. Gork stepped forward to the edge of the

chamber deck. He could clearly see the *Caesar* standing off at some distance where it had been previously but the Gazelle had disappeared. Recalling the unintelligible noises in his helmet receiver, he adjusted his transmitter and called the *Caesar*. He learned from Col. Sukril what had transpired but no explanation was given.

"Stay where you are, Sergeant—I'll send reinforcements. We'll take care of Germa later."

"But . . . ."

"Did you hear my order? Alright then! Wait!"

Gork gritted his teeth. He was standing here uselessly while something weird was happening to Germa. Cadet Wilkovski was only a few steps away from him when he suddenly cried out. In their headphones were the same distorted and hideous sounds again.

"The hatch . . . !"

Gork saw it himself. The lock door began to close, slowly but steadily. However there was no accompanying rumble or vibration of running machinery. The great launch gate was lowering as tho it were being moved by invisible hands. It was closing without any help from the motor drive.

Without thinking, Gork ran forward and dove thru the narrowing gap into the emptiness of space. He chose to try getting to the *Caesar* this way or take his chances on getting fished out of the void rather than remain in a haunted ship.

Cadet Wilkovski stayed where he was. He was no hero, which was why he hadn't moved. It was better here, he reasoned, than to take the risk of running out of air somewhere among the stars.

The launch hatch closed.

* * * *

A few seconds before this, Pucky had teleported to the Control Central of the *Caesar*. He had given Iltu strictest orders to remain in her cabin and keep in telepathiccontact with him. It had not taken long but each moment was precious now.

Col. Sukril almost jumped when the mousebeaver made such a sudden intrusion right next to him but then he remembered and was willing to dispense with regulations for the moment. And Pucky also forgot the rule books. Sukril's rank was a side issue now.

"Well, here's your backstop, buddy! I knew right away there was something wrong about those ships. Why didn't you let me go with Germa . . . ?"

"Quiet!" roared Sukril, turning red in the face. But he still kept his eyes on the viewscreen. "Who's the commander here—you or me?"

Wanting to be polite, Pucky ignored the question. "Shall I make the jump?"

"What are you still waiting for? Open that main hatch so a fully-manned Gazelle can fly in there. Do you know the robot controls enough to make the switch to manual?"

"I took a course in it!" Pucky muttered angrily. Without another word he dematerialized.

In his haste of course he had forgotten to put on his Arkonide combatsuit. He merely wore his normal uniform, which only allowed him to remain in a breathing environment, and it afforded him no protection against an attack of any kind.

He materialized in the launch chamber. A dim emergency lamp shone from the ceiling, which was enough to reveal Cadet Wilkowski. He was back against the wall, staring at him out of a fear-whitened face and holding a beamer in his hand.

"It's me, Pucky! Where's Gork?"

Wilkowski lowered his weapon. "He jumped out," he said shakily. "Before the hatch closed."

Pucky looked around. It wasn't hard for him to locate the controls. But no matter how much he labored with them the launch gate failed to move. It was as if it were held fast by invisible forces.

After his telekinesis also failed him, Pucky gave it up. "You stay here, Wilkovski. I'll make a try in the Control Central. Maybe it'll work when I cut out the robot circuits. As soon as the gate opens, tell Col. Sukril to send the troops. Tell him to man all 11 ships at the same time. Did you get that?"

Wilkovski nodded. "Yes—but what about Germa?"

"I'll worry about him as soon as there's time. He's not in immediate danger. So you wait here!"

The ship was of the same model series as the *Caesar* but since it hadn't been planned for use by living crews it was devoid of every human comfort. The cabins included in the design were empty but in case of operation by organic intelligences the ship could be made livable at any time by means of the appropriate installations.

Pucky teleported directly into the Control Central. When he materialized he remained in one spot, motionless. Here, too, was a burning emergency light altho it might appear superfluous to the untrained observer. Pucky recalled that such lights were always provided on robotships and that they were designed to turn on automatically in the presence of radiated heat from living beings.

The giant control board and countless meters and rows of instrument consoles were not confusing to Pucky. He knew exactly what he had to do because now his previous experience was an advantage. He had been thru this in the Blue System when the Terrans had stolen a robot fleet from the Akons that Atlan had unwillingly turned over to them. All he had to do was remove the tiny capsule from the activating circuit. Once this was done the ship would respond again to manual controls.

He took only a step or two toward the controls before he suddenly froze in his tracks again. Here it was again—the strange awareness of horrible danger.

His sensitive brain registered incoming thought impulses that had no fixed pattern and certainly didn't make any sense. Basically all they transmitted were emotions and they were anything but friendly. A wave of hate flooded in upon him, apparently from nowhere. For a moment he had to struggle against a feeling of panic but his instinct of self-preservation won out. He jerked the energy gun from his belt and released the safety. The deadly weapon was ready for firing.

He looked slowly about him in every direction in search of the enemy who had to be hiding somewhere very close by. But he saw nothing altho he could sense something present. The waves of hate came at him from all sides and threatened to pull him into unknown depths. Yes, that was it—it was as if he were caught in a whirlpool.

The enemy was here with him in the Control Central but he was invisible!

Pucky backed up slowly until he stood with his back to the control panels. From this position he could see the entire room. Of course there were places of concealment here if one were to crawl into the narrow recesses between the consoles and cabinets. But Pucky knew the enemy wasn't hiding. Moreover, there wasn't just one but many of them. They were all invisible and in his immediate vicinity.

Now he realized bitterly that he had forgotten his Arkonide combatsuit. With that he could have also made himself invisible by merely turning on the deflector-field. Also he would have felt more secure under the protection of its defense screen. But it was too late now for such considerations nor was he thinking in terms of teleporting back to the *Caesar*. As long as Cadet Wilkovski was down in the launch lock there was simply no retreating.

For a moment he thought of Lt. Germa, who was racing at an incredible speed into the starless void. He would have to fetch him back—later when he had time.

The streams of hostile thoughts became more intense. They were still exhuding hate, nothing else—or perhaps also a touch of curiosity. The thought patterns were alien yet Pucky couldn't rid himself of the notion that he had encountered them somewhere before. His memory was usually excellent but this time it failed him. No matter how hard he tried he couldn't recall when or where it had been.

At least not yet!

Close in front of him there was a sudden blue flash. The energy beam emerged from emptiness. It missed him by only a few centimeters but the thermal effect was strong enough to singe his arm. He felt a terrible pain that almost made him blank out. Without thinking he returned the fire, aiming at the exact spot that the shot had come from. At the same time he dropped to the deck in order to concentrate. He had to get out of here or he was done for.

He sensed a note of satisfaction in the hateful thoughts.

When he dropped down he had fallen on his wounded arm, which shot a wave of maddening pain thru his body. *Scram out of here!*—he thought. He saw the objects around him begin to blur and disappear —only to rematerialize again.

He was in a completely empty room. The hostile

thoughts were weaker here, more distant. He had escaped—but for how long?

Iltu, he thought, *can you hear me?*

Pucky! Can I help you?

Her answer came sharply and clearly to him. She must have been in constant contact with him and was probably aware of everything that had happened.

Iltu! In my cabin, in the cabinet! The combatsuits! Put yours on and bring me mine! Hurry!

No answer. Had Iltu understood him?

He straightened up and felt of his injured arm. The pain hadn't lessened but he began to suppress it mentally. Only a burn, he hoped. It wasn't anything worse but it was very painful.

While he was waiting something suddenly occurred to him that he had not thought of until now. Everything had happened too swiftly for him to fully register his observations but he recalled that he had seen something. When he had shot at the invisible nemesis he must have hit him, judging from 2 impressions he had received. The thought emanations of hate and satisfaction had changed to a sudden surge of pain. Secondly, he had caught a fleeting glimpse of a shadowy form.

The shadow had appeared only very briefly before disappearing again. The agent from nowhere had been visible for the fraction of a second. The outline had been somewhat humanoid but was so transparent that he had been able to see thru it.

Agents from nowhere . . . ?

Pucky suddenly knew where he had encountered them before. It was that time on the wandering planet of Barkon which was rushing thru the starless reaches of the intergalactic gulf on its long course back to the Milky Way. There an attack had occurred. The enemy then had also been immaterial and could only be made visible or could only be destroyed under a concentrated energy fire. They seemed to be thought forms only —invisible and bodiless entities with telepathic abilities but with such alien thought forms that they could not be comprehended. They always made bold and deadly attacks.

No one had known where they came from or where they had fled later because even their ships were invisible. Only a special instrument capable of graphing energy emanations had made them visible—elongated torpedo shapes more than 100 meters in length. They had taken off and disappeared into the infinite depths of intergalactic space.

And now they had returned! Pucky knew that they were the most dangerous entities that humans had ever encountered, especially because they were unknown forms of life. It was as if they lived in a different plane of existence.

The thought patterns became stronger again. They were looking for him. They were getting closer.

Pucky knew he had to avoid teleporting back into the launch lock area where Wilkovski was waiting. It would expose the cadet unnecessarily to danger. But where was Iltu?

Iltu!

The answer came at once: *I'm just about ready. Think of your surroundings so that I can find you. Where are you?*

Pucky teleported. The hostile thoughts became weaker again. He had landed precisely in the spot he had concentrated on—in the robotship's observation dome. Naturally the normal equipment was missing here for full observations of the outer void because robots were more instrumentally oriented than visually. But Pucky wasn't ready for astronomy at the moment.

I'm in the observation dome, Iltu. Same as on board the Caesar. Teleport over here—and hurry!

He waited. Seconds passed.

Once more the mysterious thought impressions were weaker but there was no doubt that the aliens were looking for him. He had vanished before their eyes—or did they have eyes? Even that time on Barkon he had seen that they were not capable of teleporting and that their movements actually were fairly slow. He could always manage to get away from them, again and again—but was that the answer?

Who were these beings who came out of invisible realms and attacked everything that entered the intergalactic abyss? They apparently didn't venture into the galaxy itself. Their habitat seemed to be in the vast emptiness between the universes. They were unassailable and represented the greatest menace that the Terrans had been confronted with thus far.

The air shimmered in front of Pucky and then Iltu appeared. She wore her combatsuit and carried a second outfit with her.

"Terrific, girl!" chirped Pucky, and he immediately pulled on the suit over his uniform. Then he picked up his raygun and thrust it into his outer belt. "Turn on your defense screen so that they can't hurt you. Ow —speaking of hurt . . . !"

Iltu had helped him with the suit because he could hardly move his left arm. Concernedly, she stroked his sleeve where the wound was located.

"Does it pain you a lot, Pucky?"

He nodded and smiled appreciatively. "Only when I laugh. Ps-s-t! They're coming again!"

She listened inwardly. "Yes, I'm picking up their thoughts. But how strange they are! It's just like you were thinking when I was in contact with you. Where do they come from? Who are they?"

"Nobody knows," muttered Pucky, and again he sensed the immediate presence of the sinister intruders. The fact that they had found them here indicated strongly that they were telepathic. "We'll try to make them visible. Let's hope our screens will stand up against their weapons."

Iltu nodded bravely. She took up a position next to Pucky with her back to the wall and drew out her beamer. Her normally gentle eyes gleamed venturesomely. It wasn't supposed to be in her line of duty to—

The blue energy beam flashed not 2 meters away and struck Pucky's defense screen. It divided there and glanced off of him without doing any damage.

"Fire!" shouted the mousebeaver as he activated his weapon. Iltu complied.

The 2 streams of energy intersected and glanced from an invisible obstruction. Back on Barkon, 3 such beams had been necessary to make the unseen creatures visible. But now it also succeeded with just 2. Of course the effect was not as penetrating or lingering.

The flame-lined outline of the enemy became dimly discernible. His body was resistant enough to reflect the beams of energy. A small onslaught like this couldn't hurt him but the force of 4 or 5 simultaneous shots could kill him. This Pucky knew from his experience on Barkon.

But nothing more.

The invisible entity assumed a shape for several seconds before it ducked out of harm's way. The figure was entirely human altho no face could be seen. Two arms, a torso, 2 legs—that was all. But it was enough. Judging from that it had to be a material form.

With gun in hand, Pucky sprang forward and tried to grasp the shadow phantom. He clutched at emptiness. His hands encountered no resistance. Evil thoughts streamed into his mind, so filled with hate and rage that he drew back involuntarily. Never in his life had he encountered such venemous thoughts.

He sprang back next to Iltu, where his neutralizer field enabled him to join his defense screen with hers. He took her by the hand. ''I'll teleport and take you with me. You don't have to do a thing.''

He jumped—and landed directly in the concentrated blue fire of 6 or 7 energy weapons. Altho the mousebeavers' doubly strengthened screens were able to deflect the deadly beams, their micro-generators were strained to the limit. Pucky was much too flabbergasted to react wisely. He raised his own weapon in order to return the fire.

Then it was Iltu who saved both their lives. Instead of thinking uselessly of a counter-offense she concentrated on making a short teleport jump. A fraction of a second before their screens could collapse, the 2 mousebeavers vanished and rematerialized in one of the peripheral corridors of the ship.

''That was close,'' muttered Pucky, releasing her hand. ''Well done, little one!''

Iltu was about to retort something but she decided to remain silent. It was enough that Pucky praised her deed, even tho he called her ''little one''. Perhaps that, too, was a mark of esteem.

''I have to switch over the controls, Iltu. Only then can the boarding crews operate. If the shadows are faster than we are, they'll rob the ship and we'll be in a fix. Do you want to wait here or are you coming along?''

The question was unnecessary. Iltu went along.

As far as Pucky could make out, the Control Central was empty. The invisible ones were apparently all engaged in the search for him and Iltu—which could mean that there weren't very many of them.

The main circuits were in an adjoining room. With a

certainty which was surprising even to Pucky, he found the interface capsule behind the proper access panel and removed it. From that moment on the mighty ship was dependent upon the manual operations of living intelligences. Even tho there were other independent automatic systems on board, as of this second they had been cut off.

Another jump brought them into the launch chamber where Cadet Wilkovski was still standing, weapon in hand, with his back to the wall.

"Call Col. Sukril!" Pucky ordered, while turning off his defense screen. "Tell him to start the takeover operation—for this ship and the others. We'll try to divert the shadow spooks. There can't be many of them."

Cadet Wilkovski passed on this information over his helmet radio and then made a new attempt to open the outer hatch. This time he succeeded. The heavy lock gate swung into its retainer well and the *Caesar* became visible. There they could see the great hangar locks of the battleship opening up to disgorge a swarm of auxiliary craft and Gazelles which promptly headed for the various robotships.

The actual operation had begun. The die had been cast. As long as the men wore their combatsuits and kept their screens up, they would be relatively safe from the invisible enemy. Moreover, they could defend themselves with concentrated fire from multiple weapons.

But Pucky did not yet realize how greatly he had underestimated the unknown opposition. "Iltu, you stay here," he said. He was watching some of the other robotships in the distance as the boarding commandos opened their locks and entered them. Evidently his switching over this flagship put the rest of them on manual control. "I have something else I have to take care of," he added.

"I'll go with you!"

"No—you stay here. It's too dangerous. You aren't ready yet for the real precision jumps. And the distance is too great."

"What are you going to do?"

Pucky looked straight at her. "Look for Germa. He's our friend."

"Then I've got to go with you!"

Pucky remained adamant. "It's not only the danger of it, Iltu. I have to know I've got somebody here I can depend on." He swallowed with difficulty. "I *can* depend on you, can't I, girl? Somebody had to stay here to divert the shadow people from the commando crews. It's a rough job and you'll have to keep on the jump all the time. Depend on the troops and make sure they use a concentrated fire against the spooks whenever they show up. You're the only one who can tell when they're around."

"Alright, Pucky, as you wish. But—I'll come if anything happens to you."

"I'll call if I need you," he reassured her. "But don't forget that you represent me here now. Col. Sukril is depending only on me, not you. He mustn't see that we've switched places. But I can't leave Germa in the lurch."

She pressed his paw. "You can depend on me." She smiled and revealed her pretty incisor tooth. "Until later, Grandpa."

Pucky was forced to admire her tooth for a moment. Then he raised a threatening finger to her, finally thought better of it—and vanished.

But Iltu had overcome her secret awe of Pucky in that moment. She watched the oncoming transports, which were carrying more than 2000 troops. Her task would be to protect these men.

3/ GALACTIC ALARM

After the *Caesar* and the 11 robotships had dropped from sight, nothing else changed. The distances were too great for that.

Lt. Germa slumped in the pilot seat and stared at the useless flight lever. During the past 20 minutes he had tried often enough to move it back. Even the navigation controls were blocked. Invisible hands had manipulated the machinery—but to whom did those hands belong?

He looked about him again but outside of himself and his 3 companions there was no one else in the control room. By now the weird presentiment of lurking menace had disappeared, which they had all sensed so clearly before. It was as if the invisible ones had left the ship, having accomplished their objective.

Once more he attempted to make contact with the *Caesar* and this time he succeeded. The com system was still intact.

Sukril sounded somewhat impatient with him. "No, we haven't forgotten you, Lieutenant! I just haven't had time. The operation's started. The men are boarding the robotships."

"Where is Pucky?"

Sukril suppressed a bitter remark. "Also on the mission," was all he said. "Be patient, we'll pick you up soon enough. We have you on the tracking scanners and can locate you at any moment. But first I have to know that everything here is in order. We seem to be up against some very unusual opposition. The enemy is invisible and possibly even disembodied."

"Invisible!" gasped Germa as he felt his hackles rising. "How is that possible?"

"To be invisible isn't so impossible," replied Sukril. "The unusual part is that they are apparently immaterial. I've already sent a report on this to Terra so that Rhodan will know what's going on."

Germa nodded to himself. "Well then, thank you, sir. We'll wait and depend entirely upon you."

"You do just that," Sukril admonished, and he cut off.

It seemed that at the moment he had plenty to do. Germa felt better about it because he realized that he himself was not in immediate danger. Later it would be child's play for the *Caesar* to trace him and find him.

But in the meantime the Gazelle was racing onward into the depths of the intergalactic void. The velocity of light had been reached, which was the limit of speed in the Einstein universe. Brado, Hansen and Lester sat silently at their stations to Germa's right and left. In spite of the fright they'd been thru they had become fascinated by the aspect of empty space. The white band of the Milky Way still marked the location of their home but the Gazelle was hurtling directly in an opposite direction. They were moving toward the distant nebula which hovered far ahead in the infinite vastness. For one horrible moment Germa had the thought that the shadow beings might stem from there but then he rejected the idea.

A race that could fly at will from universe to universe would not be lingering around the edges of a galaxy and attacking stray robotships. They wouldn't be out to conquer a planet or star but an entire galaxy.

What was keeping Pucky?

His thoughts returned to the mousebeaver. He liked him very much, that was for sure. He liked all animals—but was Pucky what one might commonly refer to as "animal"? Wasn't he actually more than that? In this cosmic age, outer differences of form and color of skin ought to be a thing of the past. In fact when men first encountered extraterrestrial beings, the concept of racial barriers was shattered. Humanity itself melted into a single unity. People learned to judge others by character rather than by outward appearances. This was the only way they could adjust themselves to a contact with other intelligences.

Thru his deeds and comportment, Pucky had contributed much to this kind of understanding. He had lost his home world and his own kind but had found a new home on Earth among humans. He loved humanity but he was immensely proud of being a mousebeaver.

"Lieutenant!"

Cadet Hansen had chanced to turn around to search again for signs of the unknown invaders in the control room. He had not yet gotten rid of the feeling of being under constant observation.

Germa forgot his philosophical contemplations and whirled around, instinctively grasping his beamer, which lay on the flight panel. But then he breathed a sigh of relief. He had just been thinking of Pucky—and here the mousebeaver was, emerging out of nowhere.

"Pucky! At last!"

"Man—that wasn't so easy!"

Pucky released the helmet of his combatsuit and shook himself. He nodded encouragingly at the 4 men and then, as far as he was able to determine by telepathy, he assured himself that the invisible foe was neither in the control room nor on board the Gazelle.

"I was tracking your brain impulses, Germa," continued Pucky as he took over the last remaining seat, "but that alone wasn't enough. The distance was so great that I couldn't zero in exactly. I simply jumped and naturally I materialized immediately in the middle of nothing." He shuddered again at the memory of the unpleasant experience. "Man, I can tell you, that was

something creepy! There I was in the middle of nowhere, out of sight of the *Caesar* and the Gazelle. Only
the thought impulses were left. I could pick out Sukril's
thoughts, alright—strictly military. After all, he was
running the mission. But your thoughts, Germa, were
something else. They were very good ones." He produced a friendly smile, which caused his incisor tooth
to gleam brightly. "That's what made it easy to find
you. So here I am!"

"Where is Iltu?"

"A brave girl!" exclaimed Pucky happily, altho he
added immediately: "Of course she's a bit young and
inexperienced but all the same . . . "

Germa made no further comment, of course not
knowing what had happened in the meantime. He
pointed to the controls. "So now what do we do? The
flight controls seem to be welded in place. I can't
change the speed or the course. Can you bring us back
to the *Caesar* all by yourself?"

"That could be a possibility but I don't want to have
Sukril chew me out." Pucky started to laugh and then
gave a pontifical imitation of the commander: "That
mousebeaver! He was entrusted with a ship and left it to
an uncertain fate!"

Germa had to grin, as did his 3 companions. It was
really comical the way the mousebeaver imitated the
colonel's speech characteristics. Of course he couldn't
reproduce the Skipper's deep deep tone of voice but
otherwise it was a good try.

"How can you free up the controls?" he asked.

Pucky promptly forgot Col. Sukril. "I don't have
any idea, Germa. I'll have to look them over."

It wasn't actually what he meant because there
wasn't much to see. There was only one way to find the
probable obstructions—he had to put his telekinetic
faculties to work. He carefully probed along the length

of the flight lever with his psychokinetic emanations. In this way he penetrated deep into the control mechanism until he encountered a resistance.

"That's probably it," he muttered, while trying to determine the shape of the obstruction. It had an uneven shape but there was no doubt that this was what kept the lever from moving. Pucky took a deep breath and grasped it telekinetically. Now that he had found the cause, the damage should be easy to correct. It all depended upon whether or not his powers were greater than the energies which held the obstruction in place.

"Shift the level to neutral!" he said suddenly.

Germa reached out to it. The lever was quite easy to move. It clicked audibly to the intended slot. The velocity of the Gazelle did not lessen due to the force of inertia. At light-speed it made no difference whether the propulsion system was working or not.

Then Pucky got busy on the frozen nav-controls. He succeeded only after a number of trials, again encountering an unknown type of resistance. It seemed to be something that had been melted down and then hardened again but there was no explanation of how it had gotten there. Was it possible that the invisible ones could penetrate into solid matter?

"You can try it now."

Germa moved the controls testily and when the Gazelle actually changed course and responded obediently to every manipulation he shook his head in amazement. "Wow—we'd all better take up telekinesis! How did you do it, Pucky?"

"To tell you the truth—I don't know exactly, myself," the mousebeaver admitted. "I'm a boob in arms compared to those aliens. They seem to be able to do anything."

"Haven't you just outsmarted them?"

''Well, not really, Germa. I had to search a long time to clear the obstructions out of the way. But they put them there in seconds. I'm afraid we're still in for some surprises with those spooks. They aren't material substance in our sense of the word. Maybe you could go so far as to say they are bodiless, even in their own dimension. I don't know, Germa, when we first ran into them that time on Barkon, we racked our brains trying to figure them out—with no results. We thought then that it was a one-time contact and we almost forgot them after that. And now . . . '' Pucky fell silent, having become very pensive.

Germa spoke up. ''Col. Sukril should ask Rhodan for support.''

''I'll recommend that to him,'' said Pucky, pointing to the control board. ''Do you want to try locating the *Caesar?*''

Germa turned on the radio and put out a call to the flagship. There was a 2-minute delay before the *Caesar* answered.

''I already told you, Lt. Germa, that I would send somebody——''

Germa interrupted the angry voice. ''We're already on our way back, sir. The phantoms have let go of us. I only wanted to inform you that Rhodan would be very interested in their presence here because he met them once before. May I recommend, sir, that you get into personal contact with him at once——?''

''I've had an appropriate message sent,'' replied Sukril in a rigid tone of voice.

''Did it describe the phenomena we've just experienced?''

''Would you care to explain that?''

''Yessir. These shadow people are not only a local menace to us here but for the entire galaxy. Pucky told me about them. It's absolutely necessary to bypass official channels on Earth and go directly to Rhodan. The red tape would take too long . . . "

Sukril did not seem to realize that Germa could not have spoken to Pucky—since he wasn't aware of the mousebeaver's present location. "Alright, Germa, then you take care of getting back here on your own. I'll get into direct communication with the Administrator. Does that satisfy you?"

Germa sighed his relief and glanced briefly at Pucky. "Thank you, sir. I believe you'll be doing us all a big favor. Don't worry about me, I can find my way back without help."

Sukril grumbled something unintelligible and cut off the connection. Germa also shut down the com unit and looked at Pucky.

"The Old Man seems to be taking it pretty calmly. Do you think he knew about the danger already?"

"It looks like it," Pucky nodded. He stared at the Milky Way and pointed in their direction of flight. "It's my guess that you'll catch sight of the *Caesar* and the robots in about 5 minutes. Better start decelerating."

The Gazelle responded to the retropulsion controls. The ships came into view after 15 minutes. After arriving at the *Caesar,* Germa flew the Gazelle into the wide-open hangar and landed it gently. He had hardly done so before the mighty lock gate started to close.

Germa had gotten up and was about to leave the Gazelle when Pucky suddenly tensed and grasped his arm.

"Wait, Germa—something's fishy! Why are they closing the hangar hatch? The action can't be over with yet. Besides, I'm picking up the spook thoughts again." He looked about but couldn't see anything suspicious other than the fact that the hangar itself was strangely deserted-looking. "Stay in the Gazelle,

Germa. Turn on the energy screen! And don't turn it off until you see me over by that wall and I give you a signal. Have you got that?"

"Yes—but what gives?"

"Don't ask me now. Just a precaution, that's all. OK, I'm making the jump. Turn on the screen in 10 seconds. See you later." He dematerialized before the eyes of the 4 men and vanished.

Germa made a reassuring sign to his men. Of course he didn't know what was on the mousebeaver's mind yet but he trusted him blindly. After the prescribed 10 seconds, he switched on the screen. Now the Gazelle lay under a protective dome of energy which isolated it completely from the outside world.

Only then did Germa note how unusually quiet it was on board the *Caesar*. There was no sign of the hangar personnel. No crews had hurried forward to receive the Gazelle.

He sat down. "Let's wait," he said.

And they waited.

4/ GHOST SHIP

Iltu's hour of trial had come.

When the special troop carriers landed in the giant hangar and the commandos leapt out with ready weapons to swarm into the corridors, she was immediately spotted by Maj. Borovski who led the mission.

"Oh there you are, Pucky!" he cried out as he ran past her.

"I am Iltu!" she chirped indignantly, trying in vain to keep up with the towering major. "Wait a minute! I have something important to say to you!"

Borovski stopped. "Oh—Iltu?" he said wonderingly. "The other mousebeaver!"

"A girl mousebeaver!" she corrected him, coming to a stop beside him. "Pucky is fetching Germa. I'm here in his place."

"Fine!" retorted Borovski. "Then do it!"

He was about to take off again but Iltu furiously grasped him by the leg of his trousers.

"Wait, I said! Do you want to listen to me or don't you? Pucky has left some instructions for you. They have to do with the invisible enemies who are here on the ship."

Borovski kept a straight face and stood still. The men running passed him were seen to grin as they noted Iltu holding him by the pants of his combatsuit. Only a few of them came to a stop.

"Alright, Iltu, tell me."

She gave him a brief report on her experiences with the shadow people and how they could be combatted. She advised Borovski to keep his men in groups of at least 5 and to keep their screens turned on. As soon as anyone fired at them out of the emptiness they should set up a crossfire. They should keep it up until the enemy became visible and died. Then of course he would vanish back into the nothingness he had emerged from.

Maj. Borovski had a good faculty of perception. "And you can pick up their thoughts? I mean—you can tell when some of them are close by?"

"Yes."

"Good!" he decided. "Then you come with me. You can ride up here on my arm."

Iltu didn't hesitate long. She climbed up his lanky form and established herself in the crook of his left arm. Borovski carried his beamer in his right hand. He turned on his defense screen and then beckoned to the men who had remained with him. The search of the robotship began.

Not everyone had come equipped with combatsuits so they formed in groups around those who were so protected. They sent the protected men ahead of them to lure the phantoms out of hiding. As soon as there was any firing out of the air, the others were to close in and join in the answering fire.

Maj. Borovski's group achieved the first results altho he was honest enough later to explain that it was actually due to Iltu. There were 7 men in the group. The major was leading the way with his activated defense screen. Iltu sat on his arm and searched for the enemy's thought impulses, which she knew must be able to come thru their own protective screens. The other 6 men were a few steps behind and covered all sides with their weapons ready to fire.

The first impulses that came to Iltu were very weak. The aliens were approaching slowly but steadily. It seemed as if they were especially attracted by Iltu's own brainwave patterns.

The small commando group was moving along a wide passageway. To their right and left were the doors of the empty cabins. The dim emergency lights were still coming on automatically as they progressed but all they revealed were the naked deckplates of the corridor, since on such ships there was no plastic floor coating or carpeting.

Borovski came to a cross passage and stopped. "Where to?"

"To your right," whispered Iltu and pointed into the narrower corridor. "The impulses come from there. We should be meeting them any minute."

"Let's go!" the major whispered to his men.

Iltu felt the impulses getting stronger. She wondered anxiously if she would be safe here under Borovski's defense screen. What would Pucky have felt in her place? Was he really as fearless as he always acted or could he also sense fear?

"Stop!"

Maj. Borovski complied at once. "Do you see something?"

"You can't see them," she whispered tensely. "But I sense somebody. One of them is here."

The 6 other men had come to a stop and taken cover. At the first sign of attack they would charge forward. Borovski couldn't rid himself of a very uneasy feeling. He was accustomed to facing an enemy he could see but here there was no one visible. Iltu couldn't even tell him where the phantom was standing. She only knew that he was here—that was all.

"He's thinking—hate! Now it's still more hate! He's going to attack!"

She had hardly spoken before a blue-white energy beam flashed out directly in front of Borovski. It struck his screen and was deflected harmlessly in a spray of pyrotechnics. The major aimed his weapon and pressed the trigger. Simultaneously the other men joined him and opened a furious counterfire against the phantom. Within fractions of a second his outlines became visible under that sheet of flame but the Terrans kept on firing. As the figure sank to the floor they followed it with their beams and saturated it with energy.

During the fighting a fairly human outline had been seen. It was a colorless silhouette against the background of the wall and then the floor except that it was 3-dimensional and seemingly material since the energy beams virtually encircled it as it went down. Borovski closely observed the phenomenon while he was firing. Now the thing lay on the deck. The blue-white flashes from its weapon had ceased. The phantom offered no further resistance because it was dying. Then it faded back into invisibility.

Iltu could sense that the thought impulses also died away. At first they had been emanations of pure hate, then rage and a will to attack. Finally there had been anguish and pain—followed by the calm of death.

At any rate, the uncanny foe could be conquered. That is—on an individual basis, for the invaders as a whole were far from being beaten. Nor was it all to be as easy as this.

*   *   *   *

Maj. Borovski learned over radio that the enemy was not present on the other robotships. According to plan, each vessel was taken over and manned. They waited within 2 km of the *Caesar* for the further instructions of Col. Sukril.

But the colonel did not respond to any of their radio calls. The *Caesar* hovered silently and motionlessly in space. It seemed as if Sukril had withdrawn from the operation and preferred to leave everything in the hands of the commando leaders.

Maj. Borovski gave up trying to make contact with the commander; he had more important things to do. With help from Iltu he was able to track down 3 more phantoms and kill them but then there were no more impulses. It was as if the invaders had been swallowed up by the ethers of Eternity.

On the other hand, up in the Control Central the troops of Sgt. Bering ran into a well-prepared death trap.

Bering was no telepath so he was not sensitive to the thought emanations of the aliens. Unsuspectingly he came into the Control Central and occupied it with his men. There was no sign of hostiles here so they began to feel secure. In the adjacent Com Room an operator took over the radio console and reported in to the *Caesar*. He received no answer.

Bering deployed his men in groups so as to offer the required defensive pattern. The only mistake he made was to think in terms of only *one* attacker. It was thus a deadly surprise to see blue energy beams emerging simultaneously from 3 different directions.

Iltu had slipped out of Maj. Borovski's arm when she picked up the thoughts of the hard-pressed men. She oriented herself swiftly and cried out: "In the Control Central—it's a concentrated attack! I'll jump ahead —you follow!" And with that she vanished.

Borovski comprehended at once. He and his men stormed into the nearest antigrav lift and arrived 2 minutes later in the Control Central. What he saw there he would never forget.

3 men in the pastel green service uniforms of the Terran spacefleet were lying on the floor. There could be no doubt that they were dead. Out of sheer nothingness the blue energy beams were sweeping thru the room in search of new victims. Under cover of their defense screens, Sgt. Bering and Iltu opened fire on the

invisible enemy but their 2 weapons were not enough to kill them or even to drive them away. Three or 4 men had thrown themselves to the deck and crept into various niches, from which cover they fired haphazardly at the invaders.

"Get the one on the left!" yelled Borovski and he signaled his men to take cover before retaliating.

Bering caught on. He concentrated on the spot, in the middle of the air, where an energy beam was emanating from the left. Seconds later the enemy became visible under their combined attack. He sank to the floor and ceased firing.

The second one was also put out of harm's way but the third phantom disappeared without leaving a trace. Nobody knew it but at that moment all of the aliens withdrew at once. It was as if they had obeyed a silent command to retreat. It came 5 minutes too late because 3 Terrans lay dead in the Control Central of the vast robotship.

The enemy casualties were both invisible and immaterial. They could not be counted but it was certain that their losses had been greater than those of the Terrans. It was a poor consolation in spite of their victory.

"Call the *Caesar!*" shouted Borovski after the various group leaders reported that there were no further signs of attack. "Looks like the ship is ours." He signaled into the Com Room at the operator who had already turned on the equipment again. "Make contact with Col. Sukril—on the double!" After that he paced restlessly back and forth while his men took care of the fallen ones.

"Sir, the *Caesar* still doesn't answer!"

Borovski's brows shot up. "What the devil's that supposed to mean? Are they sleeping over there? Try it again!"

Iltu felt strangely alerted by this. In the past few minutes she had gained still more self-confidence and knew that she could depend on her faculties. Pucky had been an excellent task-master. She tried to establish contact with Sukril's mind but was blocked by the confusion of hundreds of other impulses. For a moment she thought she caught an emanation from Pucky but then she lost it again. It was equivalent to trying to pick out one person's voice in the shout of a thousand-man multitude—and also attempting to identify him.

The Com Man came back. "No contact, sir. They don't answer."

Iltu spoke up. "Should I have a look, Major? All I have to do is teleport."

Borovski looked about him uncertainly. "And if they show up again—the shadow people?"

"I can be back right away."

He nodded. "Alright—but hurry it up! If I only knew where Pucky was! He ought to be here."

Iltu said nothing. She was beginning to worry about her fellow mousebeaver. She concentrated and vanished without attempting to answer the major's unexpressed question. No one could say that she was a weak and uncertain teleporter. She had only to think of the *Caesar's* Command Central—and there she materialized.

Col. Sukril was slumped motionlessly in his flight seat before the controls. The Nav Officer, Capt. Henderson, also seemed to be unconscious or dead. His head was resting on the chart table. The finger of his right hand was curled around the butt of his weapon. Three other officers were stretched out flat on the deck. The door of the Com Room was standing wide open. There was no sign of life from the chief operator.

Iltu took all this in within seconds. With a shrill whistle of alarm she pattered over to Col. Sukril. He was breathing weakly but steadily. His brain convolutions gave out an abstract pattern of dreamlike communications. At any rate he was alive.

Iltu didn't deliberate for long. For the moment there was nothing here she could do and Maj. Borovski was waiting for her. He must be informed of this at once. So she teleported back into the robotship. She briefly described what she had seen. For about 10 seconds Maj. Borovski stared at her in disconcerted amazement. Then he turned to the radio operator in Bering's detail.

"Are you familiar with the com equipment?"

"Yessir. It's the same as on the *Caesar*."

"Including the hypercom?"

"Yessir."

Borovski took a deep breath before giving his order. "Make a hypercom connection with Perry Rhodan. Straight to Terrania. But make it fast—we've no time to lose!"

He leaned back against the control panels in the Com Room and waited. In his right hand he still held his de-safetied weapon. Iltu sat on his left arm and used her *esp*. She was to warn him if the phantoms were getting ready to make another attack.

But there were no phantoms present. At least not here.

* * * *

Sgt. Gork ran into some real trouble.

When he had panicked and leapt into space he had not given any thought to how he was going to reach the *Caesar*. The main thing was to get out of the terrible ghost ship. He somersaulted slowly and some seconds went by before he could orient himself. Naturally he had missed his mark and ended up drifting past the *Caesar* just as its locks opened up.

Laboriously he drew his handgun and fired it carefully. His turning motion became slower and finally stopped. He had to fire another shot to get out of the way of the commando craft that were emerging from the *Caesar's* launching locks.

His freefall course brought him above the *Caesar* and the formation of robotships. He could observe everything quite clearly. In his helmet phones was a confusion of orders and answering confirmations mixed with reports and conversations. The special commando details were boarding the robotships.

Gork altered his direction of flight again but just when he was about to give himself a boost of speed the energy weapon slipped from his fingers. He tried in vain to reach for the slowly drifting gun but it receded irretrievably into the void. He himself hovered motionlessly in emptiness. Beneath him the *Caesar* reminded him of a vast planet with robotships for moons.

It took him 10 minutes to realize that the warship's artificial gravity had caught him in its field and that he was sinking toward it with exasperating slowness. Another half hour passed before his feet touched the hull. He moved carefully in order not to launch himself into space again. After a few steps to the nearest open hatch, he entered the hangar inside.

It was empty.

Which in itself wasn't so extraordinary. The commando units had left the *Caesar* and gone to man the robotships. Everything appeared to have operated according to plan and schedule. He, however, had more or less deserted his post.

The thought struck him for the firstime that he could only have fled from a phantom. In one sense it was a relief to know this but in its final consequences the possibilities were not so pleasant. An explanation would be demanded of him. Well, maybe the disappearance of the Gazelle with Lt. Germa would help to explain it—or the launch gate of the robot battleship.

But where the devil were the usual hangar personnel?

Gork looked around. He was alone. No other crewmen were in evidence. Some of the doors leading into the corridors were standing wide open. The air must have escaped from the pressure-equalizing chambers. That was completely against regulations and was unexplainable.

He stirred himself and, choosing the nearest door, closed it behind him and turned on the air supply. When the pressure was equalized he took off his space helmet. Of course he no longer carried a weapon but he didn't see any reason why he should need one now. He still didn't realize what had happened.

Out in the main corridor he ran across the first unconscious crewmen. They were men from the hangar who must have been called from their regular posts by the alarm because they had even forgotten to close the outer launch gate. Some of them had only partially put on their spacesuits before they had fallen unconscious.

Gork sniffed the air testily but could smell nothing suspicious. Had they all been knocked out with some kind of gas?

He bent down to look at several of the men but then gave it up. There were too many of them and he couldn't help them right now anyway. It soon became clear to him that no one was left on board the *Caesar* who was still in an able-bodied condition. They were all unconscious—if that was what one might call a condition that left them still breathing with their eyes staring wide open. Their limbs were stiff and unmovable. Some of them were beginning to stir but they seemed not to hear when they were spoken to.

Gork scolded himself for his frantic desertion of the

robotship. He had to get to Col. Sukril, to the Commander! He had to reach the Control Central!

He found his way thru the passages and corridors and lifts but it was some minutes before he finally stood before the door of the Inner Sanctum. He knew that entry here was forbidden. Only the Commander himself could authorize it.

But—was Sukril still the commander of the *Caesar* . . . ?

Gork pressed his palm against the heat-sensing release. The door slid to one side into its niche. The hatchway was open.

When he entered he saw several figures lying apparently dead on the floor. Two officers sat slumped motionlessly before their control consoles.

Over at the chart table something moved. The captain there slowly raised his head. He stared at the instruments with unseeing eyes. His hands moved wearily. Then he turned and looked at Gork. His lips moved laboriously as he uttered a broken sentence . . . "Course BJ-97-UK . . . build up the screens . . . increase velocity . . . "

Gork clenched his teeth together. He intuited rather than cognized the fact that he was not facing a whole man. What sat there at the chart table was Capt. Henderson or at least that was who he looked like. Yet it couldn't be he. Just his eyes alone betrayed him! They stared vacantly, just slightly past him. They were empty of any spark of life. Or else this was the look of a madman.

Gork pulled himself together and acted almost as quickly as he had when the lock gate had started closing on the robotship. He came to attention and saluted. "Yessir. Increase velocity! Shall I wake up the Commander?"

He received no answer but Col. Sukril began to

move. His right hand picked up his weapon from where it had been lying and shoved it into his holster. He straightened up. His eyes were exactly as empty and dead as Henderson's.

Ignoring Gork he turned to the controls and prepared for a flight—which had been ordered by whom? Certainly not by Capt. Henderson?! Gork began to grasp the whole truth of the situation and he had a prickly sensation of the scalp. The Commander and the Navigation Officer were being guided by alien powers and this was the only reason they had been roused from their states of unconsciousness. The aliens needed them in order to maneuver the *Caesar*.

And what about himself? Wasn't he within this uncanny sphere of influence? Wasn't it only due to his belated return that he was still in command of his senses? Perhaps he was even the only man on board who was now able to think normally.

He had to do something! But in no case must Col. Sukril—or that which Sukril was now—become aware of his intentions. He had to play along in order not to appear suspicious.

"Your orders, sir?" he asked, coming to attention again.

Col. Sukril turned around slowly and looked at him thru dead eyes. He spoke slowly and tonelessly. "Take over the defense screens and turn them all on as soon as the *Caesar* gets underway."

Gork nodded. "Very well, sir. Screens on after we get underway."

He went to the designated control console not far from Sukril, who had already ceased to be concerned with him. As Gork seated himself the activating levers protruded at him from the cabinet panel. Once he moved them forward, the *Caesar* would be hermetically shut off from its outer environment. None of the commando teams would be able to return. The men presently on board would be lost if this unknown power were to steal them away under protection of the screens.

He must not turn them on, or at least he'd have to hold off as long as possible.

Sukril waited until Henderson told him that the coordinates had been calculated and fed to the computer. Then he turned on the ship's mighty engines and started to accelerate. On the viewscreens the robotships fell away swiftly. They grew smaller until they disappeared from view.

Gork saw to his horror that the *Caesar* was being guided into the gulf of intergalactic space. Where was this sector BJ-97-UK . . . ?

Col. Sukril looked over at him. Altho his eyes still remained expressionless his physical attitude seemed to be menacing. His right hand moved slowly toward his gun holster. Gork tensed. Had Sukril's invisible controllers gotten suspicious? Were they about to eliminate him? Would it be better to dash to safety somewhere while he still had a chance or should he continue his present role so that at least one normal man would be in the Control Central? Maybe if he betrayed himself they would knock him unconscious like the others.

He took a deep breath and placed his hands on the levers.

Sukril remained motionless in his seat. He made no further move to draw his weapon. Sgt. Gork dragged it out another 10 seconds but when he saw Sukril's hand start moving again he finally activated the screens of the *Caesar*.

Now inclosed in an impenetrable shell of energy the great warship hurtled away into the absolute vacuum between the galaxies, increasing its distance from the robotships and in a direction which was exactly opposed to that in which Terra lay.

Sgt. Gork stared with widened eyes at the viewscreen where a dim nebula had moved into the crosshairs of the automatic target sighter.

Was *that* sector BJ-97-UK . . . ?

5/ LOST IN THE ABYSS

Pucky sprang first into a number of the smaller robotships but could detect no trace of the phantoms. After he had determined that his help was not needed there, he decided quickly to go to Iltu. He had picked up her thought trace and was able to teleport directly to her. The fight with the shadow people on the main robotship had just ended.

"They're all gone now, Pucky," chirped Iltu wearily. She was still perched on Borovski's arm. "We drove some of them away and killed the rest."

The major briefed Pucky also and didn't forget to point out that without Iltu's courageous help it might not have gone so well. He repeatedly praised the "young" mousebeaver girl and petted her silky fur. Which of course was very pleasing to Iltu. She cuddled comfortably in the crook of Borovski's arm and winked contentedly at Pucky.

"We had 3 casualties," the major concluded. "They've already been taken to the launch lock. As Iltu says, the ship has been cleared of the enemy. She can't detect any more of their impulses."

"Neither can I," Pucky confirmed. He then reported how he had helped Lt. Germa to bring back the Gazelle. "They're over on board the *Caesar*." He paused, apparently recalling something else. "Incidentally, something isn't right over there—on the ship itself."

Borovski nodded. "Iltu found the crew in the Control Central unconscious. Were you there too?"

"Yes but I didn't stay there long." Pucky pointed to the flight consoles. "Couldn't we get this crate into action? The viewscreens and so forth . . . ?"

Borovski beckoned several officers to him. "Man the stations. Turn on the defense screens and test-run the engines. Please hurry it up!"

Within 2 minutes the viewscreens flashed to life. Deep inside the vast warship the main equipment began to vibrate, finally responding to human commands instead of being dependent upon lifeless data pulses from the robot Regent.

Someone called out from the Com Room. "We have contact with the *Ironduke*, sir. The Administrator!"

Borovski moved so quickly that Iltu might have fallen if she had not clung desperately to his sleeve. Pucky waddled slowly after him, thought better of it and turned back to the main room.

The mousebeaver tensely watched the viewscreens. A premonition of disaster had seized him. The *Caesar* remained unchanged in the same position. The movements of the other robotships indicated to him that they had been properly taken over and were now under control of the special commando teams.

The *Caesar* was his main interest at the moment.

Suddenly Pucky was startled to see a tiny figure land on the hull of the mighty ship. It was a man in a spacesuit. Concentrating on the weak thought impulses from that direction, he discovered that it was Gork. So he, too, had gotten to safety. But then he saw him enter one of the empty hangars, which was ironical. He would have saved time if he had gone to the one where Germa was.

He ignored Gork for the time being and sought to pick up other thought streams from that direction. But nobody appeared to be thinking on board the *Caesar*, altho of course he might be mistaken. In the total area of the operation there were too many thought streams impinging on his consciousness—more than 20,000 at least.

He could hear Borovski's calm voice in the adjacent room as he reported to Rhodan. There were pauses while the Major also listened to the orders coming thru.

Pucky looked at the screens again and stiffened in alarm. The *Caesar* was moving! It picked up speed, suddenly hurtling past the robot formation and receding. As he watched, it dwindled away into the starless abyss beyond. Seconds later it was a tiny speck of light in the distance and then it was gone.

Pucky made a short teleport jump into the Com Room—and there was Rhodan looking down at him from the hypercom screen. Without bothering about Borovski he interrupted with a shrill cry. "Perry—they've stolen the *Caesar!* I'll try to overtake them—but we need you fast!"

He swiftly closed his space helmet and then vanished, leaving Borovski, Rhodan and everybody else in considerable confusion.

When he materialized he was in the empty void. Once more he experienced the lonely feeling of being in an infinite gulf without any point of reference, struggling to orient himself. He could only do that if he could pick up thought impulses from the *Caesar*—but the only one there who could think was Sgt. Gork. Lt. Germa and his 3 men sat under the energy screen of their Gazelle and were isolated. Pucky desperately applied his *esp* faculties to locate Gork but in vain.

Then, not 10 meters from him, a figure appeared out of nowhere. It happened with no warning shimmer because here there was no air.

Iltu!

"Are you out of your mind!" he yelled instinctively altho it wasn't necessary. Iltu could understand him without the need for words.

"I followed you. Maybe you can use my help."

Pucky gasped, beside himself. "Help?! When I myself don't know what I should do?"

Iltu flailed her arms but didn't come any closer. "Let's get out of here—why not jump to the *Caesar?*"

Pucky answered her heatedly. "Where are you going to jump to when you can't locate it? I've been trying all this time to find Gork but the donk is blanked out mentally or something. He has to be on the ship! Wherever he is, that's where the *Caesar* is."

Thru her faceplate he could see her faint smile.

"Gork is in the Control Central—been there for quite awhile. He keeps talking to Col. Sukril but Sukril has no thought patterns just now. When he answers, I can't pick up his words."

Pucky gasped again in his irritation. "You say you have Gork? Wait—I'm coming over there to you. Then you make the jump and take me with you."

He knew there was no more time to attempt his own tracking. If Iltu had contact that was enough. This little mousebeaver gal was not to be underestimated.

With a short transition he was next to her. He grasped her hand tightly in both of his. "Jump!" he said quickly.

She jumped.

Meanwhile the *Caesar* had traveled more than 100,000 km but with Pucky's reinforcement Iltu made it. In the fraction of a single second the 2 mousebeavers covered the incredible gap and materialized exactly at the source of Gork's mental emanations.

In the Control Central.

In a glance Pucky grasped the situation. It wasn't the first time that men had been taken over by extraterrestrial influences and forced to obey an alien will altho the methods varied. What was going on here was certainly new but the result was the same.

It was in that moment that Gork activated the energy screens. He was not yet aware of the mousebeavers but they knew that he did it consciously if against his will. He had to do it if he didn't want to betray the fact that his will was still his own. He had delayed the action —fortunately just long enough.

Pucky had not let go of Iltu's hand. He teleported into the hangar, where he knew Germa was located. Iltu came with him. He only let go of her after they had both arrived safely.

The Gazelle was still in the same place. Meanwhile the hangar had automatically filled up with air again and the small scoutship's energy dome shimmered strangely in the dim illumination.

Pucky signaled with both arms and the screen disappeared. Moments later he and Iltu were on board and were received by Germa and his friends with great relief.

"I was really afraid!" admitted the lieutenant unabashedly. "What the devil's going on? Where's the crew? When the *Caesar* got underway again I was on the verge of leaving the Gazelle and reporting back to the Commander. I assumed that everything was OK. But then I got this funny feeling again—like a warning."

"It's a good thing you listened to your instincts," said Pucky. "It would have gone badly for you if you had left the Gazelle. The *Caesar* has been taken over by the spooks!"

Lt. Germa stared at Pucky in horrified alarm. "What are you saying! The shadow people? Here—on board the *Caesar*?"

"Yes but they're being extra careful. So far I haven't been able to trace their thoughts. Maybe they can shield their minds."

"And the crew? Is it . . . ?"

"No, not dead, merely unconscious. Of course some of the officers and the Commander are conscious in a way but they are under the influence of the phantoms. They were used so that the ship could take off and be captured."

"How is it possible?" Germa was not to be pacified. Brado, Hansen and Lester stood facing the mousebeavers in helpless perplexity. On their faces were expressions of incipient panic. "What are we going to do?"

Meanwhile Pucky had taken off his helmet, following Iltu's example. "Just now I can't answer either of those questions," he said. "The robotships are alright—they've been taken over. Rhodan has been alerted. He'll come and get us. If I only knew how to stop the *Caesar* in the meantime! Pretty soon she's going to reach light-speed and more. If we can't get to the communications gear, nobody will be able to track us or find us."

"What's wrong with the com equipment here on the Gazelle?"

Pucky looked surprised for the moment. "That's right—I didn't think of that. But we need a good outside antenna. Without that there can be no signal tracking."

Here, too, Germa had a solution. "We'll tie the equipment to the outer hull of the *Caesar*. That will make an excellent antenna. Now what about Col. Sukril? We can't just leave him in the power of the aliens. Who knows how long he can stand it?"

"Pucky!" It was Iltu, who had not taken part in the conversation. Instead she had been listening inwardly. "I'm getting Gork's thoughts. He's trying to figure how he can overcome Sukril and Henderson without harming them. I hope he doesn't try anything foolish!"

"That youngster isn't so dumb," muttered Pucky

grimly but then he added: "How is he planning to do it?"

He followed Iltu's example and concentrated for awhile on Gork's thoughts. Then he explained what was happening to Germa. "He wants to knock out Sukril—also Henderson—and then he hopes to bring the *Caesar* back to its starting point. I still think he's about to make a mistake. Those phantoms are here on board. Hm-m . . . One other thing, Germa: do you have any weapons, like hand beamers?"

"Sure, I've got a whole cabinet full of them. But you're not saying you're going to—?"

"What else? How else can you bushwhack those spooks? Iltu and I can tell they're here even tho they've been trying to conceal themselves. But first let's connect that antenna. Who's the radio tech?"

"Lt. Hansen knows enough about it—Lester and Brado, too."

While the 3 men worked, Pucky stood guard, but no matter how hard he tried he couldn't actually detect any of the enemy nearby. On her part, Iltu kept in contact with Gork, who was still desperately seeking a way to overcome the hypnotized officers in the Control Central. It seemed that the hidden ones still thought that he was under their general influence.

"I wonder if the propulsion system can be knocked out," said Germa suddenly. "Even if we make contact with Rhodan he won't be able to help us if the *Caesar* is inside the Kalup absorption field—and that's where she'll be if she goes into linear drive."

"The absorption field, hm-m . . . " thought Pucky aloud. "If it collapsed the *Caesar* would automatically come back under the speed of light. Also if the defense screens broke down. Yup, that would be one way. Just cripple the absorption field and everything would be kosh. But it won't do to just shut it off. We'd have to damage the generating equipment so that it couldn't be fixed so easily. Those spooks mustn't have any chance to escape. I'm half convinced they want the secret of linear spacedrive—otherwise they wouldn't have swiped the *Caesar*."

. Sgt. Brado came into the Gazelle's control room. "Antenna's ready, sir," he told Lt. Germa. "Let's hope it works. We've shot another one outside the defense screens."

"OK, get going! Hypercom the *Ironduke*— non-directional. Maybe they'll hear us!"

Pucky left this task to Germa and his men. He took Iltu to one side. "Listen, Iltu, we have to do something about Gork. The poor guy is in a heck of a fix. He still doesn't know how close we are to him and he might do something stupid. We'll take the paralysis beamer with us and try to put Sukril and the other officers out of the action. We'll take the energy guns with us, too, in case we come up against the spooks."

Dispensing with teleportation they went on foot toward the Control Central. It wasn't until they were in the main corridor that they picked up their first weak thought patterns from the aliens. They were coming closer at a steady and menacing pace.

"Watch out!" whispered Iltu, raising her weapon. "They're waiting for us." The fur on the back of her neck bristled as she pointed ahead into the curved passage. "They are there—but why don't they fire at us?"

Pucky had also raised his weapon. "I don't know —they may have something else in mind. Remember the other crewmen. Maybe they want to take the *Caesar* together with its entire crew. They're not killing anybody anymore."

"What are we waiting for? Come on—let's fire at them! If we don't they'll also try to bring *us* under their control!"

Their 2 energy beams crossed at a point 5 meters ahead. Immediately it became unbearably hot in the corridor but a vague shadow appeared where the beams were intersecting. Seconds later it vanished.

"2 weapons aren't enough," grumbled Pucky. "But at least we can hold them off. Let's keep going—to the Control Central. Now we know anyway that they're aware of us."

They did not have far to go. Almost soundlessly the hatch door slid to one side. Sgt. Gork was still sitting before the controls of the defense screens. He was not yet aware of the 2 mousebeavers. His brain was too busy with a number of wild plans which he was rejecting as fast as they occurred to him.

Col. Sukril turned around slowly. A chill ran thru Pucky when he looked into his empty and lifeless-seeming eyes. They were the eyes of a zombie or a corpse. Without any sign of recognition, Sukril raised his weapon and aimed at him. His finger tightened on the trigger.

Pucky exerted his telekinetic powers. Cautiously his mental force stream grasped the raygun and removed it from the Commander's fingers. After floating away from him, Pucky released the weapon and it dropped to the floor. Capt. Henderson was not armed.

The sound of the falling weapon caused Gork to turn around. He was nonplussed when he saw Pucky and Iltu. It was as if he could not believe his eyes.

"Relax, Gork, it's us alright. Stay seated there and turn off the defense screens. Hey, Sukril—can you hear me?"

The Commander stared at Pucky, still giving no sign of recognition. Then his head sank suddenly and he slumped in his seat, completely unconscious. The phantoms had simply "turned him off". Also in that moment, Capt. Henderson slumped into the same state.

"Pucky!" called Gork. "The defense screens! They can't be turned off!"

Pucky spun around to look at him but finally nodded. "I thought as much! They're blocked. Same as in Germa's Gazelle. Well, then maybe the only way out is to disable the absorption field setup. Iltu, you stay here with Gork. If the spooks come in here—shoot! I'll be back as soon as possible."

There was hardly any ship-type better known to Pucky than a superbattleship. Once on Zalit he had spent days with one of the crews in operations drills. On board the *Caesar*, while training Iltu, he had also gone thru every room via teleportation. So he naturally knew where the main power and machine rooms were. He didn't know too much about the technical aspects but what he knew was enough. This wasn't the firstime he'd been called upon to cripple a large propulsion system.

Meanwhile the *Caesar* had been racing toward its unknown destination at many times the speed of light. Second by second its velocity increased. In the time it would take to breathe in and out, the ship covered many millions of kilometers. Soon that would increase to billions of kilometers—perhaps light years.

While Pucky was cautiously approaching the machinery section of the giant ship, with his parafaculties sharply tuned to weak thought emanations from the invisible enemy, Iltu and Sgt. Gork did not remain idle.

"Do you believe," said Gork, "that they can just take over an unconscious person and make them move as they will them to? Wouldn't they have to slip themselves into such a person's body?"

"We don't know, Gork," answered Iltu. She was constantly on the alert and was doing 2 things at once. She was mentally following Pucky and was also keeping her senses open to any signs of the shadow people. "But one thing I do know: we have to find a way of bringing the men out of their state of unconsciousness."

Gork nodded eagerly. "Maybe we should try bringing a medico around first. The ship's clinic! I know something about that kind of thing because we all had to go thru a course on the subject. Shall I go and see what I can do?"

Iltu shook her head. "We have to stay together because one weapon isn't enough to handle those phantoms. Take my hand. I know where the hospital section is. Maybe we'll find something." She telepathed to Pucky to brief him on what they were intending to do. Then she made her jump.

It took her 3 jumps to find her objective. The hospital personnel were still lying or sitting where they had been at the moment of the attack. One of the doctors had collapsed in front of a medicine cabinet. He had evidently softened his fall by supporting himself against the cabinet, which stood wide open. Hundreds of hypodermic ampules, medicine packets and bottles were standing there, row upon row.

Gork let loose of Iltu's hand and approached the cabinet. "If I only knew what to use," he mumbled as he carefully inspected the supplies. "Something to increase the circulation maybe?"

"Don't ask me about it," chirped Iltu in a shrill voice, looking about her searchingly. "I don't understand anything about this kind of thing."

"But you can surely make an injection?"

"I think so," she nodded uncertainly. "If you show me how."

He didn't answer her but kept on rummaging thru the cabinet. Finally he held one of the bottles in his hand to study it more closely.

Gork read the label carefully. "I think this is it. Adrenalin serum KHS-stimulant. We always used this for fainting cases. Let's try it. Where the heck are the hypodermics? Ah, here . . . !" He extracted a flat case from a lower shelf. "It's quite simple. You only have to hold the point against a vein and press the button here. I'll fill this one. The medicine is transferred thru the skin under pressure and it goes right into the blood stream. That's all there is to it. One filling is enough for 20 injections. Do you think you can do it?"

Iltu nodded silently. Gork filled one of the transparent high-pressure hypo-guns. "Let's check it out first. Here—this attendant. I'll do it to show you. Now watch . . ."

Iltu watched tensely as the sergeant placed the instrument and pressed the release. There was nothing to see except that the colorless liquid in the glass tube went down a notch on the scale.

Gork straightened up with a sigh. "If it works we won't know for at the most 5 minutes or so. We have to wait before we do any more."

Iltu used the waiting period to get in touch with Pucky. *"How far along are you, Pucky?"*

"Don't bother me now, Iltu. I think I've located the machinery I'm looking for. Its controls are blocked like everything else. The Kalup just keeps on working. If I can't get rid of the obstruction, nothing's going to stop it. How is it with you?"

"Nothing's happened so far."

Pucky did not continue the telepathic conversation. Iltu still kept a loose contact with him while giving her major attention to the dim and distant thought impulses of the shadow people. They had not tried to make any further attacks. Perhaps they assumed that these 3 conscious beings on board were not a threat to them.

Gork suddenly leaned over the attendant again. "He's moving—just look at that!" He seemed to be surprised at the success of his medical experiment but he was still more pleased when the man sat up and looked at him questioningly.

"What happened? I—I felt so lousy all of a sudden."

"How do you feel now?"

"Thanks—OK now I guess." He looked around then at the other unconscious men. "Glord—what hit us!"

"They all got the same," said Gork, avoiding the details. "I have to know if you're back in shape again. Get on your feet. Do you know your medicine? I mean, could you take the place of a doctor—at least in theory?"

"Sure! Why would I be stationed here if I couldn't? Why do you ask?"

Gork showed the attendant the adrenalin bottle. "You familiar with this? That's what I injected you with. Was I right?"

The attendant read the label. "Exactly right. Why?"

Gork turned and filled 2 more hypo-guns, one for Iltu and one for the attendant. "OK, get to work! Wake everybody up—and then let those phantoms try attacking us again! They'll be in for a surprise."

Within half an hour the entire staff of the clinic was equipped with hypo-guns and energy weapons. They deployed out thru the ship in groups so that they could defend themselves against any ambush by the aliens. But no ambush came. Thus they were able to continue undisturbed while they resuscitated the entire crew of the *Caesar*.

Iltu went with Gork to the Control Central and woke up Col. Sukril as well as Henderson and the other officers. Two minutes later, 1st Officer Maj. Brokov rushed into the room. It seemed that the rescue work had succeeded and that the *Caesar* was saved. However it was quickly discovered that such was not the case.

When Col. Sukril ordered the course changed, the ship did not respond. It seemed as if all the controls were blocked. With ever-increasing acceleration the *Caesar* continued to race thru the intergalactic gulf toward the distant nebula. One glance at the instruments revealed that they were already traveling at 10,000 times the speed of light. With each passing second, this velocity was increasing. One light-year in less than an hour! Soon it would be a lyr every 30 minutes—then one every minute.

The great milky Way behind them didn't change visibly because they were too close to it and still relatively too slow.

Col. Sukril turned and saw Iltu. "Now listen, Lt. Puck . . . !"

"I am Iltu, Commander!"

For a moment Sukril was confused but then recovered irritably. "We ought to be able to tell you two apart. Alright, then were is your friend Pucky?"

"Oh he's trying to knock out the propulsion system."

Sukril turned blue. "He's doing what?! Knock out the—has he lost his mind?"

Now Iltu revealed that she had absorbed some of Pucky's personality. Her self-confidence had grown considerably and she also knew that without her and Pucky the situation here might be much worse. "For your information, sir, Pucky has not lost his mind! Do you happen to have a better idea? How is Rhodan ever going to catch up to us if we keep on shooting away from the galaxy at top speed?"

Sukril's normal color gradually returned. Maj.

Brokov grinned, not envying his superior for this un-answerable rebuff.

Sukril gasped. "Rhodan?"

Iltu nodded triumphantly. "That's right—who else? Didn't you inform him about the aliens?"

Sukril turned back to stare at his useless instruments and controls. "I contacted him, yes, but he doesn't know our present position. You in the Com Room —what about the transmitter?"

"Forget that," said Iltu. "How are you going to transmit anything when you can't shut off the screens? Anyway, Lt. Germa is already trying to contact Rhodan or at least to send out a tracer signal. We've shot an antenna line thru the outer defense screen so that the transmission wouldn't be blocked. If that doesn't work . . ."

Sukril regarded Iltu with a more kindly expression. "Don't be angry if I've underestimated you, Iltu. But is Pucky really doing the right thing, trying to knock out the Kalup? Without the absorption field and the screens we'd be defenseless . . ."

"The aliens aren't threatening us from outside —only here on the inside. Wait—I think Pucky has located the obstruction. Yes, he has! It won't take long now!"

But it took 2 full hours while the wandering resuscitation crews were attacked three times by the aliens, of whom two were killed. At least they assumed that the phantoms were killed because as they faded from view they went thru all the symptoms of dying.

Then without any warning the *Caesar* suddenly dropped back into the normal Einstein universe. The tremendous shock of slowing down was not too great because the inertial absorbers hadn't been cut off. Nevertheless a sensible jolt ran thru the ship as if it had suffered an explosion somewhere in its depths.

At the same time Pucky appeared in the Control Central. He looked exhausted. Without paying any attention to those present in the room he waddled directly to the nearest cushioned seat and jumped into it. With a satisfied sigh he closed his eyes and comfortably stretched his limbs.

For a moment Col. Sukril was transfixed by astonishment and disbelief but the shameless grin of his First Officer reminded him of the regulation discipline that was expected on board every ship of the Terran spacefleet. "Lt. Puck! Might we be informed of where you've been all this time? What happened to the propulsion system?"

Pucky didn't so much as raise an eyelid. "Ask Iltu—she's got all the latest poop. Good night!"

Sukril gave a masterful demonstration of self-control. His hands trembled slightly but otherwise he suppressed his agitation. "I want the report from *you*, Lt. Puck!"

Pucky finally opened his eyes and looked at the commander. Then he slipped out of the chair obediently. With dignified gravity he strutted straight across the room, drew himself up before Sukril and even attempted to keep his bowed little legs straighter than usual. With his right hand he almost executed a perfect salute. "Propulsion put out of commission, sir! Absorption field and screens down, sir! And now if you don't watch out and let me do my *esp* in peace, you and your whole crew will soon be sleeping again as you were before. Good night, sir!" Having said his speech, he marched right back to his chair. He sprang into it and promptly closed his eyes again.

Col. Sukril didn't move. Finally, after almost 10 seconds of tense expectancy, he spoke. "Major, see to it that Pucky is not disturbed. Keep all weapons ready. Iltu, you warn us if the aliens try another attack. We can't do anything else except wait for Rhodan or the robotships. Is the crew alerted and in shape?''

''They're briefed and ready, sir,'' said Brokov.

In his chair, Pucky still had his eyes closed but he suddenly called out: ''Watch out—! I've picked them up! They're trying another attack! Two of them are entering now. Even if you wreck the place—fire! Get going—what are you waiting for? *Shoot!*''

6/ FAR NEBULA, LONG SHADOWS

"What do you say, Brado? Any contact yet?"

"I'm sorry, sir—none at all. But it's possible that the tracer signal got thru which may help them to track the *Caesar*. The antenna is too small, tho, to receive any possible return tra smissions."

"But could they pick up our distress call?"

"That's quite possible, sir."

Lt. Germa sighed with relief. "We can't ask for anything more. But maybe it'll work better now that the *Caesar's* screen is gone. Keep trying, Brado."

Meanwhile the hangar personnel had returned. They reported that some hours before an order from the commander had called them all into the main corridor and that was where they had lost consciousness. They had no explanation for it.

They deployed themselves strategically with ready weapons and waited for the enemy. But the enemy didn't come.

The enemy was attacking the Control Central.

* * * *

Pucky had leapt from his chair. "There—near the entrance!"

7 or 8 energy beams concentrated on the indicated area. The shadowy outlines of the alien became visible so that they could see him sink to the floor. He almost completely materialized before fading away.

"Iltu, you stay here!" said Pucky. "I'll cover the defenses of the rest of the ship. In any case they'll try to get the Control Central back in their hands."

He dematerialized before Sukril had a chance to give

his permission. The colonel was gradually getting used to the idea that Pucky operated independently—and operated correctly.

Iltu took over the task of detecting the approach of the aliens and warning the defenders of it. The system of concentrated fire proved effective as usual. During the ensuing hour they were able to eliminate more than 7 of the uncanny invaders. At any rate the previous catastrophe was not repeated. Nobody fell unconscious or came under control of the aliens.

In the Control Central the viewscreen was still operating. It was apparently the only thing that did work. All other equipment had ceased to function or to respond to controls. The *Caesar* was moving in freefall toward the distant nebula but only at the normal speed of light. If anyone were to track them now from the direction of the galaxy, they would be easy to overtake.

"Turn on the communications equipment!" ordered Sukril. "Now we should be able to make contact!"

While the Com Room crew was trying to put out a call to the small fleet of robotships, the shadow people attacked again. They had changed their tactics and came in groups of 4 or 5 at a time. And this time they used a new type of weapon. The energy beams that suddenly shot at the officers out of emptiness were now orange instead of blue.

Capt. Henderson was the first victim. He had followed Iltu's warning and gone for cover with his weapon ready to fire but he couldn't know where the scattered phantoms were located. Before he could make a defensive move an orange beam struck him squarely. He remained standing where he was. He neither collapsed nor turned to smoking cinders, he simply became rigid and didn't move a muscle. His eyes stared fixedly but there was life in them. Henderson was not dead but only immobilized.

Sukril let out a shout of surprise which was cut off abruptly when he too was enveloped by the weird energy and rendered motionless.

Iltu screamed a warning and jumped forward with a gun in either hand. She knew exactly where the nearest alien was standing. Both of her weapons fired simultaneously at maximum intensity. She hit the phantom, who immediately withdrew. Without stopping she continued her fire, turning slightly to hit the next one. But the third one was faster.

He got her.

* * * *

Somewhere in the ship, Pucky was frightened nearly to death when Iltu's thought stream suddenly faded out. He had been aware of events in the Control Central but had hoped that the officers and his little friend would be able to handle the aliens. But now Iltu wasn't in contact with him any more.

Without any further deliberation, he teleported into the Control Central, immediately traced the presence of a phantom, tore a weapon away from an officer and opened fire against the enemy. Even while he was noting with satisfaction that the nemesis had disappeared, a human figure materialized in the room. He was wearing a rather cumbersome combat suit—an old SHK model—and in his hands he carried an oversized energy gun which he lowered as soon as he saw the officers and Pucky.

It was Ras Tschubai, the African teleporter.

Pucky yelled out in astonishment: "Ras! Is it really you? I thought you were on the *Ironduke* . . ."

"You thought right," replied Ras, and he looked about him searchingly. His gaze rested momentarily on Iltu, then wandered on to Col. Sukril, who had also not moved from his position. "What's wrong with them?"

Pucky ascertained that the Control Central was free of enemies. It seemed that the phantoms had decided to leave the scene without further resistance. "You mean you've come for us?" he asked.

Ras nodded. "The *Ironduke's* alongside. We tracked you on that tracer signal. It was very weak but we picked it up. I made a jump over here as soon as we arrived but Rhodan and his men will be coming on board any second now. They're at the outer locks."

Pucky sank into the nearest chair. "Not a minute too soon! I still don't know how we're going to handle the spooks." On second thought he jumped up again and ran to Iltu. He carefully touched her and looked at her closely. "She's warm—normal temperature! She's alive. Look! She's starting to move again!" He heaved a great sigh of relief and even began to laugh. "It was only a temporary paralysis. There—even Sukril is moving and so is Henderson!"

It was like a miracle. The officers and Iltu appeared to be waking up from a deep sleep. Their brains and their memory had been turned off when the paralysis beams had struck them but now they were turned on again simultaneously. What had occurred between must have been a blank for them.

Iltu finally lowered both of her weapons. Their charges had been exhausted in this spirited battle. Sukril looked around for further signs of the enemy but couldn't discover any.

Then the door of the Control Central slid to one side and Perry Rhodan entered.

In one sweeping glance he took in the scene, nodded curtly to Pucky and then looked questioningly at Col. Sukril. Several other men pressed past him into the room carrying some strange-looking equipment, which they deposited on the deck with obvious relief.

Rhodan smiled faintly. "It seems we got here in the

nick of time," he said. "Pucky, were those aliens really the same phantoms of Barkon?"

The mousebeaver had taken Iltu by the hand and led her to a chair. He carefully helped her into it before turning around to Rhodan. "They're the ones, Perry. All the same phenomena and reactions."

"So they've found us again," muttered Rhodan gravely. "I've been afraid this would happen, for a long time." He nodded to the men who were standing by the mysterious instruments. "Might as well get to work. First, here in the Control Central. We have to know what's happened."

Meanwhile Col. Sukril had regained his presence of mind. "Sir, if you wish my report . . ."

"Thank you, Colonel—I've been briefed on the situation. You were not to blame. You and your men have handled yourselves very well. The robot fleet is on its way to Terra. You had already accomplished your assigned mission. A confrontation with the invisible invaders was not foreseen."

Capt. Henderson had finally overcome his sense of awe at being in the presence of the highest Commander-in-Chief. He had returned to his station and was trying to pick up the *Ironduke* on the viewscreen. To his surprise the tracking system responded immediately. The instruments functioned without any difficulty. The 800-meter hull of the battleship moved laterally into the field of vision. Small units were streaming in a steady stream from the great launch-lock hatches, bringing extra crewmen to the *Caesar*.

But the tracking equipment picked up something else as well.

Vaguely discernible in silhouette, another spaceship was hovering nearby. The instruments gave a distance of 3 km. Rather than spherical in shape, the ship was reminiscent of a missile or torpedo. It was more than

100 meters in length but this was relatively small by comparison.

"Sir . . . we're tracking an alien ship! The indicators must not be working right because it's not showing up very clearly . . . "

In 2 long strides, Rhodan was beside him, staring at the screen. "There's nothing wrong with your equipment," he said grimly. "It's the ship of the phantom people. That configuration is the same we saw on Barkon." He turned to Col. Sukril. "Colonel—get the *Caesar* ready for combat—but fast! Don't lose a second!"

Sukril raced to his commander seat. He switched on the intercom and gave the necessary orders. He didn't even have time to be surprised that the intercom was working.

Rhodan turned to Pucky. "Did you knock out the Kalup absorption generator?"

"Yes—there was no other choice."

"Alright, so we'll repair it. I've brought the whole tech team along. I assume all we have to do is replace the generator itself. Hm-m . . . How did Iltu work out? I was afraid she wouldn't match up to the assignment. She's so young. Actually, I should have let her stay on Mars . . . "

"Knockitoff!" muttered Pucky, so softly that only Rhodan could hear him. "Without Iltu I wouldn't have made it, to be honest with you. And—well—she's not such a child, you know; she's quite a young lady, if you ask me."

Rhodan smiled and bent down close to the mousebeaver's ear. "Tell me now, are you maybe in love with her?"

Pucky drew back as if a snake had bitten him. "In love?!" he gasped indignantly. "That's too much! I could never fall in love with such a stupid little moose—pah!'' But he suddenly fell silent for a moment while he cocked his head and looked at Rhodan confidentially. "You won't tell on me, will you?"

Rhodan shook his head. "Why should I? They'll be able to guess the truth, the same as I did.'' He grinned and added: "Especially Bell!"

Pucky stamped his foot and grimaced. "Did you bring him along by any chance?"

"At the moment he's commanding the *Ironduke*, along with Claudrin of course."

"So I even have to put up with that now!" moaned Pucky as he waddled away.

The gunners of the *Caesar* reported battle readiness. Meanwhile Pucky and Iltu announced that there were evidently no more shadow people on board the giant warship.

Rhodan concluded swiftly: "They've given up and are trying to escape in that ship out there. We have to stop them! Col. Sukril, open fire! Give your crews the coordinates from here because I don't think their target scopes can see the ship anymore. Hurry—before they get away!"

After the *Ironduke* had withdrawn from the danger zone the *Caesar* opened fire from all gun positions. The attack could only be directed from the Control Central because the opposing vessel's outlines could only be detected on the special tracking equipment. The normal screens revealed nothing but the distant light patch of the unknown stellar nebula.

The energy lightnings darted into emptiness—and struck the unseen objective. While the beams sprayed off it in all directions, they brought the outlines of the enemy ship into 3-D clarity for all to see. Whether or not the aliens had a defense screen couldn't quite be determined because of the rapidity of events. Or if they had one it was very weak. Five beams struck in one spot and that was the end.

As the concentrated fire penetrated the armorplate hull, a blinding explosion forced the Terrans to close their eyes. When everybody looked again there was an expanding gas cloud where the invisible ship had been. The glowing mass was attenuating in all directions.

Pucky was next to Rhodan. He whispered: "Their thought patterns—they've dropped off. I'm not getting a trace of them." He turned around. "How about you, Iltu?"

"No—nothing more. Do you think—they're all dead?"

"They must be if your *esp* doesn't pick them up. Did you hear that, Perry? They've been wiped out. We did it!"

Rhodan didn't take his eyes from the viewscreen. There was a deep cleft between his brows as he gazed pensively at the spreading atom cloud which was still glowing and even obscured the distant stellar nebula.

Pucky had followed his thoughts and suddenly spoke up again: "Yes, I think they come from there, too, but how will we ever really find out? Could it be that that whole island universe is subject to other laws of nature? Maybe the spooks simply live in a different dimension than ours. Maybe in the 6th or 7th—but then what would I know about that?"

Rhodan gave him a quick nod. "Precisely! What would you know about it? But at least we'll find out what they were after here and what they planned to do with the *Caesar*." He turned to the men who were working with the new equipment. "How far along are we?"

"Just about ready, sir. All that's left is to determine

the wavelength of the heat radiations so that we won't make any mistakes.''

Col. Sukril was standing nearby in helpless perplexity as he watched the experts manipulate the equipment, making meter adjustments and turning little dials under miniature screens. A movie camera was coupled to the largest screen on the control panel.

Pucky had joined Ras Tschubai to watch. "What is that?" he asked.

The African shrugged. "New-fangled gadgets, little one. Unfortunately I haven't the slightest idea of what it is. We were going to test it while underway but then came your call for help. As it seems, we can also check out the invention here."

Rhodan joined them. "The infra-red delayed tracking process isn't all that new," he said with a faint smile. "All we did on Earth was to make some advanced developments on the basic principle. Ordinarily the equipment is large and terribly cumbersome —difficult to transport. What you see here used to take up a small assembly room. Now it only takes 4 men to carry the whole thing."

"Infra-red relayed trucking process?" Pucky struggled with the long name, not understanding a word of it. "What the heck is that?"

On the larger viewscreen a blur of shadows flitted briefly and was gone.

One of the technicians said almost apologetically: "They're human types, after all—have to adjust it finer."

"What?" said Pucky, flabbergasted. "Human types?"

Rhodan put a finger to his lips, ordering silence. He motioned Col. Sukril and Capt. Henderson to get out of the line of sight between the infra-red tracer and the ship's flight controls. Everyone waited breathlessly while the main viewscreen continued to reveal the spectacle of the glowing cloud of molecular residue from the annihilated ship. It was dispersing more and more and growing dimmer.

Pucky watched the tech team for a while as they worked with their new equipment. Then he took Iltu's hand. "Let's go—this is too way out for me. I'm hungry."

They teleported into his cabin and for the next few minutes dismissed the fortunate outcome of the adventure from their minds. Pucky scrabbled around in his luggage and finally produced a plastic bag containing some carrots. He gallantly offered to share them with Iltu and sat down next to her on the bed.

"Terrific, aren't they? From my own garden by Lake Goshun."

Iltu nibbled a carrot reluctantly. "But I don't find it as good as all that."

Pucky stared in amazement. "What—! Not good? I must not have heard you right!"

Iltu shook her little head and revealed her incisor tooth. "Yes, you heard me. Whenever I get the chance I'm going to cultivate a field of cabbage turnips."

Pucky's eyes widened as if they were going to come out of his head. "Cabbage turnips?!"

Iltu licked her lips with gourmet appreciation. "The most gorgeous ones you can imagine. Your tiresome old carrots couldn't come anywhere near them, Old Boy."

"What did you say?"

Iltu nodded for emphasis. "That your carrots couldn't compare with——"

"No, I don't mean that! Did you say 'Old Boy?' "

She nodded again, this time in mock surprise. "Yes—so?"

Pucky slipped off the couch and placed his arms on

his hips, striking an almost threatening pose. He took a deep breath and was about to launch a tirade when Iltu burst out laughing. Her pink incisor came into full play as she held her stomach in mirth.

"How can anyone be so conceited, Pucky? You don't see me get insulted when you call me 'little' or 'too young', as you just did in front of Rhodan. On the contrary, I'm pleased to know—"

Pucky appeared to shrink about a centimeter as he stared at Iltu in consternation. "You listened when I was talking to Rhodan?" He fumed angrily. "That was mean and nasty of you—besides being low-down shameless imprudence!"

She stopped laughing. "Now why do you say that, Pucky? After all, you were telling him such *nice* things . . . Or did you forget?"

Pucky closed his eyes. He grabbed one of the carrots and began to gnaw at it desperately. "Anyway, you *are* too young!" he confirmed in the midst of his chewing.

She nodded while also resuming her meal. "But you are not too old," she retorted with equal conviction.

If possible, Pucky shrank a tiny bit more.

*   *   *   *

The officers who were present in the Control Central stood tensely watching the infra-red tracer. Rhodan stood in the background and spoke now and then to Col. Sukril. He also received Lt. Germa's report which helped to round out the picture.

"Now we've got it!" cried one of the technicians excitedly. He looked at one of the meters. "Two hours back, sir."

On the main screen of the tracer console could be seen shadowy figures which moved swiftly about in the room. The camera began to hum as it captured these events from the recent past. What the men were looking at had happened 2 hours before. The invisible invaders had emitted heat rays from their bodies, which were now rendered visible. Each of the movements they had made 2 hours ago could now be observed and carefully studied. Earth scientists had developed this astounding equipment for the purpose of obtaining evidence in criminal cases.

"They're looking over the controls," muttered Col. Sukril. He stared in utter amazement at the visible heat imprints of the now dead intelligences. "Those look like human silhouettes. They seem to be interested in the engines."

"You mean our linear propulsion," said Rhodan. "Look! They're also taking pictures! You can't see the camera but their movements are unmistakable. I just hope the photographs were destroyed with their ship because now we know what they were after." He turned to one of the specialists. "That's fine, Professor. Now will you be so good as to repeat the process down in the Machine Center? We have to know what they were doing there."

The tech team packed up their gear and left the Control Central. Their films would be evaluated later. Once the intentions of the aliens were known, conclusions might be drawn with regard to their character, their mode of living and possibly their origin.

The absorption field assembly was replaced and a test run indicated that the *Caesar* was able to return under its own power back to Earth, where it was to have a general overhaul.

Rhodan said goodby to Col. Sukril, wished him a safe journey home and returned with his men to the *Ironduke*. He took the 2 mousebeavers with him. They waited until the *Caesar* started off. It quickly accelerated and was finally only a tiny star against the silvery band of the Milky Way. Then it vanished entirely.

Col. Jefe Claudrin, Flight Commander of the *Ironduke*, also gave orders to get underway. Rhodan's flagship followed the *Caesar*.

Rhodan and Bell sat at a small conference table at a slight distance to one side of the viewscreens. Pucky squatted in a chair beside them and repeated his report in detail. Both men listened intently, frequently interrupting with questions and attempting to dig out every possible clue concerning the aliens.

"It would be almost impossible to tell they were present without telepathy," Pucky emphasized again. "Of course they finally tried to screen their thoughts but didn't work entirely. If they're really telepaths they're pretty poor ones. A good telepath can isolate his thoughts. And there's another thing I noticed: under a heavy attack they back off pretty fast. They're not too keen about fighting. As soon as the *Ironduke* showed up they ditched their plans and simply gave up the *Caesar* when it was just about in their hands. They escaped—even tho it was only to go up in smoke right afterwards. Then all the blocked controls suddenly came free. Is it possible that they locked the controls by telekinesis?"

Rhodan shook his head negatively. "No, they don't use psychokinesis or we would have noticed that during our combats with them. I'm more in favor of your first idea. They penetrate matter, which offers them no resistance. On the other hand it can be assumed that there are obstacles for them which offer no resistance to us. We know for sure, tho, that they can cover short distances in space without a ship. All in all they're quite amazing—a very dangerous race. I'm afraid they're still going to make trouble for us."

Pucky looked up at the viewscreen. "That stellar nebula there—do you think it's where they come from?"

Rhodan and Bell looked over at the stern screen. The blurred nebulous spot appeared to be small and insignificant. The unknown galaxy looked harmless—and very, very distant. But that dim blob happened to be the Andromeda Nebula in sector BJ-97-UK—the target zone that Capt. Henderson, the *Caesar's* Navigation Officer, had been ordered to steer his course for. If the shadow people were intent upon stealing the *Caesar* it could be assumed that they were planning to take it to their homeworld.

Bell had been silent for some time but he suddenly spoke up. "Wasn't that little Iltu a pain in the neck for you?"

Pucky was caught off guard. "A pain? How come?"

Bell grinned. "Well, I seem to remember how badly you complained about her once when we made a visit to the colony on Mars. Isn't that the fresh little guy who was always so impudent—the one who tossed the camp commander thru the air?"

"Iltu isn't a 'guy', Fatso—she's a girl!"

"A mousebeaver's a mousebeaver," retorted Bell somewhat disdainfully. "Anyway, you were really sore at her. That's why we assigned her to you without giving you any previous warning. It was to be a surprise so that you wouldn't have time to complain . . . "

"She was a surprise alright!"

"Oh?"

Pucky nodded. "Yes, a pleasant one. Without her help I wouldn't have been able to handle those spooks. Iltu is a first-class teleporter."

"Well, so what?" said Bell in mock disparagement. "She's still just a child—you said so yourself."

"She's no child now!" fumed Pucky angrily, and he bared his incisor tooth. This time it was not a sign of pleasure. "She's a grownup young lady mousebeaver! Anybody who insults her is also insulting me. Just get that into your head, once and for all, or something could happen to you!''

Bell caught a warning look from Rhodan. He had almost failed to realize that the situation had changed. Previously he had always had Pucky's support whenever he had complained about Iltu—or any of the other mousebeavers of the colony—but today such an approach produced the opposite effect. Strange.

''OK, little buddy. I didn't mean it like that.''

''Well that's what it sounded like,'' grumbled Pucky, although he was already half-consoled. ''I will admit, though, that I underestimated Ilty . . . ''

''Who?''

Pucky's mouse ears twitched in a sign of embarrassment. ''Oh I often call her that. It fits her better than Iltu.''

''My, my!'' said Bell, grinning broadly. ''You already have a pet name for her?'' He winked at Rhodan. ''When will congratulations be in order?''

Pucky seemed to be exceptionally slow on the uptake today. ''Congratulations? What for?''

''Don't hand me that! You know very well what I mean. You've gone off the deep end for Ilty—or haven't you?''

''You dare to call her Ilty?'' chirped Pucky in new irritation.

''Don't dodge the subject. Do you love her or don't you?''

Pucky gasped under the shock of the other's merciless suspicion. ''For that—she's too young. She's only just a child . . . ''

Bell burst out laughing. ''You know you change your opinion like I change my shirt! Only now you were just saying . . . !'' He broke off suddenly.

The air was shimmering in the middle of the table. Then Iltu materialized from nowhere. She stood there and looked about at everyone triumphantly until her gaze rested on Pucky.

"So!" she chirped menacingly. "After all, now I'm such a youngster again, am I?"

Pucky was noticeably cowed. Rhodan and Bell couldn't remember ever having seen him so humbled. "Well now . . . I *mean* . . . !" He pointed to Bell. "Fatso's talking out of his head, Ilty—Iltu. I was only defending you, that's all."

Iltu came closer to him. "So I'm so young, am I? Then you know what *you* are!"

Pucky cast an imploring glance at Rhodan. He was caught squarely on the horns of an awful dilemma. If he insisted that Iltu was young, then it was a guaranteed certainty that here in front of Bell she'd give him the title of "Grandpa". And if he should admit that after all she was not "*too* young", then the other trap would close!

Women!—he thought bitterly. One shouldn't get mixed up with them. Men always came out on the short end of things because they were dumber!

But it wasn't all quite that bad. "Listen, Ilty, do we have to discuss this right out in public, for the ears of this nosey Fatso? Just look at his ears bending forward! What business is it of his what the two of us . . . I mean, the way we two . . . " He became hopelessly confused and slumped disconsolately. "Take it any way you want to!"

Iltu went over to Rhodan and slipped into his lap. She looked at him guilelessly and took his hands in hers. "Don't you agree, Perry—when I'm grown up I get to marry Pucky?"

A choking sound came from where Pucky had been sitting. The mousebeaver had lost his balance and fallen under the table. On all fours he came scrabbling out again, trembling in all his limbs.

"No! I will not get married! I'm too . . . no, not now anymore! I won't!"

"You don't mean to say, perhaps, that you're too old?" said Rhodan as he stroked Iltu's silky hair reassuringly. "But Pucky, who would want to admit a thing like that?"

"I didn't admit it . . . but all the same . . . "

"Grandpa!" whispered Iltu affectionately.

Pucky went rigid.

Rhodan tensed.

Bell began to laugh uncontrolably. "Grandpa!" he exclaimed, at the same time groaning with mirth. "That's a good one! Grandpa!" And he kept on as if he would never stop.

When Iltu saw what she had wrought by her remark, she got quickly out of Rhodan's lap, pattered over to Pucky and took his hand. "You know I didn't mean it like that . . . !"

Pucky remembered his manhood. "Leave me alone!" he snapped, and shook her hand away. "You . . . you infant! You babe in diapers! You . . . you . . . you . . . " Words failed him.

Iltu stared at him and then drew herself up until she was almost taller than Pucky. She shouted at him in a shrill voice: "Oh, so now you're getting smart, are you? Well, I'll fix that, you just wait!" She took him by the hand again. "You come now, right now. The two of us alone! Are you in for a surprise! Pah! Too old! Too young! That's an excuse! Now will you *please* come along?"

They dematerialized.

The last thing Rhodan and Bell saw of Pucky was his sorrowful look of reproach.

Rhodan spoke first. "You can stop laughing now, Bell. You should have respect for the feelings of our little friend. He's fallen in love."

Bell ceased laughing abruptly. He stared at Rhodan in astonishment. ''You don't mean it's for real, do you?''

''Of course I do. Haven't you ever been in love?''

Bell turned red and shifted uncomfortably. ''But Iltu is only . . . ''

''A mousebeaver? So? For Pucky I'm sure she's the most beautiful and attractive maiden in the universe. What would you say, for example, if one day Pucky were to become—not a grandpa, that's still too far away—but let's say a proud father? The father of 3 or 4 tiny, cute little mousebeavers? When I think of it——''

''No thank you!'' groaned Bell, horrified. ''That I couldn't take! All I have to remember is my visit to the mousebeaver colony on Mars. The little rascals sat around on my head and my stomach and my legs, scratching me and making a big game out of it where I was ticklish. No! Pucky's pups will be the death of me!''

Rhodan looked thoughtfully at the dwindling blob of light in the middle of the viewscreen. ''Maybe it will be just the opposite—for the Earth.'' He was still watching the spiral nebula, which was many millions of light-years distant and was perhaps the home of the invisible foe. ''Maybe one day Pucky's children will determine the fate of the human race.''

TIME-VAULTING TO THE FUTURE

10 ADVENTURES FROM NOW
Beware the
Beasts of Subterrania

25 ADVENTURES FROM NOW
Be alert for the
Signals from Eternity

50 ADVENTURES FROM NOW
Hold your breath for
Moment Penultimate

100 ADVENTURES FROM NOW
He'll lead you a merry chase—
The Parasprinter

200 ADVENTURES FROM NOW
It's Monsterrific!
Pucky & The Golem

300 ADVENTURES FROM NOW
Prepare to meet
The Moon Thing

400 ADVENTURES FROM NOW
It's a tale of
Galactic Mercenaries

500 ADVENTURES FROM NOW
Craniums clash in
War of the Brains

600 ADVENTURES FROM NOW
Excitement reigns in
The Dakkar Zone

THE PERRYSCOPE

LOUIS LaSALLE of 319 Maple, Anaconda/MT 59271 has
some interesting comments to make:

I want you to know Star Trek is my favorite series,
not Perry Rhodan. Altho PR on a scale of 1-10 is
19.999999 etc. to Star Trek's 20!

I've learned my lesson, you can't tell a book by its
cover. PR 92 (my first) had a great cover but only
average story, while PR 90 had a fair cover but just
about the best story I've ever read.

On John Wagner's letter in PR 95 I don't mind a
thousand year jump but what will happen to Pucky,
Bell, and Marshall? Will they still be around. And what
will happen to and/or on Earth and Arkon? Also, don't
forget Atlan!

Getting back to PR 90, did you have to destroy
Vagabond, sorry FJA, you're totally right—the monsters did it. I especially liked "Og tille u?" repeated
Pucky "Joe that means he has to . . . " which I believe
lightened the story just enough for that just great touch-
ing ending.

BILL MACHURE of 21 Elm St., Yarmouth, Nova Scotia, puns a letter to the Perryscope as follows:

Dear Forry,

(I hope you will be Perrymissive enough to let me call you that) I am writing to compliment you and Wendayne on the swell job you're doing with the PR series.

I really liked stories 91, 92, & 93. In 91, you showed Khrest just as he should have been. I knew eventually Khrest would have to die but I really liked the way you did it. You could have had him assassinated by a fanatic or something like that, but that's not good enough, he goes down helping mankind to the end.

92 was a good story, but not as good as 91 & 93. I liked the way that Rhodan and company found Akon. 93 was a funny yet still had an air of danger. I liked the encounter with Rambugle. The idea of a planet covered by an organic creature is interesting.

Now that I have Rambulled on about books, I will talk about something else.

I am beginning to think that I am the only Perry Rhodan fan in Yarmouth. If any one wants to write to me to talk about PR I would sure appreciate it.

Keep the Peace, Perry.

MARK WILLIAMS of Philadelphia/PA has his small say:

The PR series is getting better all the time. The stories are improving very much (not that they weren't great before).

My favorite author is Clark Darlton (who else). His adventures have more action than the other authors. But all the other ones are great too.

THE INDEFATIGABLE HENRY DAVIS JR. writes from Baker Station Rd., Goodlettsville/TN:

#106 and #107 set the stage for Cardif's death in #108. I'm still surprised that Pucky in particular and the telepathics among the mutants have been fooled so easily by Cardif. It surprised me Atlan joined with the Akons, apparently forgetting Phantom Fleet. He'll probably have trouble getting out of his alliance with the Akons, it'll probably cause Atlan and Perry some trouble eventually. Also I detected another conflict; I'll call it Spaceship of Ancestors-Atlan's Rule conflict. In it the Arkonides rescued by Pucky and the Terrans in Blazing Sun and to be used to assist Atlan ruling the Empire are suddenly forgotten—they become nonexistent. I believe there were over 100,000 of these colonial Arkonide ancestors. But they've been forgotten, and Atlan falls back on Toseff and 43 other Arkonide commanders. It's almost *ridiculous*. It makes the series seem 'pulpy', as one *German* fan described the 'leaving out' of alien races *without explaining* what has happened to them. I hope things like this aren't typical of future episodes.

Indications are Trakarat *will* be found. No doubt Cardif dies here and the real PR is rescued from the clutches of the Antis.

The drawing of Atlan was good but I intensely dislike the 'outfits' of the Terrans. Do you go about barechested? I doubt it. The interior artwork is good, almost excellent.

Experiment in Genius. I dislike this serial, it's dull and uninteresting. Good riddance.

Ms. Reid's story wasn't bad. Just retribution for plantlife (esp. trees) if they do outsurvive us.

Gold was so so. It seemed to lack, how can I say it, the ability to entertain the reader.

Tunnel is a spectacular story! Beautiful! So they shrank (or shrunk); not a nice predicament to be in.

Inflexure seems to have potential. Not as good as Heinlein's To Build A Crooked House or By His Bootstraps, or even the story Hall of Mirrors by Geoffrey (or was it Fred?) Hoyle (I think). But enough of criticism. I enjoyed it very much, I've never heard of a 4-D star (a man, but not a star). I do doubt the ability to transfer characteristics from one star to another, however. The time angle should bring back all sorts of dinosaurs, prehistoric men and monsters, revolutionary heroes, cowboys and Indians, etc.

It was good to see you finally express yourself. You haven't really done that since Ross Paluak's letters. I admit I've felt the same way as Mr. Bunch at times. We for the most part know you try to conform to our wishes. It seems obvious you are subservient to the people at Ace/Grossett-Dunlap. What is important is that you realize how hard it is to know the Germans are almost 800 books ahead of us and by the time PR in America reaches 800, the sun will be a burned out cinder and the earth lifeless. It almost seems that way. I know you're trying but it'll always seem to some of us that you're not trying hard enough, I'm *sorry* to say. The reason Rhofans aren't showering you with money (even $1.00) for the Ackermuseum is simple. Why should they give you money for something most of them will probably never see?

To answer your question: for the same reason since 1939 science fiction fans have been buying Supporting Memberships in World Science Fiction Conventions not all of them can attend; for the reason I supported rocket research in the 30s altho I never expect to go to Mars; for the reason I have poured money & effort into the promulgation of Esperanto—the artificial interna-

tional language—since the 30s, altho I am not going to live to see it universally accepted; for the reason that I contribute to charities for the blind, the black, brain-diseased children (tho I have no children of my own), cancer research (tho I hope never to have cancer); have a care for Israel, tho I am not Jewish nor have any guarantee I'll ever visit there; etc. The other day I received a thank-you letter from the head of the Institute of Science Fiction in England for my donation of 4 boxes full of sci-fi–including a set of PERRY RHO-DAN. I may never see that Institute but I like the world a little better to know it's there & prospering (the Institute, not the world; I know the world is there, whether it's prospering or not is another matter). If your explanation is correct, Henry, and 99.99% of PR's readers refrain from sending me $1 to get the mortgage on the Science Fiction Museum off my back and to help pay for the $4200-a-year property tax, then I'm faced with the prospect of working on & on till I'm 82 in 1998 so I call my home my own–and leave it & its contents to posterity. Then all I'll have to worry about will be the Death Tax. Isaac Asimov, bless him, sent me $100; Roger Aday, bless him & his, sent me $100 he collected from a lot of Rhofans; Mike Le Vine, R. Laurraine Tutihasi, Mark Gregory, Ricky Uhlenkott, Nathan Brindle, Brian Jordan, James K. Woosley, Dan Oakes, Henry Andruschak, Karen E. Weber, Donald H. Degnan, and the IFC, among others, have contributed above & beyond the call of duty—bless' em all! If, after reading the foregoing, any one is moved to make a donation to my Foundation (and miracles can happen: out of approximately 135,000 potential contributors–the readership of ANALOG—28 did! the month A.E. van Vogt's appeal on my behalf was pub-

lished) the address to send your dollar to is: Forrest Ackerman, 2495 Glendower Ave., Hollywood/CA 90027. Forvala & Shahntel in advance!—FJA

THE RETURN of HENRY DAVIS JR! (Does it seem to you he's hardly been away?)

Dear FJA;

My comments on that fantastic issue, #108 (Duel Under the Double Sun) by Herr Scheer.

The cover wasn't bad, Wilson seems to know how to draw Atlan, if not Perry.

Your dedication to Neil R. Jones was an appropriate one. Fondly I remember Professor Jameson, the Tripeds, the Mumeds (if spelled right), metal eaters and shrieking fear causing monsters from a parallel universe. Do you realize how hard it was for me to find all the old volumes and the exorbitant prices I paid in con huckster rooms for them? Ace should reprint them.

Well, I'm happy to say Cardiff got his. Explosion incredible—and out burst the cell activator, attaching itself to Perry under the gaze of Perry, Pucky, Atlan, and the High Baalol, while IT's laughter rumbles on. Good riddance!

One thing puzzled me. On page 118, quoting "Marriages could only be consummated on Trakarat and only between the Baalols themselves." We all know that's so much balloon juice, Mr. Ackerman. Mr. Scheer must have changed his mind. So much for the future.

As for Stolen Spacefleet, it seems obvious Perry will never marry Auris. It saddens me; I wish he had married her, rather than Morry Ahro, whom I've heard some unpleasant things about. It just seems those German authors love to kill off the hero's spouse. Did Jane, Duare, Dejah Thoris, Helen, Dian, Eve Hendron, Tavia, Thuvia, Dian the Beautiful, or most other space opera heroines ever die? Hardly ever.

The Banning wasn't terrific but was entertaining in its own way. As usual earth gets punished—for simply being human.

A Fragment of Diamond Quartz reminds me of a story I once read in Asimov's SF anthology a couple of years ago. Altho the name of the story eludes me, I recall the power, the vision, within it. The Cummings' story wasn't too bad itself. Toler got what he deserved; Lawton should be pitied for his stupidity.

Orhelein's *Extenuating Circumstances* seemed out of Asimov's robot tales. But he (Robert) wasn't bound by those laws of robotics, which I've always considered somewhat silly anyway.

The cast of a Rhodan film submitted to to the Perryscope was an interesting one. Except Pucky could be played by Michael Dunn, who played Dr. Lovelace in the old Wild Wild West series (*Sorry, he died several years ago—FJA*) or by one of the drone robots in that movie—oh, what was its name?—anyway the movie in which all the plants and animals were in a fleet out in space—anyway by one of the guys who played one of those robots. Boy, you're in a sad state when you can't even recall the name of a movie as famous as that one was. (*SILENT RUNNING*). I agree that Borgnine could be the pugnacious Reggie. If you could get William Conrad (of Cannon) to play one of your ''Super heavy men'' you'd be in ''good shape''. Basically I agree with the list provided by Ms. Mondragon and Mr. Concepcioun. It would cost a million solars, even with the changes you and I suggested. But wouldn't you love to see it happen? Well done, it would be a success and break the backs of the enemies of Rhofandom—people like Ellison.

EDITOR EVALUATED by M. CLARK, POB 5, Gleneden Beach/OR 97388:

I feel that PR is the best sf series anywhere, and shall say so very loudly. PR IS THE BEST!

And at least some of the credit goes to Mr. Ackerman, the editor. Mr. Ackerman, I feel that you have done PR a great service by making it what it is. For now, not only is it the best sf series in the world, it is also a library of science fiction (with such features as the Shock Shorts, Serials, and Time Vault, which bring back many otherwise forgotten stories).

And the other features that you added. They are good, too. The editorials. The Ship of Things to Come. Scientifilm world. The occasional features such as Ray Bradbury's ''Where are the Golden-Eyed Martians?'' and ''The Atlantean Chronicles'' by Henry Eichner.

AND THE PERRYSCOPE!

So, PR is great. You've done a good job, Mr. Ackerman. Thanks. But, though it is the best, can I in my impatience leave it that way? Of course not. Here are some suggestions (to make PR even better!):

1. Hurry up and get someone to write the ATLAN series.

2. Possibly install another section dealing with new sf books and series.

3. Compile a few PR dictionaries. A FEW. The accumulated slang, events, people, places, and developments of nearly 2 centuries would be too confusing for JUST ONE book. So you could have one dictio-

nary dealing with books 1-50; one for 50-75; one for 75-100; etc. . . .

I hope I haven't taken up too much space, but I had to get my 13¢ worth.

So, in signing off—PR IS GREAT—
LET IT LIVE LONG & PROSPER!

THE SHADOW KNOWS

YES, The Shadow Knows what a Great Deal it is to be a Subscriber to **PERRY RHODAN**.

Jack Shadow, that is, of Niagara Falls, Arizona.

This Issue ANTHONY CARACCIOLO of Brooklyn discovers to his surprise & pleasure that the subscription he sent in is being *doubled*. Nextime it could happen to you.

Regular subscriptions now 5 months for $10.50, 10 months for $21. That includes postage—and remember! You get TWO novels in one volume so for $10.50 you'll be reading 10 of Perry's adventures, while you can make it 20 booklength Rhodan novels in 10 exciting volumes for $21.

NB: *These rates good only during month of issuance and until next price change (if any). IF this is a back number, check CURRENT number's ad.*

Check or Money Order—and don't write anything on back of either—to address below. Canadians must send POSTAL MONEY ORDERS ONLY payable in U.S. DOLLARS.

KRIS DARKON
2495 Glendower Ave.
Hollywood/CA 90027

PERRY RHODAN #119 thru . . . etc

NAME (Print Clearly) . . . .

AGE . . . .

ADDRESS . . . .

CITY . . . .

STATE (Spell Out) . . . .

ZIP . . . .

COUNTRY . . . .

KRIS DARKON
2495 Glendower Ave.
Hollywood/CA 90027

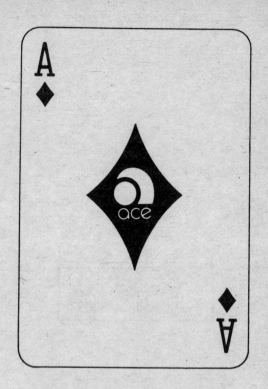

There are a lot more
where this one came from!